ZRLG

OCT - - 2021

Waiting on Love

Books by Tracie Peterson

★with Kimberley Woodhouse
★★with Karen Witemeyer, Regina Jennings, and Jen Turano

For a complete list of Tracie's books,
visit her website www.traciepeterson.com

Waiting on Love

TRACIE PETERSON

BETHANYHOUSE

a division of Baker Publishing Group
Minneapolis, Minnesota

© 2021 by Peterson Ink, Inc.

Published by Bethany House Publishers
11400 Hampshire Avenue South
Bloomington, Minnesota 55438
www.bethanyhouse.com

Bethany House Publishers is a division of
Baker Publishing Group, Grand Rapids, Michigan

Printed in the United States of America

Library of Congress Cataloging-in-Publication Data
Names: Peterson, Tracie, author.
Title: Waiting on love / Tracie Peterson.
Description: Minneapolis, Minnesota : Bethany House Publishers, [2021] | Series: Ladies of the lake
Identifiers: LCCN 2021015651 | ISBN 9780764232404 (trade paper) | ISBN 9780764232411 (cloth) | ISBN 9780764232428 (large print) | ISBN 9781493433889 (ebook)
Subjects: GSAFD: Christian fiction. | Love stories. | Sea stories.
Classification: LCC PS3566.E7717 W35 2021 | DDC 813/.54—dc23
LC record available at https://lccn.loc.gov/2021015651

Scripture quotations are from the King James Version of the Bible.

Cover design by LOOK Design Studio
Cover photography by Aimee Christenson

Baker Publishing Group publications use paper produced from sustainable forestry practices and post-consumer waste whenever possible.

21 22 23 24 25 26 27   7 6 5 4 3 2 1

Dedicated with thanks to Brendon Baillod, an award-winning Great Lakes maritime historian based in Wisconsin. He has appeared on the History Channel, the Discovery Channel, the National Geographic Channel, and the Travel Channel, discussing Great Lakes shipwrecks, and is an avid collector of antiquarian Great Lakes books, maps, and ephemera. And yet he still took the time to help me with facts and a myriad of questions regarding the Great Lakes and sailing. He is the author of *Fathoms Deep but Not Forgotten: Wisconsin's Lost Ships* as well as the creator of the Great Lakes Shipwreck Research Group on social media, where he hosts the weekly podcast *Great Lakes Shipwrecks LIVE!* Thank you so much, Brendon, for your help. I'm sure I probably still managed to get some things wrong, but it won't be your fault if I did.

Thanks also to Mark Sprang, archivist of historical collections of the Great Lakes at Bowling Green State University, for his hours of researching files for me. A good historian is an amazing blessing to an author.

Chapter 1

Oswego, New York
Late June 1872

Elise Wright watched her sister, Caroline, as she greeted the wedding guests. Caroline was five years her junior, and Elise wanted to be happy for her but found it difficult. Caroline hadn't sought their father's advice, or even Elise's, about her marriage. Of course, her sister was so distanced from the family that when Mama died the year before, Caroline hardly even seemed upset. Elise had tried not to hate her for her callous attitude, but it required a great deal of prayer. Now Caroline wanted Elise and their father to be happy about her marrying into New York society to a man none of them really knew.

Still, Caroline seemed happy as she moved

effortlessly in her ivory wedding gown of satin ruching and lace upon lace. The long train didn't seem to slow her in the least, nor did the trailing tulle veil. She was radiant and full of energy. Maybe she truly had married for love rather than money and position.

"She is beautiful, isn't she?" their father whispered against Elise's ear.

"She is. And she seems so happy. Nelson must be the right man for her." They'd met Nelson Worthington only a few days ago.

Her father nodded. "I had my doubts, but your uncle James assured me he was from a good family. They're in church every Sunday. Your mama would be happy to know that."

"I don't know that it would be enough. Mama used to say that Satan himself is in church every Sunday. The purpose in being there is what really matters."

Her father smiled. "You're so like her. How I miss her." His joy seemed to fade.

"I do too, Papa." She let him hug her close despite her very tight corset and uncomfortable clothes. She knew her father was just as miserable in the fancy suit that Uncle James let him borrow. As if reading her thoughts, Papa loosened his tie.

"It's been a little more than a year, and yet it seems like she was here just yesterday," her father whispered. "Other days it feels like she's been gone forever."

"I know, Papa. It's that way for me too."

He gazed out across the garden reception. "She would love seeing your sister get what she wanted for her wedding."

"It would have been nice if Caroline had given more consideration to what you and Mama wanted." Elise struggled with the anger she felt toward her sister. Caroline had hurt their parents so much with her choices. She never seemed to think of anyone but herself.

"We used to talk about you girls getting married. We worried about having enough money to give you a nice wedding. I regret that your uncle is paying for this. I offered him money—what I could—but he said it was their delight to give this wedding to Caroline. What could I say?"

"Well, you won't have to worry about giving me this kind of wedding. I can scarcely breathe, much less enjoy myself, in restrictive gowns like this." She looked down at the lavender creation she wore. "I feel completely out of sorts. Especially with this bustle. Goodness, whoever created such a thing?" She glanced over her shoulder and then gave her father a smile. "Besides, I don't intend to marry. I'm married to the *Mary Elise*," she said, referencing their ship.

Her father roared with laughter, causing many of Oswego's social elite to look their way. It would no doubt be a terrible embarrassment to Caroline, who hated that she was from a ship captain's family and spoke very little of it. Elise had heard from her cousins that Caroline told people their father was quite wealthy and chose to captain a ship for pure pleasure. Elise herself had heard her sister say their father took to sailing because it was his favorite thing to do, and he was very eccentric.

The truth was, however, that Elise and her sister had both grown up on ships, and money was often scarce. When Uncle James got into the shipping business six years ago, he had helped Papa buy the *Mary Elise*—a three-masted schooner named after Elise and Caroline's mother and grandmother. Elise loved life on the lakes and had helped their mother in the galley, but Caroline had enjoyed when they stayed with Uncle James and his family. She had taken to the life of a wealthy socialite and never wanted to return to their shipboard life. More than once, Caroline had made their mother cry, and Elise hated that Caroline had been so heartless. Her sister was only a child at the time, so Mama had encouraged everyone to be patient with her, but as the years passed, the tantrums only increased. Caroline would cry for hours. She would take to her bed and swear that ship life was killing her. By the time she was fifteen, Mama and Papa had given up. They allowed her to live with Mama's wealthy brother and his family.

Uncle James had been Mama's support throughout the years. Even when she ran away to elope with Papa, he had been the one to make it possible. When he'd offered to let the girls come live with him and his family, it wasn't a surprise. He had told his sister that the girls would never get good husbands if they weren't trained properly. Mama and Papa left it up to Elise as to whether she wanted to join her sister. She didn't.

"Are you enjoying yourselves?" her cousin Louis asked, interrupting her thoughts.

"It's everything I expected it would be." Elise gave him a smile. "What about you?"

"I'd rather be anywhere else in the world," he answered, returning the smile.

"You mean you don't like dressing up in tight-fitting suits?" Papa asked.

"As much as any fellow ever has at these occasions. Being here just reminds every would-be bride that I'm eligible to marry." Even though he was three years younger than Elise, at twenty-two, Louis seemed to have a very stable outlook on life.

Elise giggled. She had watched a bevy of frilly young ladies flock around her male cousins all day.

"Go ahead and laugh, but it's torment for me. At least Caroline and her young man seem happy. A father could hardly ask for more." Louis looked at Elise. "She did, however, step out of line and marry before her older sister."

"Oh, I am not finding her position enviable," Elise replied, hugging her father's arm. "Besides, being married hasn't seemed harmful to your brother Randolph. He looks quite content." She nodded toward the tall, handsome man who stood smiling into the face of his wife.

"They're absolutely gone over each other. It's so embarrassing, but our mother's greatest triumph. Well, at least until now, with Caroline. Mother just loves pairing us all up." Louis grinned. "If Elise sticks around, Mother is convinced she can get her married off as well. She loves having people to fuss over. I suppose they're like china dolls to dress up and arrange."

"Well, I'd just as soon Elise stay with me awhile longer," her father declared. "After all, if she were gone, who would cook for the men on the *Mary Elise*?" He winked at her.

"Also," Elise said, trying to keep her tone

sweet, "I'm afraid I would make a very poor china doll. Besides, the *Mary Elise* is my life. I don't intend to add a man to that equation."

"You are a strange one, just as Mother said." Louis bit his lip. "I didn't mean to say that. It's not exactly what Mother meant."

"It's all right. I know I'm not what passes for a normal female in her world." Elise did her best not to reveal the hurt his words had caused. Why should her aunt call her strange just because she enjoyed life on the lakes with her parents? Since Mama died the year before, however, Aunt Martha had nagged Elise to come and live with them.

"It looks like that dashing Mr. Casper is coming our way," her father whispered. "No doubt he wants to dance, Elise."

"Oh, please send him away. He stepped on my foot three times in our first dance. I have no desire to repeat the performance, and I'm sick of dancing."

"I'll take care of it," Louis declared. "I know Charlie. I'll take him to see my new horse. He loves horses more than anything else on earth. Charlie! Wait until you see my new mare." He headed off to intercept the man, whose face lit up as Louis explained his plan.

"What a sweetheart." Elise would have to find a way to pay Louis back. "How much longer will this go on?"

Her father shrugged. "I have no idea. In my experience, the party's over when the liquor runs out, but since these folks have enough money to keep that flow steady, I'm not sure what will bring things to an end."

"Perhaps someone will announce it, as they do for dinner." Elise smiled, imagining a well-dressed butler announcing that the party was over and everyone needed to vacate the property.

"They seem to have announcements for just about everything else. Why not the end of a party?" her father replied.

"Do you suppose if we just sneak off to our rooms to change, they will leave us to our rat-killing?" Elise asked with a grin. *Rat-killing* was her mother's favorite phrase for any odd task that needed to be done. "We could slip upstairs when no one is looking."

"I honestly don't expect we'll be missed. Not even by your sister." There was an edge of regret in Papa's voice. "Besides, I need to check on Joe and see what the doc said about his leg."

Neither of them expected the news to be good. The *Mary Elise*'s first mate had injured his leg nearly a month ago, but no one had known about the wound until he started limping. By that time, the leg was putrid, and red streaks were moving up the thigh.

"Let's just go, then. We can tell Caroline good-bye and pray with her on our way out the door."

Elise pulled Papa in the direction of her sister. She didn't want to give him a chance to refuse. He didn't even try.

Elise waited for her sister to finish speaking to some guests before tapping her shoulder. "Caroline, we must be on our way."

"But you can't! Not until you help me change. I was already looking for an excuse. Nelson said we had to keep to our schedule."

Elise looked at her father with a shrug. "I guess Caroline needs my help. I'll be back as soon as possible, and then we can go."

Caroline all but dragged Elise up the stairs. "Everything was beautiful, wasn't it?"

"Yes. Quite lovely."

"The garden was perfect for the reception. I was so afraid there'd be no roses because of the cold spring, but they were in full bloom, and the gardeners were able to buy additional flowers to weave in." Caroline opened the door to her bedroom suite.

Elise gazed around the large room. There was a sitting area by the fireplace, a dressing area, and, of course, a beautiful four-poster bed with elegant gossamer curtains draped from its frame. It was hard to imagine calling such a place home.

"Unfasten the buttons in back," Caroline commanded as she removed her veil.

"What about *please*?"

"I'm used to servants, and you don't say *please* or *thank you*. It's their job."

"But Mama always encouraged us to be polite, even to the lowliest servant."

"Well, you aren't Mama," Caroline snapped.

"I'm also not a servant."

Silence hung heavy for a moment. Caroline gave a little huff. "Would you please undo my buttons?"

Elise began the task of unfastening thirty-six pearl buttons. "Why did you make that comment about Mama?"

"Well, ever since you and Papa arrived, you've done nothing but mother me. You've even talked to me like Mama. I'm sure you must feel the need to step into her shoes, and while that might be acceptable regarding cooking for Papa and the boys on the ship, it's not for me. I'm perfectly capable of seeing to myself."

"Including your back buttons?"

Caroline sighed. "Very well. Etta!" she called, not seeming to notice whether Elise continued with the buttons.

The uniformed maid appeared. "Ma'am." She gave a curtsy.

"Bring my new traveling suit and help me dress." Caroline glanced over her shoulder as Elise finished with the last of the buttons. "Please."

Elise smiled and watched the maid hurry away. "That wasn't so hard, was it?"

Caroline rolled her eyes. She worked at undoing the buttons on her sleeves. "Etta can help me now. Why don't you go downstairs and wait with the others? I know they plan to throw rice."

Elise waited as Caroline finished with her buttons. Stepping close, she surprised Caroline with an embrace. "I just want you to know that I love you. I hope you have a wonderful trip . . . and marriage."

Caroline hesitated, then finally returned Elise's hug. "I'm certain I will, so you can stop fretting." She stiffened and gave a little push. "Now, let me get back to this."

"We were close once." Elise hadn't meant to whisper the words aloud.

"We were children," Caroline countered. "And we had no choice. There was no other person to confide in or play with. We had only each other."

In that moment, Elise saw her sister not as a wealthy bride but as a little girl. "I liked it that way. We knew we could always count on each other to be there. Now you have other obligations. I will continue to miss you."

"Oh, bother. Where is that girl?" Caroline went to the open door that led to her bathing room. "Etta?"

"Coming, ma'am." Etta returned carrying a forest-green traveling suit. She placed the outfit carefully at the end of the bed, then went immediately to Caroline and helped rid her of the ivory gown.

Elise slipped from the room, knowing that neither woman needed her nor cared for her company. Her sister's attitude only stirred her anger. How could she be so cold? Didn't Caroline have any feelings of love toward her family? Maybe money and prestige were all she loved now.

An hour later, Elise waited in her uncle's borrowed carriage outside of Joseph Brett's apartment. Her father's first mate lived in a modest part of town. Elise knew that despite Joe being a better-paid seaman who didn't drink or gamble, he was still hard-pressed to keep his family fed and clothed, so the tiny duplex came as no surprise.

Joe had a family of five children and a wife who had once been quite pretty. Since Mrs. Brett had been on her way out the door when they'd pulled up to the curb, Elise had decided to wait outside and let her father and Joe visit privately. The two women had exchanged hellos, but then Joe's wife had to be on her way to retrieve her children from her sister's house.

Mrs. Brett had at least shared the news that Joe was doing better. The doctor had given him medication for his wound and strict orders for tending it. She was certain he'd be back on his feet soon.

It was good to hear. Joe had been her father's first mate for as long as Elise could remember. Papa relied on him heavily. It was hard enough to be without Mama on board, but losing Joe would be sheer misery. Her father would be relieved to hear the good news.

While she waited in the carriage, Elise fidgeted with the bodice of her gown. At least it wasn't as fancy as her wedding clothes, but it was just as snug. Probably much smaller than she usually wore, thanks to the tightly tied corset beneath it. She could scarcely draw breath, and given the day's heat and humidity, she worried she might faint dead away. How ridiculous! Why did women put themselves through such torment? A well-fitted corset tied in a reasonable manner was a useful thing, but the practice of securing them as tightly as possible was absurd.

There was some sort of commotion going on down the street, and Elise looked up just in time to see a freight wagon veering out of control. The horses pulling the wagon were driverless and headed straight for her. All she could do was brace herself for impact as her uncle's driver struggled to get the carriage out of the way.

⁓

"Miss. Miss, are you all right?"

Elise slowly opened her eyes and gazed straight up into the worried expression of a very handsome man. His face was freshly shaved, and the cologne he'd used had a pleasant aroma.

"What . . . what happened?" She was lying on her back, and her vision seemed blurred.

The man smiled. "Your carriage was hit by a freighter. It threw you to the street. You have a few scrapes on your chin. Are you hurt anywhere else?"

"I don't know." Elise put her gloved hand to her chin.

"Are you able to sit?"

She tried with his help, but pain cut through her back. "Oh, I don't think so." She was grateful when he lowered her back to the ground.

"My father . . . he's in number twelve-twenty-three." How had she remembered the address? "He's visiting Joseph Brett."

"I know Joe," another man said. "I'll fetch her father."

The man who'd tried to help her sit up glanced around. "I think I'd best lift you rather than leave you lying here in the street."

"Yes. Thank you." With a jolt of fear, she asked, "How's the driver?"

"He jumped free at the last minute. He's just fine and busy trying to calm the horses."

The stranger put one arm behind her back and another under her legs. He was so very gentle.

"What is your name?" she asked.

He smiled. "Nicodemus Clark, but most call me Nick."

"Nick. Thank you again."

He frowned. "You might want to wait to thank me. This will probably hurt."

"I know." She drew a deep breath. "Go ahead." She gritted her teeth, determined not to cry out.

"Elise!" Her father appeared. "Bring her in the house. I'm sure Joe won't mind." He instructed Nick where to go and turned back to Elise. "They said a freight wagon hit you. How do you feel, darlin'?"

"Confused, dizzy, and in pain." She smiled. "How are you?"

Her father chuckled. "Much the same without the aid of a freight wagon."

Nick carried her into the house and placed her on the empty kitchen table. The pain wasn't quite as bad as before.

"I'm a doctor," a man said, pushing past several of the bystanders who'd followed them inside. "If you aren't related to this young woman or live here, then I want you to leave." Several people filed outside.

Elise's father grabbed her hand. The look on his face nearly broke her heart. He looked at the doctor. "Can you tell if her back is broken?"

"My back isn't broken," Elise assured him. "It hurts, but look—I can move my legs and arms, and with a little help I can sit up." She looked to the right and found the same man who had helped her earlier. "Would you lend me a hand?"

"It's best you don't stress your body at this time, miss," the doctor declared. "I've already sent a man to bring 'round the ambulance."

"That was hardly necessary." Elise knew her protest fell on deaf ears.

"The carriage was totally demolished, Elise," her father added. "We'll need some form of transport for you. The young man who helped you has no wagon either. We can't very well expect him to carry you home."

Elise tried to swallow her embarrassment. She shrugged, and it hurt from the base of her neck down the back of her legs. She didn't so much as grimace, however. Papa was already worried, and she didn't want to give him something else to worry about.

The doctor forced a large spoonful of medicine into her mouth. "Take this. It will help with the pain."

She swallowed the bitter medicine and couldn't hide her displeasure. "I don't know what that was, but I believe the pain was less difficult to bear. That tastes terrible."

Her father laughed. "Good medicine often tastes bad."

"It will make the ambulance ride more bearable," the doctor said.

She felt a wave of dizziness. "Well, I've never ridden in an ambulance. I suppose there are first times for everything." She forced a smile and looked at the man who'd helped her. "What did you say your name was?" The medicine was making her sleepy.

"Nick."

She fought to keep her focus. "Yes. Nicodemus. Such a wonderful name." She closed her eyes. "Thank you for helping me."

"I would say it was my pleasure, but I'm not sure that's exactly the right word."

She smiled. "Nor would I. But I appreciate no longer lying in the middle of the road."

"The ambulance is here," someone called from the open door.

Elise wasn't sure how long she'd been unconscious in the street, but now she felt like falling asleep for a good long time. Two men with a stretcher appeared. They spoke to the doctor, then maneuvered the stretcher beneath her without any apparent concern for her comfort and lifted her from the table. She couldn't help but moan.

Her father gave them Uncle James's address, then followed them. She had no chance to bid good-bye to the man who'd rescued her. And he'd been so nice.

After her aunt's personal maid undressed her and cleaned her up, Elise was again examined by the doctor as she faded in and out of sleep. Finally she heard the doctor tell her aunt to bring in her father.

"I do not see nor feel anything that indicates her back is broken, but I believe she should remain bedfast for at least two weeks. I will come tomorrow and check on her. There's a great deal of swelling, no doubt.

After fourteen days, we can expect the swelling to go down, and then we can reassess the situation."

"But we planned to leave tomorrow," she murmured, looking at her father.

"Well, you clearly cannot go." Papa's voice was firm, and even in her stupor, Elise knew there would be no arguing with him.

"She will remain with us," Uncle James said from the open bedroom doorway.

"But Papa needs me to cook on the *Mary Elise*." She tried her best to ignore the pain.

"We'll get by, girl. We can take turns cooking for ourselves. I'll lay in more cheese, fruit, and bread," her father declared. "I'm just happy to know you aren't permanently injured. Or worse yet. You could have been killed."

"Indeed," her aunt said, shaking her head.

Elise knew by the expressions on everyone's faces that she wasn't going anywhere. She tried to sit up, but the pain was too much, and she fell back. Maybe they were right.

Chapter 2

That evening, Nick Clark made his way down a stately avenue to the estate of James Monroe. He carried all his worldly belongings on his back in a large canvas duffel bag. This way, if he managed to find a job on a ship, he would have no reason to delay the captain. It hadn't always been this way. Years ago, he'd lived with his family in a place not so different from the Monroes' grand house.

Standing in front of the three-story brick mansion, Nick could only imagine that the wealth of these people came close to that of his father's—and maybe exceeded it. The gown worn by the young woman he'd helped was worth more than he would make in a year working as a ship's mate.

He chuckled. Who would expect a twenty-eight-year-old seaman to know about expensive women's fashions? But he had two sisters, and such things had always been enormously important to them. How could he not know?

The groomed walkway bid him forward. There were trimmed shrubs on either side for about ten feet, and then the yard opened up. Groundsmen were working on the far side of the front yard. One man was on his hands and knees, trimming the area beneath the flowering bushes. Everything was lovely and perfect.

Nick made his way to the door and knocked. It seemed to take quite a while, but an older woman wearing a mobcap appeared with a frown. She looked him up and down to determine whether he was worth her time, then started to close the door.

"We aren't looking to hire," she said. "Don't need any knives sharpened nor chimneys cleaned. Good day."

"I'm here to see Miss Wright. Or her father," he added, knowing it was hardly appropriate for him to visit a young woman of such high society.

The woman stared at him for what seemed an eternity before relenting. "Mr. Wright is in the parlor. Please come in." She stepped back and let Nick enter, but she wore a definite look of disapproval. "I'll tell Mr. Wright that you've come." She paused a moment. "I don't suppose you have a card?"

"No. Just tell him Nicodemus Clark would like a word."

Her frown deepened. "Very well. Wait here."

Nick nodded and lowered his duffel to the black-and-white tiled floor. He gazed around the circular entryway. There were mirrors hanging at every angle. They were in matching gold frames and nearly as long as he was tall. In the center of the room stood a round table bearing a huge bouquet of mixed flowers. Large white blooms the size of a man's fist were trimmed out with pale pink roses and something delicate and lacy looking in a darker shade of pink.

There was a very grand staircase— Brazilian cherry, if he wasn't mistaken. It rose from a singular point, then split off to the left and right, while arched entryways led out of the foyer to halls on either side of the stairs. It was from the left side that Mr. Wright appeared.

"Nick, good to see you." Mr. Wright strode into the foyer. He wore a casual suit with a white shirt and tie. He looked just as uncomfortable as he had earlier that day. "What can I do for you?"

Nick laughed. "You could give me a job.

God knows I need one. But I actually came to check on your daughter. Was she very badly hurt?"

"No. The doc believes she's just strained her back. She had a slight concussion from hitting the back of her head, but he wasn't overly concerned. So thanks be to God, nothing is broken."

"Indeed. I'm glad to hear it. Well, I won't keep you."

"Wait, now. You mentioned being in need of a job. What can you do?"

"Well, I was told you are a ship's captain. I've ten years' experience on the water." Nick grinned.

"I'm in need of a first mate on the schooner *Mary Elise*. It's temporary. My man is down with an injured leg."

"I'm more than qualified. As I said, I've been sailing for over ten years—ocean and the lakes. I worked my way up on commercial schooners and served as first mate on two different ships."

The older man rubbed his bearded chin. "I'm impressed."

"I'd be grateful for any position, even one that's only temporary."

"And I'd be grateful to take you on." He extended his hand to Nick. They shook.

"When do we sail?"

"Tomorrow at dawn."

"Thank you, Mr.—uh, Captain Wright."

"Most of the men just call me Captain. I've had my crew for years."

Nick could imagine the difficulty of being a new man on a loyal crew, even if it was only a temporary position. "You mentioned the schooner is called the *Mary Elise*."

"Yes, she's named for my wife and her mother. My daughter too. The young lady you rescued yesterday."

"Yes, I heard her name mentioned. A very pretty name." Nick didn't want to overstay his welcome. "Well, thank you again for your time. I'll be on the *Mary Elise* before dawn."

"Why don't you head over today? You can talk to Sam Matthews. He's my second mate. Tell him I've hired you on to fill in for Joe. He'll give you a tour and acquaint you with our operation and show you where you'll sleep. I don't have a regular cabin for my first mate, but there is space set aside from the men in the forecastle. I hope that will work for you. And before you go, why don't you come upstairs with me to see Elise? I was just heading up. You can see for yourself that she's just fine."

Nick nodded. "Of course." He left his duffel beside the table and followed the older man up the stairs and to the right.

"Knock, knock," Captain Wright called when they reached the open door. "I've brought you a visitor."

"Come in, Papa." Elise sat propped up on several lace-trimmed pillows. "Who have you brought?"

"Your rescuer, Mr. Nicodemus Clark."

Nick popped his head around the doorjamb. "I just came to check on you. Your father thought I should see you for myself."

She smiled, and it warmed him from the top of his head to the bottom of his toes. "Hello, Mr. Clark."

"Please call me Nick. Everyone does."

"Very well. Nick it is. Thank you again for what you did for me. I still shiver at the idea of lying unconscious in the street with terrified horses threatening to bolt and run over me."

"I've just hired Nick to fill in for Joe," her father said. "He has a lot of experience."

She nodded at him. "Welcome to our family—at least temporarily."

"Thank you." Nick found her smile infectious. "How are you feeling?"

"My back hurts, but my head is clear. I disagree with the doctor wanting to keep me on bedrest for two weeks, and I hate that nasty medicine."

"But we are going to follow his orders,"

her father interjected. "Your Uncle James and Aunt Martha will take good care of you."

Nick wasn't sure how this family was related. Captain Wright was a ship's captain—a laboring man who obviously worked hard, from the look of him. Then there was James Monroe, one of the wealthiest men in Oswego. He must have been Elise's mother's brother, since his last name wasn't Wright. He supposed there'd be time later to sort it out.

"I know they'll take care of me, but who will take care of you?" Elise asked.

Captain Wright laughed, and it was so genuinely full of joy that it made Nick smile as well. He looked at Elise, who folded her arms across the ruffles of her white robe.

"I suppose you're on his side," she said.

Nick shrugged. "He's the man who just hired me. Don't you think I should be?"

She pushed back her long black hair, and Nick found himself wishing he might do the same. Her hair was a thing of beauty. It was long and straight and dressed only with a simple ribbon tied in a bow atop her head.

He glanced into her eyes. He couldn't forget their deep blue color. She was watching him and looked curious, as if she had unspoken questions.

"I suppose you must be loyal to him," she finally replied. "I still think the doctor is daft for making me rest. I'll be fine in another day or so."

"Two weeks will pass before you know it, darlin' girl," Captain Wright said. "You take a rest here, and we'll leave at first light. Then soon enough I'll be here for you, and you'll be back in the galley, cooking up a storm."

"She cooks for the *Mary Elise*?" Nick asked, surprised. He had assumed she lived here with her uncle.

"She does, and we're known for having the best meals on the lakes. But for the next ten days, we'll have to make do cooking for ourselves. I've laid in extra bread and cheese. It's always good for a quick breakfast or lunch."

"It's hardly enough to give you the energy you'll need for the work you do," Elise countered. She shook her head. "You'll all starve."

Her father again roared in laughter and rubbed his muscular midsection. "I'm sure that won't be happenin' anytime soon. Now, you get your rest. I'll be back to see you later." He leaned over and kissed her head. "I love you, my darlin' girl."

"I love you too, Papa. Oh, and Mister . . . Nick, it was very nice to meet you under less painful circumstances."

"You too." Nick followed Captain Wright back downstairs. He picked up his duffel and headed for the door. "I'll head on over to the *Mary Elise*."

"If you give me five minutes, I'll come with you. I just need to leave word with the housekeeper. I'll be right back."

"Of course, Captain."

Nick again found himself studying the foyer. It definitely boasted the trimmings of the very rich. He wondered for a moment if the little porcelain statuettes and miniature paintings of landscapes on the highly polished tables made anyone happy. Did they even notice them? For a moment it brought up visions of another time and place. Such things had never made anyone happy in his childhood home.

"All right," the captain said as he returned with his hat in hand. "I'm ready now." He pulled on his coat as they went.

Halfway down the street, Nick was still pondering how Captain Wright fit in with James Monroe. It seemed as good a time as any to ask.

"Is Mr. Monroe your wife's brother?"

"Aye. She was the baby of the family, and he doted on her. My wife passed away just last year. We were all worse for it."

"I can only imagine. I lost my mother when I was fourteen. Nothing was ever the same."

"She held me together—held us all together. A good woman like no other. She and Elise cooked for the ship. She grew up in wealth like what you saw back there but never regretted her decision to leave it for life on a schooner. At least, if she did, she never said a word." Captain Wright sighed. "She's definitely missed."

"My mother too. Her passing sent my father into dark times."

"Are you his only son?"

"I am. I'm the oldest of the family with two sisters. My mother gave birth to a boy after that, but he only lived a few days. My mother died giving birth to another son who was stillborn."

"That's a lot of sorrow to bear. Not only the loss of a wife, but of children as well. Your father must have been devastated."

"Yes, I suppose so. He never shared it with me, however. He was cold and indifferent to my sisters and me. Business consumed him, even before Mother departed."

The neighborhood of the wealthy faded away as they moved closer to the city proper. A sense of anxiety mixed with joy motivated Nick's every step. He longed to be back aboard a ship.

"And did your mother know the Good Lord as her Savior?" the captain asked.

"She did." Nick couldn't help but smile. "She used to tell me Bible stories when I was young, and she taught me to pray. I was always amazed at her faith in God."

They started down the street that led to the waterfront, and the captain threw out another question. "And what about you? Do you have a faith of your own?"

Nick nodded and missed his mother even more. "She led me to the Lord when I was ten. She cried so much, I thought surely something was wrong, but she told me she was weeping for joy. She said she could almost hear all of heaven rejoicing for another sinner set free. I like to imagine she hears that heavenly rejoicing all the time now."

"Aye." The older man nodded. "I'm sure she does. Probably joins in. My Mary would."

After that they walked in silence, but the words they had shared seemed to bond them in a way Nick had never felt with another man. It was a spiritual joining that made him feel he had gained a brother and not just a job.

He thought of Elise and wondered at her faith. Nick imagined it was probably a strong one. She seemed so kind and at peace. There was nothing pretentious about her.

And even more amazing, she loved the sea.

Nick liked the crew of the *Mary Elise* almost immediately. The men were friendly and open about their duties and what they thought of the captain.

"Cap'n isn't one to accept second best," the youngest member of the crew declared after the captain left Nick in his care. Just turned fifteen, Tom Mallory was years ahead of his age. He explained he'd been orphaned at only six and had lived his life on the streets until he got himself in trouble. Some time ago, a local judge had asked Captain Wright to take him on, giving him a job in lieu of going to jail for breaking into a local grocer to steal food.

"I'll give my all," Nick assured him. The boy looked him up and down and gave a nod. Apparently Nick had passed muster. Besides Tom, there were another six men, plus the captain and Elise. Of course, she wouldn't be able to join them until later. It seemed like all the men knew their jobs and were good at them. They had been with the captain for some time and worked as one body to ready the *Mary Elise* for departure.

The captain showed up after having been gone an hour or two. A large man trailed behind him. The captain was at least six foot two and two hundred thirty pounds, but this man was bigger still.

"Men, this is Booker Duran. I'm hiring him on for this short run. It'll let me see what kind of worker he is."

Nick looked Duran over. The man was huge, but Nick had worked with big men before. More worrisome was the coldness that edged his expression. There was a hardness about him that suggested he was used to being in control. That could cause problems when working with a crew.

"Seamus, show him the ropes. Nick, you come with me. We need to talk."

Nick startled at this. He wondered if the captain had found out the truth about him. It bothered him something fierce not to be completely honest with his employer about his background. It wasn't that he wouldn't be honest if asked, but Nick was hesitant to just offer up the truth. He comforted himself that he hadn't and wouldn't lie to the older man, but it nagged at him nevertheless.

Captain Wright stopped abruptly and turned back to the men before they could disperse. "By the way, you may have noticed Elise isn't with us. She was nearly killed when a freight wagon collided with the carriage she was in. This young man saved her." He patted Nick's shoulder. "So for the time being, we'll be cookin' for ourselves. I'll even go first." He called to his second mate. "Sam, you assign and write down who's going to cook tomorrow and all the days after that."

There was a bit of grumbling, but most of the men said nothing.

Booker Duran made his protests known. "I didn't sign on to cook."

Captain Wright walked to where he stood, and despite Duran being a bit taller, the captain looked him in the face. "Mr. Duran, on this ship we do as ordered by the captain or first mate, or in your case most any other man on board the *Mary Elise*. If that's a problem . . . there's the gangplank." The captain motioned toward the side of the ship.

Duran scowled. "I don't think anyone will care for what I cook up."

"That's not the point. Not one of these men can cook as well as my daughter, but we eat what we're served or go hungry. Do you understand?"

"Aye aye, Captain." The words sounded sarcastic and insincere, but Nick knew that the captain would have his way.

"I suggest you have a last meal in town tonight. It might be the last edible thing you get for a while." Captain Wright laughed and gave Nick's back a nudge. "You too." He motioned for Nick to follow him. "I know I told you about young Tom earlier, but I'm gonna ask you to keep a special eye out for him with regard to Mr. Duran. The man clearly has a chip on his shoulder and a desire to take on the world. I don't want to see Tom influenced to do something stupid."

Nick breathed a sigh of relief that the captain didn't yet know about his past. "I'll definitely do what I can."

"Duran has his issues, but I believe in giving every man a chance to right his wrongs."

With that, the captain headed to the stern. Nick thought about his comment and wondered if that would extend to someone like him. Someone who had caused the death of so many.

The next morning, Nick awoke in the darkness of the *Mary Elise*'s forecastle. Most of the men were pulling on their boots.

"You better get a move on, Nick," young Tom declared. "We'll eat our breakfast and then get right to work."

Nick nodded. He was more than ready to be back on the water. Most of his sailing had been spent on the Great Lakes. He had worked on an ocean-going schooner for a couple of years, then traded life on the Atlantic for that of the Great Lakes. Now, with ten years of working experience in every area of responsibility, Nick felt confident, yet he wasn't too proud to fill in for any man. He had always believed it was a good thing to use his skills and keep them up to date.

After a rushed breakfast of overcooked oatmeal, fresh fruit, and lots of hot coffee, they were underway. A tug helped get them out of the harbor while the crew saw to last-minute tasks. Once they were clear of the breakwater, the real work began.

"Raise sails!" Captain Wright called to the crew.

The sails were unfurled on all three masts and released to catch the wind. It was a beautiful sound as they snapped into place.

"First mate, take the wheel," Captain Wright barked, relinquishing control.

Nick threw his heart and mind into the work, but he found it impossible to shake off the feeling that he had wronged Captain Wright by not admitting his past to him. He had been raised by his Christian mother never to lie and never to avoid the truth in order to save yourself embarrassment. Yet here he was, keeping the truth from a good man who had taken a risk to give him a job.

Nick hadn't said a word because he worried Captain Wright might rescind his job offer. Other captains had, so why would this man be any different? Of course, Nick had saved Elise from harm. It might be enough to keep the captain from changing his mind.

I have to tell him.

Nick glanced around. They were now in open water. He couldn't imagine the captain would waste time turning back to port. Besides, the job was just a temporary one. Captain Wright needed him as much as Nick needed the job. Didn't he?

~

The next day, the issue was still nagging at Nick's conscience. He had to be honest and let the captain know exactly who he was and what he'd done. He worked while contemplating exactly how he'd manage his confession.

He saw Duran leaning against the rail doing nothing and approached him with a smile. "You'll be helping with the painting, Duran. Sam will see that you get the tools you need."

Duran's eyes narrowed. "I know about you. I spent a lot of time on the Lakes and know all about the *Polaris*."

Nick stiffened. "Right now I hope you know all about sanding and painting. Less talk and lounging about would serve you well."

"I wonder if the rest of them know you were responsible for killing your crew."

Nick wanted to punch the man in the nose. He stared hard at Duran, trying his best to show no emotion whatsoever. "Get to work, Duran." He turned and spotted Sam coming toward him. "Sam, Mr. Duran needs help finding the sandpaper. Would you please assist him and then instruct him on his duties?"

Sam smiled. "Of course."

"Cap'n said to join him in the galley. He wants to go over the ship's upkeep."

Nick hadn't heard Tom approach. He turned to look at the boy as Sam ordered Duran to follow him. "You're pretty stealthy."

"You learn to walk soft when you live on the streets."

"Understandable. Say, would you mind getting to work sanding the deckhouse? Captain wants to repaint it today."

Tom gave a two-fingered salute. "I'll see to it, Mr. Clark."

Tom struck Nick as a hard worker with a guarded heart. No doubt the boy had been through a lot in life.

Nick opened the deckhouse door and went down the few stairs into the galley. He hadn't seen it since breakfast, but already it was clean and orderly.

"You asked for me, Captain?"

"Indeed." Captain Wright pointed to a chart on the table. "Are you familiar with the area?"

"I am. I've sailed many a time from Oswego to Chicago and beyond. I've even managed the trip to Duluth a few times."

"Well, this time it's just Detroit, but that's enough." The captain smiled. "Looks to be clear sailing today."

Nick couldn't stand it a moment longer. "Look, I have to say something. I should have spoken up sooner." Nick lowered his head and breathed a prayer that the older man would extend grace. "I've made mistakes in my years on the water. I didn't tell you, but I once captained my own ship. I made a big mistake just a few months back. A lapse in judgment." He shook his head. "No, it was more than that. My pride got the best of me. It cost many lives, but even if it had only cost one, it would have been too many. I saw that a storm had formed to the southwest. It was moving to the northeast across Lake Michigan. I was certain I could stay clear of its path, so rather than take shelter, I kept moving. I had a schedule to keep, and we were already behind."

Nick looked up and found Captain Wright staring straight ahead, his expression stoic.

"The storm shifted and back built. By that time, I realized it was too late. While trying desperately to seek shelter, the wind and waves broke us apart. Eight men drowned. Only me and two others managed to survive."

He waited for Captain Wright to say something, but the captain remained silent.

Nick continued. "My bad judgment cost the lives of those men. It's not something I will ever forget or forgive myself for."

"The book of Matthew says we must forgive others or God won't forgive us. I tend to think that goes for ourselves as well," the older man finally said.

"I'm sorry I didn't tell you, Captain. I was afraid you wouldn't hire me if you knew. I was so anxious to prove myself again, and no one would give me a chance." Nick looked away. "I deeply regret it now and completely understand if you feel the need to put me off the *Mary Elise*."

The older man studied him for a moment, then gave him a smile. "Nick, I knew about the *Polaris*. I remembered it the moment we met and I learned your name. I did ask around about you after I dropped you at the ship that day. I wanted to know if there was anything beyond that I should know. You had a stellar reputation prior to that storm."

Nick tried to swallow the lump in his

throat. The captain had known all along. It was hard to imagine he had known and said nothing. Perhaps it was a test.

"I'm glad you worked up the courage to tell me. That says a lot about your character, son. I've always been a good judge of a man. I credit God with giving me that gift. I like to give a fella a chance to redeem himself, because God knows He's given me enough chances. You're a good man, Nick. I've no doubt of it, just as I've no doubt that Duran is trouble. Still, I feel everyone deserves a chance."

"So I can stay?" Nick asked, feeling a huge sense of relief wash over him.

"I need a mate, and you need to find forgiveness." The captain scratched his graying beard. "I think we'll be a good match." He paused and glanced at the door. "Duran, on the other hand, is more troubling to me. I have a feeling he may cause problems for more than Tom."

"Why did you take him on if you discerned he was trouble?"

"I just felt I was supposed to. I can't really explain it, but he came begging for a job, and I felt the nudge to hire him on. He hadn't eaten in days and was positively desperate." The captain shook his head. "Sometimes it's like that. I want to give him a chance, but at the same time I don't want him causing problems for the men. Just keep an eye open."

"Will do."

"Now, I want to go over what we'll be doing in regard to maintaining the ship. The men were already busy with the hold while we were delayed with the wedding. They did a good job, and no doubt we'll pass any inspection. Besides the painting, there are sails that need mending and ropes that need to be changed out or repaired. I'll leave that to your care."

"Of course."

The captain gave further instructions, but Nick was so relieved over his knowing the truth that he didn't mind at all. There was always a lot of work to do, and frankly, in that moment, Nick felt so happy and grateful that he could have taken it all on himself.

Chapter 3

Elise stretched in bed. The pain was minimal. She'd been certain it would pass quickly, and she was right. Unfortunately, it was too late to prove her condition to anyone. Her father was well underway on his trip to Detroit.

From the look of the light shining in through her window, it must be nearly eight o'clock. She wasn't used to sleeping so late, but the doctor had plied her with medicine again, and it had made her drowsy. There would be no more of that.

She sat up and listened for a moment. The house was very quiet. She sighed, overcome by a sense of mourning to know the *Mary Elise* and her father had sailed away without her yesterday. It left her with such a sense of loss. She'd felt this same sense of emptiness when her mother died.

Mama loved living on the water almost as much as she loved Papa. She'd thought life on a ship to be an amazing and adventurous life—even the close calls. Mama had told Elise once that the storms were terrifying and energizing all at once. It gave her a determination to live each minute to its fullest because one never knew when they'd be called home. She'd been right. God had taken her nearly without warning. One day she was fine, and the next sick with a fever and dying. By the time they'd reached port, Mama was dead, and Elise and her father were left to grieve.

Elise thought again of Caroline and her accusations. Had Elise been trying to mother her sister? She supposed it was possible. She had pledged to care for her father and to see that the crew of the *Mary Elise* had the same care and comfort her mother had provided. She had worked hard to fill Mama's shoes by being good to the crew. She baked cookies all the time, just as Mama had. She fixed the crew's favorite foods and made sure they always had clean clothes. Her workload had more than doubled after her mother's death, but that was all right. Elise knew her father needed her more than ever.

Of course, if Caroline had been there, they could have each taken on duties and shared the load. Was that why Elise felt so angry with her sister? She remembered Caroline's commands to undo her buttons. Her sister was demanding and expected to be cared for. Elise had never had that luxury, but Caroline seemed born to it.

Her sister had never liked living on ships, but for Elise it was home, and she never intended to live long on land. Her father had purchased a little house in Duluth for them to winter in. Uncle James had wanted them to stay with him in Oswego, but the idea of wearing fancy clothes from January to April left a bad taste in her father's mouth. Mother felt the same way, but more on behalf of her husband than herself. When Uncle James mentioned one day that it would be good to have a place to stay in Duluth, Papa had suggested he would get a little house and that would be their winter harbor.

Elise liked the little Minnesota town even though it had tripled in size of late. It seemed with every trip the town grew ever larger. The people were pleasant enough, but it wasn't what she desired. She loved the water—the crack of the sails, the breeze on her face. She felt more at home on the lakes than anywhere else she had ever been.

"I should have been born male," she murmured.

She sank back onto the pillows and

yawned. Maybe she would sleep just a little longer. If the doctor was going to insist on this rest, she might as well take advantage of it. Closing her eyes, she envisioned the *Mary Elise* at full sail, cutting through the water effortlessly. She could hear her father barking out orders and the crew hurrying to do his bidding.

She thought of Nick working at Papa's side. The younger man seemed quite pleasant and kind. His brown hair was sun-kissed, and he cut a dashing figure, even in seamen togs. Yet it was the thought of his twinkling blue eyes that gave her pause. She smiled at the memory of how he had looked at her. She found herself hoping Joe's recuperation would take a little while longer. She wanted to sail with Nicodemus Clark and know him better.

Elise awoke on the third day of her recuperation feeling so much better that she insisted on being let up. On the fourth day, she announced herself healed and called the maid to help her dress. It was funny how self-sufficient she was on the *Mary Elise*, but here she needed constant help. She couldn't even begin to dress herself, given all the layers of undergarments, much less arrange her hair in a manner pleasing to her aunt.

"You look most appropriate now, Miss Elise." Etta, Caroline's former maid, had been reassigned to Elise. She continued to look Elise over for flaws. "Mrs. Monroe will be pleased to see you are well."

Elise glanced in the mirror. The transformation was amazing. She looked nothing like she did when working on the ship. In the pale blue creation she wore, she looked as if she belonged in a grand salon, sharing company with the wealthy of New York. Her already trim waist was cinched even smaller to fit the beautiful gown. The neckline was thankfully modest and trimmed in white lace, and it gave the illusion of her neck being several inches longer than it really was. Etta had done an exceptional job on her hair, despite it always being difficult for Elise to work with. She had managed to create a beautiful arrangement of curls and ribbons of white. It was quite lovely.

But as beautiful as it all was, it would never serve Elise well on board the *Mary Elise*. It had taken well over an hour to get dressed. She grinned at the thought of delaying breakfast for an hour while she fancied herself up, then imagined trying to get anything done dressed like this. There were times on the schooner that she wished she dared to wear pants. How convenient that would be. She had seriously considered purchasing one of those outfits designed with bloomers. Those full, puffed-out trousers for women who wished for more freedom of movement were being marketed all over the city. It might suit her to purchase some and try them out on the ship. At the very least they would help keep her warm when the winds turned cold.

"Your aunt is taking breakfast and asked you to join her if you insisted on being up and about," Etta stated in a formal manner.

"Goodness, it's nearly ten. It seems absurd to eat this close to lunch."

"Mrs. Monroe usually takes her meals this late during the week. The gentlemen are much too noisy when they first rise in the morning. She says they weary her nerves with all their chatter and arguing over what's in the newspaper." Etta put her hand to her mouth, then slowly lowered it. "Sorry, miss. I shouldn't be speaking so."

"Don't fear. I won't say a word about it." Elise headed for the door, and Etta scooted past her to open it.

"Thank you, miss." She gave a curtsy. "I didn't mean to be so excitable."

"Etta, I'm not my sister nor my aunt Martha." Elise smiled. "I'd just as soon we be friends, and friends keep each other's secrets." She winked and chuckled. She couldn't help wondering what the maid would ever do if something truly exciting happened.

Making her way downstairs to the dining room, Elise wished her father could have remained in Oswego just a few days more. He would have seen how quickly she recovered from her injuries. Then she might have been able to sail with the others. Especially the handsome Mr. Clark.

"Elise, I still don't think you should be out of bed," her aunt said in greeting.

"I feel perfectly fine. Very little soreness and moving is quite easy." Elise took a seat opposite her aunt at the table.

A servant was there immediately. "Would you care for something to eat?"

"Yes, I'm famished. Please bring me breakfast and coffee." She smiled at her aunt as the servant went off to do her bidding. "I'm really fine, Auntie. I told Papa there was no need to leave me behind, but he worries about me."

"And well he should. A ship is no place for a woman. I suppose, though, that since you're eating, I shouldn't worry. Your sister hardly ever ate much. She's thin as a rail."

"She'd have had a healthy appetite out on the water. My mother loved being on the water, and so do I. It's a life we were both born to. My sister, however, felt like you do. I suppose there is room for each individual heart on the matter."

"I honestly don't know what to think. My friends were completely shocked by what you do, but they had to admit you handled yourself remarkably well at the wedding. They said they might never have known you were a . . . well, a . . ."

"Ship's cook?" Elise wanted to burst out laughing. Her aunt's tone suggested Elise might as well have sold her soul.

"Yes." Her aunt took a sip of her tea.

The servant arrived with breakfast and placed a plate of eggs, sausages, and fresh slices of fruit before Elise. He returned to the kitchen and came back with a rack of toast and a pot of coffee. He placed the toast in front of her, then poured her coffee. Lastly, he brought her cream and sugar.

"Thank you. This looks delicious." She beamed a smile at the servant.

He returned the smile and looked to Mrs. Monroe. "Would you care for something else, Mrs. Monroe?"

She shook her head. "No, I'm fine. Just leave us."

He nodded and gave a curt bow before exiting the dining room. Elise bowed for a brief prayer, then dug into the food with great gusto, not feeling the need to put on an act for her aunt. Meals on the ship were usually quick and without much concern for order. Her father insisted on a prayer being said before they started in, but otherwise they were hardworking men, and he didn't try to rein them in too much when it came to their mealtime and moments of rest.

Often at mealtimes Elise was given the wheel so the men could converse at the table regarding any problems. She thrilled at those moments when she controlled the ship. The feel of the wheel in her hands was like no other. She still remembered the first time her father had let her take charge. She hadn't even been tall enough to see over the wheel, not that it would have helped. The deckhouse was directly in front of the wheel, making it impossible to see what was in front. Instead, there was usually someone to call out the details in tight spaces. Otherwise, the compass was used. Nevertheless, in that instance, her father had stood at her back the whole time, giving her guidance.

"So with that in mind, we might as well set up a dinner party," her aunt was saying.

Elise put down her fork. "I'm sorry. What did you say?"

"I said that since you're feeling recovered and your father won't be back for a couple of weeks, we should arrange a dinner party for you to meet eligible young men."

"Oh, I hardly think that needs to happen." Elise reached for the cream and added a liberal amount to her coffee. "I won't be here all that long, and there's no sense in giving a false impression."

"A false impression?"

"That I'm looking for a husband. I'm not." Elise smiled, then sipped her coffee.

"But you're twenty-five. Every single young lady should be looking for a husband. It's her destiny. You should have chosen one a long time ago."

"I'm much too busy helping Father to marry anyone."

"But that isn't appropriate. I've never approved of you being raised on a ship. Why, when your sister arrived here, she was such a hoyden."

"Now, Auntie, you must surely exaggerate. Our mother was firm that we learn all the social graces she had learned. We knew how a proper table was set and how to have acceptable conversations. We could dance before we were teenagers, and we learned to embroider and speak French as well. Mama was quite thorough in our upbringing, including our religious training."

"And I've no doubt she did a good job,

given what she had to work with. No, my criticism isn't of her, but there are other things to learn as well. For example, how to stroll a garden with a potential suitor and how to ride in a carriage or use a sidesaddle. You can hardly learn those on a ship."

Elise tried to imagine riding a horse on deck. A hint of a grin formed on her lips. "No, I suppose not. Still, I thought Mama did quite well."

"She did, bless that woman. Rather than let you climb like monkeys in the ropes—"

"Rigging," Elise corrected.

"Yes, rigging." Her aunt shook her head. "Well, she did what she could, and given the circumstances, she did a good job."

"I'm glad you feel that way." Elise was very protective of her deceased mother's memory. She wanted very much to follow her mother's example and be a positive influence to all, both on the ship and off. Her mother had been a wonderful influence on the seamen. She had taught more than one to read, and she always took time to sew for them and even led them in musical entertainment from time to time. The men all loved her, and she made life on the *Mary Elise* and other ships quite pleasant.

"You must admit, however, you were deprived of certain things."

"Such as?" Elise popped a piece of sausage in her mouth. She hoped that by chewing she wouldn't be as likely to say something she'd regret.

"Well, just as I've said. You didn't learn to ride or entertain. You've never been to the opera or ballet. And you were surrounded by ruffians rather than gentlefolk."

"Did I embarrass you at the wedding, Aunt Martha?"

Her aunt put down her teacup. "Of course not. Goodness, child, I'm not trying to make this a reprimand."

Elise smiled. "I'm so glad. Perhaps we can focus on the positive, then."

"That's what I want for you as well. A few dinners and a garden party or two, and you'll see just how positive things can be."

"I wish you wouldn't go to the trouble."

"It's no trouble at all. It will be the perfect way to celebrate the summer. There are several invitations I haven't yet replied to, and I'm long overdue to host a dinner. I will see you have the right clothes to wear. Thankfully you're very nearly my size. I have several gowns I might lend you. With a little luck, you just might find the perfect suitor. Which is another thing you can hardly do on board a ship."

"There are plenty of men on our ship.

Should I have wanted a husband, I could have taken my pick. Most of them have proposed at least once."

The color drained from her aunt's face. "But those men are laborers. They would hardly suit."

Elise let out a silent sigh. The entirety of this visit, her aunt had been quite firm about finding Elise a husband. Even at Caroline's wedding, it seemed that was Aunt Martha's focus rather than the bride. The older woman had pointed out various young men who were friends of her sons Randolph and Louis, suggesting Elise might let her know if she favored any one man over another. She wasn't likely to be dissuaded from her plans now.

On Saturday night, the Monroe house was brimming with people. Many were friends of Randolph and Louis, but an equal number were young ladies accompanying their parents. Elise wore a gown of pale pink. The skirt was a silk overlay with taffeta underneath. With every step, the material announced her coming. The shoes Aunt Martha had lent her were a size too small, and her corset had been cinched so snug that Elise could barely eat two bites at dinner.

The men paid her an abundance of attention, just as Aunt Martha had hoped. Louis acted as her guardian and host after dinner, introducing her first to one friend and then another. The single young ladies, in hopes of capturing attention for themselves, hung around Elise as if they were the dearest of friends. It was comical, and Elise might have pointed it out to Louis and shared a hearty laugh but for fear of embarrassing Aunt Martha and Uncle James.

"You look quite beautiful, Elise," her uncle declared, coming to join them. "There will be some entertainment in the music room and perhaps dancing, if I know your aunt."

Elise couldn't hide her expression, and it drew her uncle's attention.

"Goodness, child, you look as if I'd suggested we slaughter puppies."

"I suppose I feel the same disdain at having to dance with all of these men. It might be just as much a misery." She glanced around the room. "It's too hot to dance, anyway."

"I must agree with you on that." He leaned close. "Just humor your aunt, and before you know it, you'll be sailing away."

Elise smiled. "I'll do my best."

A four-string quartet accompanied by

the piano struck up a quadrille for their first number. Louis brought over a young man.

"Elise Wright, this is my good friend Matthew Henderson."

"Mr. Henderson," she said, giving a slight curtsy.

"Miss Wright." He gave a small bow. "I arrived late and missed out on dinner. It's my absolute pleasure to meet you. Would you do me the honor of dancing with me?"

"Of course." She allowed him to lead her off to join the other couples.

"I was happy to hear that you're still in town," he said as they performed the dance steps. "I wanted to meet you and didn't"—he made a turn and finished when they came back together—"I didn't have a chance."

Elise wasn't certain what to say, so she smiled. "It's very nice to meet you."

The dance left little time for talking, but upon its conclusion, Mr. Henderson tried to draw her to the refreshment table. Thankfully, someone else cut in to collect his dance. Before the evening was through, Elise had danced with ten different partners and was exhausted.

"You don't move like a woman who was just in an accident," Louis teased during another quadrille.

"But I am starting to feel like one. I'm exhausted."

Louis stopped dancing and pulled her away from the others. "You should have said something." When they reached the arched entryway, he continued pulling her along. "You should have a rest. There's no sense in letting those vultures pick your bones."

She laughed. "I hadn't thought of it that way, but now that you mention it, I do feel rather picked over."

"They're all just very impressed that you're so beautiful and dance nothing like a sailor." He stopped in the library and dropped his hold. "There. You should be safe here."

"What will they say about my absence? Your mother is determined to have me married off before midnight."

This time it was Louis's turn to laugh. "That's Mother. She's working on me as well. There is a distinct desire in that woman to see us all married."

"Where you and Randolph are concerned, she probably wants grandchildren." Elise smoothed her skirt. "Whereas she just wants me off the lakes, lest I further embarrass the family."

Louis nodded. "I'm sure you're right. I have to say there is something about your life that I envy."

"You should come along sometime. I'm sure Father would be more than willing to have you on board. It's hard work, but he could certainly teach you. And it is your father's freighting company, so you should learn the business."

"He's mentioned that before, as well, but I've never really wanted to go. I have a fear of the water." He leaned in and added, "I can't swim."

Elise leaned closer in a conspiratorial manner. "I'll keep your confidence."

Louis grinned. "Thank you."

She glanced down the hall, hoping she could manage the escape. "Please tell your mother I'm sorry."

"She'll be forgiving. I'll tell her you realized that you'd pushed yourself too hard— that the injuries from the accident were making you uncomfortable. She'll be more than understanding, but you might have to stay in bed tomorrow."

Elise grinned and gave a sigh. "Well, it's not my choice, but better than dancing and carrying on with would-be suitors."

"You go ahead up the back stairs, and I'll let her know. Just ring for your maid. I'm sure it will be fine with everyone. Nobody wants to be responsible for causing you additional pain." He smiled. "Sometime when the moment is right, perhaps you can tell me of your great adventures on the lake. Maybe I'll change my mind about wanting to come along."

Elise thought of the last storm they'd been in. "Most of my adventure stories would do nothing but dissuade you, but I'll be happy to share them nonetheless."

He gave her a mock salute and went to inform his mother while Elise made her way through the house to the back stairs. She breathed a sigh of relief at being able to return to her room and put on her bedclothes. At least they weren't confining and uncomfortable.

Etta was already there, cleaning and putting away clothes. "Oh, Miss Elise, you're back so early."

"Is it early? It feels like the middle of the night. I have a headache."

"I'll prepare you a bag of herbs and lavender. The scents help so much with the pain."

"I do wish you'd help me get out of this gown first. Please." Elise kicked off the dancing slippers and immediately sighed in relief. "That feels so much better. I'm afraid my feet are not as small as Auntie's."

Etta helped her out of the gown and corset. Elise pulled on her dressing robe, then let Etta guide her to the dressing table. The maid began pulling pins from the elaborate coiffure with expert skill. It was as if she'd memorized the position of each pin. It wasn't long at all until she was brushing out Elise's black hair.

The headache had moved down into Elise's neck, and she did her best to sit still while also shrugging her shoulders up and down to ease the tension. Etta finally took pity on her.

"You get into bed, Miss Elise, and I'll fetch the herbs."

Elise did as she suggested, and almost immediately her muscles began to relax. Closing her eyes, she was surprised not to see a room full of dancing strangers. Instead, she saw the face of Nick Clark staring back at her. His smile coaxed a grin from her. She imagined him extending his hand for a dance. The thought of dancing with Nick mesmerized her.

If Etta returned with the herbs, Elise never knew it.

Chapter 4

"Thank you for coming to the funeral with me," Elise told her uncle, leaning close. "I know Papa would want me here as a representative. Joe was like a brother to him and another uncle to me." Her eyes filled with tears. "It won't be the same without him."

"I'm glad I could be here for you, my dear." Uncle James patted her arm.

Elise dabbed her eyes with the lace-edged handkerchief her aunt had lent her. She tucked the cloth away, then folded her gloved fingers together, trying her best to control her emotions. She gazed straight ahead at the front of the church. Joe's casket had been placed just below the pulpit. The pine coffin wasn't at all ornate—just a simple wooden box.

She leaned close to her uncle again. "I feel so sorry for his widow and family. Five

children will grow up without their father."
She shook her head. "I don't know if Mrs.
Brett can do anything to earn a living, especially with children who are still so little. It's
not fair."

Word had come after a week that the *Mary
Elise*'s first mate had died. Joe Brett's leg had
been gangrenous and impossible to save. Elise
knew her father would be devastated. They
were good friends. Everyone loved Joe, including Elise. He had been a good man worthy of their admiration and trust. He would
be sorely missed.

The preacher got up and spoke of Joe's
death coming much too soon. He described
Joe's good character and his faithfulness to
his family. There were murmurs and nods
from the congregation, most of whom were
from the lower levels of society. Elise felt out
of place in her aunt's black bombazine. At
least this was her summer mourning gown,
so the silk was not blended with wool. The
heat was already stifling, and in the small,
crowded church there was no breeze from
the open windows. Elise fanned herself, but
it did little good. She could only imagine that
Uncle James's suit was unbearable.

It was hard to concentrate on the preacher's words. The last funeral she'd been to was
her mother's. Elise could still hear the waves

lapping against the ship. Her father had put them out in the middle of Lake Superior. Mother had chosen it long ago for her watery grave.

Each of the men had stood at attention around the canvas-wrapped body of her mother, including Joe. Each man said a few words in praise of Mary Wright. By the time it was her turn to say something, she had forgotten all of her memorized tributes.

"She was the best of mothers. She taught me so much and led me to the Lord." A few of the men had murmured *amen*, as Elise's mother had led them to faith in Jesus as well. "I cannot imagine a world without her loving kindness and gentle smile. She will be so missed." Tears had slipped down her cheeks as she touched the canvas. "I love you, Mama."

Then it was her father's turn. Bill Wright had stood with a stoic expression on his face. He read from the Bible and then closed the book. "She was my dearest friend and love. She was a helpmate like no other, following me from ship to ship, lake to lake. She loved the sea, and she loved me and her girls." He smiled. "She loved the lot of you too."

Those who had truly known her wiped away a tear or two. Elise could feel the love they held for her mother and their captain.

Later, when they slipped Mama's body over-board into the surprisingly calm Superior waters, Joe had wept. And now Elise sat here, doing the same for him.

"Man is but a vapor, here and then gone," the preacher continued, "yet our memories will serve us long after to say of Joseph Brett, 'He was a good man.' Let us pray."

Elise took out the handkerchief again as she bowed her head. She wiped her tears, knowing Joe would chide her not to spend her time in such a manner. The pastor prayed for comfort and mercy, but Elise couldn't pray. Comfort and mercy meant very little when a family couldn't provide for itself. She'd spied holes in the shoes of Joe's eldest boy. His widow's dress was threadbare and patched. She nudged her uncle as soon as the pastor said *amen*. "Uncle, could I have forty dollars?"

He looked at her oddly as they rose to file out of the church. "Whatever for?"

She let go a heavy breath. "Joe's widow. I'm sure Papa would pay you back. It's for one final month's pay."

"Of course."

She waited until they were outside to offer further explanation. "Papa already paid him, but I'm sure the doctor took a good portion of that. I doubt Mrs. Brett even knows what she has left to work with. I know my father would want me to do this on his behalf."

"I don't doubt what you say." He reached into his coat and drew out his wallet. He gave her two twenty-dollar gold coins. "Please tell her to come see me if she has any other needs."

"Thank you, Uncle James." She kissed his cheek.

"Don't bother to mention it to your father. He needn't pay me back." His face was full of compassion. "We're partners in this, and I want to do my part."

Elise smiled. "You're a good man. Mama always said you were her rock until Papa came along."

"I miss your mother more than I can say. I was grateful your father agreed to let me put up a stone for her in the cemetery. Sometimes I walk by there and just pause to remember her. She was so very dear."

Elise nodded. "It's harder on some days than others. I wake up and I think surely it was just a bad dream. The days are so empty without her. And poor Papa . . . he misses her so." She shook her head and looked at the ground. "He hasn't been himself since."

"I could tell at the wedding. His joy is gone. He smiled, even laughed, but it never seemed as sincere."

"He says he lost a good part of his heart

the day he lost her. He moves forward without any pause, but his grief is obvious to me. Probably to anyone who really knows him. That's why I hated to let him sail without me."

Her uncle patted her black sleeve. "He'll be all right, Elise. He has a strong faith."

She knew that much was true but wasn't sure it was enough. She had heard of people dying from heartache and sorrow. She feared her father very well might be one of those.

After the graveside prayers were concluded, Elise made her way to Mrs. Brett while her uncle motioned the driver to bring around the carriage.

"Mrs. Brett." Elise smiled and extended her hand.

Joe's widow was probably no more than ten years older than Elise—if that. She looked at Elise with watery eyes. "I can't believe he's gone."

"Nor I. My father has lost his right hand. He will be truly sorry to hear of this."

"Your father is a good man. Joe always said he was the best to work for."

Elise nodded. "This is Joe's final month of pay." She slipped the two coins into the widow's hands.

Mrs. Brett's eyes widened. "I thought he had his month's wages when he came home sick."

"No. The way Papa arranged things, there's always one final accounting." Elise smiled. "If you need anything, please get in touch with my uncle, James Monroe, at the shipping office. He wanted to make sure you knew he was there for you."

Tears came to her eyes anew. "Oh, this means bread and cheese for the children. Thank you so much. I wasn't sure what we were going to do."

Elise gave her a hug. "We're family. I'm sure my father will come by to see you when he's back in port."

"I don't know how I'll live without my Joe. He was such a good man." The widow wiped her tears with a black handkerchief. "My poor children," she sobbed, and Elise embraced her again.

"You will be in our prayers, Mrs. Brett. You needn't bear this alone."

The older woman let Elise cradle her for several long minutes. It was all Elise could do to keep from breaking into tears herself. Then Mrs. Brett's mother came to comfort her daughter, and Elise bid them both good-bye. She made her way to the carriage and was grateful when the driver helped her up.

"I feel so completely exhausted." She took her seat opposite her uncle. "All of this just reminds me so much of Mama."

"I thought the same," her uncle replied. "I wish I could have been at the ship service. I know Caroline felt the same way."

"I know, but since the doctor was unsure what had caused the fever, he thought burial should be immediate."

"I do understand. As I said before, it's comforted me to have a stone that I can visit. Would you like to see it?"

Elise hadn't considered it before now, but she nodded. "I would like that very much."

Her uncle gave the driver the new instructions. "It's a beautiful location in the cemetery. A stream runs through that portion, and it has a view of the lake. I thought of how much she loved the water."

Elise thought it sounded perfect.

They reached the cemetery only moments later. The driver returned to open the carriage door, but this time Uncle James alighted first and helped Elise down.

"You can see how well-kept the grounds are. Your grandparents are buried here, and one day it will be my resting place as well."

"It is a lovely place. All of the trees keep it cooler," she said as they strolled past the tombstones and mausoleums.

They climbed a slight rise, and at the top, her uncle stopped and pointed to the stone that bore her mother's name. "This is for Mary.

Over there are our parents' resting places, as well as a plot for Aunt Martha and me."

Elise admired the lovely grassy area with engraved marble stones marking each place. "I pray it remains empty for years to come."

"Amen," Uncle James replied. He sighed and returned his gaze to his sister's stone. "I think your mother would have approved. The water is in sight, and as a child, she loved shade trees."

Elise could imagine her mother lying in the grass to stare up at the branches. "Mama once told me she loved to lie under trees and look up through the leaves to the sky. She said that when the sun shone down through the leaves just right, it reminded her of stained-glass windows in church."

"I remember her telling me that as well." Uncle James smiled.

"It was thoughtful of you to include a spot here for her. It's such a pity her mother and father disowned her after she married Papa. They didn't even give him a chance to love them."

"No." Her uncle shook his head and stared off toward the lake. "At first, I didn't want her to marry him either, but she begged me to give him a chance. I could see their love for one another was sincere. Your father never asked for money or any other form of assistance. He was too proud, I suppose. He always supported her and kept her happy, however. I once asked Mary if she missed anything from her old life, and she told me she only missed her family. I mentioned that once at dinner to Mother and Father, and their only comment was that she should never have left, then. It was clear they were unwilling to forgive her."

"They never forgave her?" Elise couldn't hide her surprise.

"On their deathbeds they did, but of course it was too late. Your mother was far away and had no idea they were dying."

"But Mama told me she never held it against them. The way she talked, I thought they had made up long before."

"That's the way your mother saw it. She held nothing against anyone. She told me as much whenever I snuck away to see her when the *Mary Elise* was in port. She gave me her assurance and love. I'll never forget when she proudly presented you. Your father had delivered you on the ship."

"Yes. He always said I was a water baby." She smiled. "I could swim before I could walk."

The older man laughed. "I've no doubt of that."

Elise felt her spirits lift. "It was such a

good life, Uncle. I don't want you ever to worry that it wasn't. I'm sure my sister told you horrible stories of her misery, but I have loved my life at sea—even if I didn't learn how to stroll in the garden or ride a horse."

"I can see my Martha has been after you. She believes it's her job to secure you a husband."

"Well, she can relax her search. I don't plan to marry. I promised Mama I would take care of Papa. Until he no longer needs me, I am bound to see to his needs."

Uncle James frowned. "I doubt your mother meant for you to forsake true love in order to care for an aging parent. Your father would feel terrible knowing you refused a chance for the kind of love he had with your mother in order to take responsibility for him."

Elise had never thought of it that way. "Well, who knows? Perhaps God will provide me with a man who will be happy to serve on the *Mary Elise*." An image of Nick came to mind. She smiled. "It is possible."

Chapter 5

After enduring three additional dinner parties and a Fourth of July celebration, Elise was more than ready for her father's return. Hearing that the *Mary Elise* was in port left her eager to return to the ship and get back to her routine. She could only imagine the mess the men had left in the galley. Donning her simpler clothes, Elise instructed Etta on packing.

"I won't need any of these fancy dresses or beautiful undergarments and shoes. Please pack them for storage in the attic or wherever else my aunt would choose."

"Yes, miss." Etta started picking up the discarded gowns that lay across the back of a chair.

"I'll put the clothes I want to take with me

on the bed and can pack them myself when
we get back."

"Yes, miss."

Elise knew Joe's death was going to shock
and devastate her father. They'd both had
such hope that, after a couple of weeks of rest,
Joe would be back on his feet. She whispered
a prayer for him and pulled on a straw bonnet.

"My father and I will be going to pay our
respects to Mrs. Brett, if anyone asks after
me." Elise knew her aunt Martha would be
appalled that she was wearing a simple serge
skirt and blouse. She didn't want her aunt
totally shamed, however, so she grabbed a
pair of crocheted gloves.

"Yes, miss," Etta said for the third time.

Elise had just reached the top of the stairs
when she heard Mrs. Cavendish, the housekeeper, greet her father.

"Good day, Mr. Wright. Welcome back."

"Thank you. How's Elise?"

"I'm just fine, Papa." Elise bounded down
the stairs in a most unladylike fashion. "I told
you I wasn't really hurt. Just bruised." She
threw herself into his arms and hugged him
close.

"It's been a long trip without you," he said
as they embraced. "Meals were definitely not
up to your standards."

She pulled back and smiled. "Well, now you have me back."

"What say we go over to Joe's and see if he's ready to be back on board?"

Elise couldn't hide her look of sadness. She shook her head. "I'm so sorry to tell you this, Papa. Joe didn't make it."

"He's dead?" Her father dropped his hold on her and seemed to search for the nearest chair.

He looked so pale that Elise feared he might be ill. She held fast to his arm. "I was going to suggest we go see Mrs. Brett right now."

He nodded. "Yes, let's do that. The walk will give me time to consider all of this."

They headed out the door. Elise pulled on her gloves while her father re-secured his billed cap.

"I can hardly believe he's gone. It's a good thing I asked Nick to stay on."

"You did?" She tried not to sound too enthusiastic. After all, Papa had only just learned about his friend and former first mate. She reined in her happiness. "That was certainly wise."

"I really like Nick. He's a hard worker and gets along with everyone. Well, most everyone. I hired on another fella, Booker Duran, as a seaman. He hasn't found his footing yet, and he's managed to make each man mad over one thing or another. I'll tell you more about him later." He shook his head and lowered his gaze to the ground. "It seems everyone I care about is leaving me."

"I'm not. You're stuck with me," Elise teased. "Oh, before we get there, I nearly forgot." She paused to make sure she had her father's attention. "I asked Uncle James to give me forty dollars for Joe's final pay. I know you already paid him his salary, but I thought this could be like a bonus of sorts. They had to pay out so much to the doctor that I was afraid there might not be anything left." They rounded the corner onto the cobblestone street where Joe's family lived.

"You're a good-hearted woman, Elise. Your mother would have done just the same."

That comment pleased her more than she could say. "Uncle James was happy to do it and said you shouldn't try to pay it back. He feels that since you're partners in shipping, he has as much a right to help as you do. He had me tell Mrs. Brett that she could come to him with any need."

"Your uncle is much like your mother." Her father paused as they reached the Bretts' house. He drew a deep breath. "This is a hard task to face, but it must be done."

After their visit to Joe's widow and children, Elise talked her father into doing some shopping for the ship. She'd have everything delivered and given to the second mate to oversee until she and Papa were back on board. Shopping with her father was something she enjoyed. He had often accompanied her mother when Elise was younger. Mother always preferred to pick out her own vegetables and fruits, as well as breads and meats.

"We're bound for Duluth on this next trip, so we'll need plenty of food. I don't want to make any stops because you ran out of something."

Elise laughed. "I've made a list while waiting for you to return. Uncle James told me we were to be back on our regular schedule, taking coal to Duluth and bringing back grain."

"It's a good living and steady work. Folks always need coal and grain," her father said.

They went to one shop after another until Elise had arranged for everything, including a pair of bloomers. Her father, despite grieving the loss of his first mate, smiled at the scene she described.

"I can even climb the rigging if need be. Can you imagine the surprise of the men when I cast my skirt aside?"

"You'll be a sight for sure. They'll no

doubt worry that you're paradin' around in your underclothes."

She hooked her arm through his. "They're full and dark blue. They look nothing like undergarments. Say, can we spare some money for a dish of ice cream?" she asked, spying a little shop just ahead. The day was quite warm, and the iced treat sounded refreshing. Plus, she wanted a little more time alone with her father.

"Of course we can. For you, I'd find a way even if I didn't have the money."

They had been at the shop for just a few minutes when Elise saw Nick walk by outside. Her father rapped on the window to get his attention. When Nick saw them, a big grin broke across his face, and he quickly joined them.

"I need to talk to you. Care for a dish of ice cream? My treat," Papa said.

"I would. Thank you." Nick took a seat between Elise and her father.

Papa went to the counter, and Elise explained the situation. "I should let my father tell you, but our first mate Joe Brett . . . passed away. You are definitely needed now more than ever."

Nick frowned. "The leg worsened?"

"Yes. The infection moved quickly to the blood. The doctor couldn't save him. Papa saw Joe's widow just an hour ago."

Her father rejoined them. "I hope you like it with chocolate syrup," he announced.

"I do," Nick replied and looked to Elise.

"Oh, he knows how much I like it. I sometimes make my own chocolate syrup on the *Mary Elise*, and we eat it on cake instead of me making frosting."

It was only a few minutes before a young lady brought three dishes of ice cream and syrup on a tray. "Will there be anything else?"

"Not for the time," Elise's father replied. The girl gave a curtsy and exited with her tray under her arm.

"I'll ask grace," Papa said. He prayed a blessing on the food, on his companions, and on the ship.

"I hope you don't mind, Papa, but I told Nick about Joe."

Her father nodded. "A total and complete surprise. He was doing so much better. I honestly expected to return and find him playing horsey with his children. They're so young to be without a father."

"What a tragedy."

"She buried him in the churchyard, so no lake burial. The fellas will be grieved over hearing of his death."

Nick stirred his ice cream as it melted. "I will endeavor to serve in his place, although from the sounds of it, I'll have big shoes to fill."

"Aye, but I know you'll manage quite well," Papa told Nick.

"I need to write a letter to my father's housekeeper. My father and I aren't on speaking terms for a reason much too complicated to go into now. Do you know if there's a stationery store nearby where I might purchase paper?"

"Come back with us to Uncle James's house," Elise suggested. "We have to go there to collect my things and tell them all goodbye. I'm sure Aunt Martha will have all sorts of writing paper. If not her, then Uncle James. Oh, and I need to cut some herbs from their garden, so you should have plenty of time to pen your letter."

"That would be great."

Nick smiled at Elise, and she felt the breath catch in the back of her throat. No other man had ever made her feel this way. She had thought perhaps she was unable to feel charmed by handsome suitors.

Of course, Nick wasn't a suitor. He was someone she would work with, like the rest of the men on the *Mary Elise*. Nothing more.

Nick hated to think that his good fortune had come at the loss of someone so dear to Captain Wright. The big man was tenderhearted and held compassion for the people in his life. He'd even been kind and forgiving toward Booker Duran, who had been nothing but difficult.

Mrs. Monroe was more than happy to help Nick out with his needs. She even invited him to stay for supper, but of course he would have to dress appropriately. She told him a servant would come and direct him to where he could change once Nick had finished writing his letter. Nick accepted, not really knowing why. The company was pleasant enough, and Elise would be there, and she had such a great disposition. But Nick had put this grandiose life behind him. How would it feel to go back to a proper table after ten years of shipboard life?

He thought of his father as he began his letter to the Clark housekeeper. She kept him apprised of what was happening in Boston. It was the only way Nick knew anything about his family. When his mother was alive, Nick and his sisters had been quite close, but his father had forbidden the girls to contact Nick or for him to speak to them. He had easily cast this demand aside, but his sisters feared the same disinheritance Nick had received and refused to write. From time to time they'd mention something to Mrs. Schmitt, but never in a direct way. He hated his father for doing that to him, all because he refused to go into his father's textile business. Remembering this only made him angry. His father had never been an amiable man, but Nick hadn't known what a tyrant he could be. Not until he put Nick out of the house and his life.

Mrs. Schmitt, on the other hand, had been like a mother to him. She had been in his father's service for over forty years, starting as a scullery maid and working her way up. When Nick's mother died, Mrs. Schmitt stepped in to offer comfort and stability in lieu of their father's cold, almost callous behavior. She had mothered Nick and his sisters and had been a connection to home long after his father had disowned him.

Dear Mrs. Schmitt,

I only have a short moment to pen you this letter. All is well with me, and I pray it is with you and the others. I was happy to learn that my sister Deborah was safely delivered of her first child. It touched me deeply that she named the babe after our mother.

The weather has been fair, and my trip to Detroit passed in safety. Unfortunately, the man I was hired to temporarily replace has passed away. It was a great loss, and I'm sure the men will be devastated to learn the truth. The captain, however, has asked me to step into the position permanently. I will take over as first mate on the **Mary Elise.** *This is a comfort to me, since I feared I might never be allowed to work on a ship in any capacity, much less as first mate. Captain Wright knows the details of what happened on the* **Polaris** *and does not hold it against me. Oh, the blessing of a truly forgiving soul.*

The young woman I wrote to you about is now to join the ship once again. Elise Wright is the captain's daughter and is such a beauty. She has coal-black hair and blue eyes that seem to take in the world at once. I hope to know her better. She will cook for the **Mary Elise.** *Unlike many of the oceangoing crews, women are not forbidden on our lake ships. In fact, many a wife or sister or daughter cooks for the crews of the ships. They aren't considered bad luck at all and instead prove themselves to be a blessing.*

He wrote a few more lines about the new job and his happiness and then asked after Mrs. Schmitt and his father. He knew she would be honest with him about the problems they were facing or the victories. Just as he was signing his name to the letter, a feminine scream split the air.

Nick went to the open French doors. The sound had come from the garden just outside. He made his way out and saw a young man trying to take liberties with Elise. He rushed forward to deal with the matter, his anger building by the second, but without warning Elise twisted the man's arm and flipped him to the ground.

"I warned you to leave me be!" she yelled.

Nick reached her side, in awe of her response. "What's going on here?"

"This friend of my cousin thought he could force a kiss." Elise turned to regather the herbs she must have dropped in the scuffle. "I'm sure Uncle James will be quite unhappy."

Louis appeared. "What's happened?" He looked at his friend on the ground. "Franklin, whatever are you doing?"

The man got to his feet and dusted off his backside. "I thought she was a housemaid."

"And that gave you permission to accost her?" Nick asked.

Franklin shrugged. "The maids are here to serve."

Elise had collected her herbs and looked

at her cousin. "I have been sailing all of my twenty-five years. Born and raised on a ship with a full crew of men, and never once have I ever been attacked by any of them. Your upper-society friend put his hands on me in a way no one has ever done before. Is this what your wealth and societal rules teach?"

"Not in this house, Elise. I'm truly sorry." Louis gave his friend a harsh reprimand. "Franklin, that was completely uncalled for. Apologize."

"I didn't know she was your cousin, Louis. Look at her. She's dressed like a servant."

"It shouldn't matter how she's dressed," Nick replied before Louis could. "She's a lady and deserves to be treated as such. Perhaps you need another lesson?"

The younger man paled. "No. I'm sorry, Miss . . ." He looked to Louis.

"Wright. Her name is Elise Wright," Louis answered.

Franklin nodded. "I'm sorry, Miss Wright. I overstepped my bounds."

"You most certainly did, but I accept your apology."

Louis put his hand on Franklin's shoulder. "Let's get you out of here." The two men headed for the French doors.

Nick turned to Elise. "Are you certain you're all right?"

She flipped her single braid back over her shoulder. "I'm fine. I learned early on to defend myself."

"Where did you learn to do what you just did?"

"Papa." She grinned. "Isn't it grand?"

Nick laughed. "I doubt Franklin feels the same way."

She giggled. "No, I believe he was much too surprised to find me rejecting his touch. I think before we leave today, I shall teach Etta how to perform this trick."

This amused Nick even more. "It's wonderful you can take care of yourself."

"But equally wonderful you were ready to come rescue me. Thank you." She motioned to her apron full of pickings. "I shall have to sort these out in the kitchen. I'll see you at dinner." She started for the kitchen door. "Don't forget to find my father. He'll help you dress in whatever clothes my aunt has laid out for you. It can be quite daunting."

Nick gave a nod. "I grew up dressing formally. I won't have any trouble with it so long as your aunt can furnish the clothes."

Elise stopped and came back to where Nick stood. "I think she has whole rooms full of clothes just for such an occasion. I believe this so firmly"—she lowered her voice to a whisper—"that should I request a wedding gown, she would simply snap for the maid to retrieve one. Probably more than one."

Nick momentarily imagined her dressed in white satin and lace. He smiled. "I'm sure you're right."

She shrugged. "So am I."

She left him with the vision of her gowned for a wedding. Nick thought it odd that such a vision should haunt him. He would need to tighten his grip on his emotions. After all, the young woman had said more than once that she never intended to marry, and to be honest, Nick had no plan for such things either. He could provide very little as a disgraced ship's captain and the disowned son of a textile-industry baron.

Chapter 6

It was so good to be home on the *Mary Elise.*
Ever since she'd departed for her uncle's
house and sister's wedding, Elise had missed
her galley and the tiny cabin she called her
own. As the grandeur and richness of her
uncle's house faded away, Elise felt her spirit
calm. This was where she belonged. Here she
didn't have to worry about wearing uncomfortable clothes or putting on airs. Here was
a world she understood and loved. Why did
Caroline so love that other world? There was
nothing there to remind her of their parents.
No pleasant childhood memories or amus-
ing anecdotes. They had stayed with their
aunt and uncle on occasion growing up, but
most of what Elise remembered was feeling
confined and limited by the rules. And while
there were also rules on the ship—life-and-

death rules—they never seemed as imposing or unnecessary.

Leaving her bags on the bunk bed, Elise went to inspect her kitchen. To her surprise, she found everything in order and clean. She smiled. The boys knew how she kept things, and they had worked to do the same. It touched her heart that they cared enough to try. She opened the ice chest and found new blocks of ice and all the meat she'd ordered.

"I got the stuff you purchased and put it away where it belongs," Sam Matthews, the second mate, announced coming into the galley. "You shouldn't have any trouble finding things."

"Thanks so much, Sam. How's it been without me on board?"

"Boring without your company and torturous without your good food." The older man smiled, revealing several missing teeth. "Although I was surprised to learn that young Tom can make a pretty decent fish chowder. Made good biscuits too. Said you taught him."

"I did." Elise reached for her apron. "He learns fast. I told him he might need those skills one day. I'm glad he remembered."

"Well, I for one am just glad to have you back. The rest of us don't cook quite so good."

She smiled. "We'll have a bunch of favorites in the days to come. I stocked up on all the necessities and then some."

"Don't I know it. I was the one putting it all away."

Elise reached over and felt his arm. "Seems you had such a workout that you developed muscles. I guess I'll have to bake you a reward."

"Peach cobbler?" he asked.

She grinned. "But of course. What other reward is there for you?"

"Hmm, chocolate cake, spice cake, cherry pie," he said, counting off on his fingers.

"Go on now." She pushed him toward the door. "I have to check things over, and then I just might bake cookies."

Sam grinned and threw her a salute. He exited the galley in haste, knowing better than to challenge Elise's orders.

Humming to herself, Elise retrieved the herbs she'd picked in Uncle James's garden. She hung them from corded twine her father had attached to the ceiling for just such purposes. They hung just low enough for Elise's five-foot-four height to manage. Seeing them reminded her of her encounter with Louis's friend. He had been absolutely appalling, the way he tried to put his hands all over her. When Louis had related to Uncle James what had happened, he told Louis that Franklin was no longer welcome, even if his father did own the bank. She was grateful her menfolk weren't like that but could only imagine that other high-society men were. People with money seemed to think there was nothing they weren't entitled to.

Elise felt the stove. It was mostly cold. She opened the firebox and found just a few dying embers and a lot of ash. She went quickly to work cleaning out the box, careful to put the ash in the ash can. She'd dump it in the harbor momentarily, but first she'd build a fire. Once that was accomplished, Elise noticed she needed more wood. She'd find Tom and get him to bring it. But before she could do that, Tom appeared, as if knowing she had need of him.

"I'm so glad you're back, Elise," the boy declared. "Things aren't the same without you."

She gave him a hug. "I missed you too. I was just coming to find you. Would you please dispose of the ashes and then fill the woodbin?"

"Sure." A mischievous grin touched his lips. "Are you gonna bake cookies?"

"I am." She chuckled at the little jig he did as he pulled out his harmonica and began to play.

Elise laughed and clapped her hands in

time. "I've missed that too," she said when he brought the song to a close.

"That new man doesn't like it when I play. He's threatened me more than once."

"New man? You mean Nick?" Elise asked.

"No, I like Nick. It's that Booker Duran. He's just hateful and mean."

"Well, you tell him to come talk to me or Pa. We'll set him straight." She handed him the ash can. "Now, hurry."

He repocketed his harmonica. "I'll be back before you even have your dishes out of the cupboard." He left, taking the pail of ashes but forgetting to close the door behind him.

Elise quickly closed the door, laughing at Tom's enthusiasm. At the stove, she opened the firebox to add what little wood she still had on hand. It wasn't long before she had worked the embers into flames. The warmth felt good. The day had been hot, but the evening had turned a little chilly.

Warming her hands like this reminded Elise of the fall and winter months. She shivered even though it wasn't that cold. Sailing in the latter months of the year was always worrisome. There were enough dangers on the lakes without adding winter's onslaught. Most seamen were superstitious and felt there were cursed months because they were when the deadliest storms occurred. Thankfully the men on the *Mary Elise* were mostly Christians who weren't quite so concerned with old wives' tales and traditions. It seemed to Elise, however, that it was impossible to free them of all superstitions.

Thomas returned with the ash pail full of kindling dangling from his arm and a stack of wood that seemed far heavier than he should manage. Still, he was strong and able-bodied and managed the entire thing without complaint or a request for help.

"I saw two rats comin' up the gangplank onto the *Mary Elise*. That's a good sign," he said as he carefully stacked the wood in the bin.

Elise was familiar with the adage that rats boarding a ship meant the crew would have good luck, while rats deserting the ship was a sure sign the ship would sink before journey's end.

"You know we're blessed because we're in God's hands." She ruffled his hair. "Thank you for the wood. Now, get on with your chores so I can bake cookies."

"Sure thing, Elise."

Knowing that the men were going to want a late evening snack after being without it for two weeks, Elise pulled out her mixing bowl and went to work mixing up a batch of cookies. She perused her recipe box and found a recipe that her great-grandmother had passed down to Mama. The men were crazy for these molasses cookies, and they were easy and quick to bake.

Elise added more wood to the fire and then went to work on the cookies. She mixed eggs and butter, then poured in the right amount of molasses. With that accomplished, she blended her dry ingredients with a variety of spices—in heavy amounts. The men loved plenty of flavor. She put everything together, stirred it thoroughly, and set it aside. The oven still wasn't quite hot enough, so she busied herself by rolling the dough into balls before adding more wood. Finally the first batch of cookies were in the oven, and Elise could move on to the next thing on her list.

After a couple of hours, her father showed up.

"Smells good in here." He grabbed a couple of cookies from the platter on the table. "I missed this while you were gone."

Elise went to him and stretched up on tiptoe to kiss his cheek. The act still required that he bend down to meet her. She hugged him close. "It's so good to be back on board."

"Your mama used to say the same thing."

"Other than winters, there's only been a

handful of times I've been gone for more than a night or two. I don't want to be stranded on land again." She pulled away and went to the oven. "Time for the last batch to come out. Then the roast goes into the oven, more wood into the firebox, and I go to bed."

Her father sat down at the wooden table and began to eat his cookies. "It's been a long day. Funny how the days spent at your uncle's house seem more exhausting than ones on the lake."

"That's because although Uncle James is family, his world is not ours."

"No, that's for certain." He frowned as she came to the table. "I heard what happened in the garden."

Elise sat down beside him. "I'm fine. I suppose Nick told you?"

"No, actually Louis apologized for his friend, and when I asked what he was talking about, he told me everything."

"I've lived all of my life at sea in the company of men other than family, and not one of them has ever acted in such an accosting manner. This young man was raised in 'proper' society and acted far more uncivilized. He thought I was a maid and therefore his behavior was acceptable. He said something like, 'Maids are supposed to serve.' I showed Etta how to do that flip you taught me. She told me the men who visit the house often try to take liberties with the female maids."

"That is appalling. If he was my son, I would have whipped him good for such behavior." Her father shook his head and started on his second cookie.

"You would have had to beat Mama to it." Elise chuckled. "She never tolerated anything but the highest respect. I remember she once had you fire a man for his lewd behavior onshore."

"I told her what the men did on shore leave was their business, but she told me it would only be a matter of time until he was trying such things on board. I couldn't have that happening."

"You've always looked after us, Papa. You've kept us safe. Now that Mama's gone, I promise I will take good care of you."

"But you should have a family of your own. A husband and children." Although he spoke the words, Elise heard no conviction in his voice. She knew he was happy to have her by his side.

"It's in God's hands, and I believe He's called me to take care of you." She did her best to stifle a yawn. "I need to be going to bed."

"So do I. Some of the men haven't returned from town, but Nick has the watch, so I'm going to catch some sleep." He got up and kissed the top of her head.

Elise waited until her father was in his cabin before gathering a handful of warm cookies. She left the galley and went outside, where she found Nick walking the deck. He looked deep in thought.

"I thought you might like some cookies. I just baked them."

"Sounds wonderful," Nick replied. He took the four cookies she offered. "Smells delicious."

Elise couldn't help but smile. Nick made her feel safe. It used to be she only felt that way with her father. Maybe it was because Nick had helped rescue her the day of the carriage accident. No matter what the reason, she was certain he was a good and honorable man.

"Tastes good too," Nick said after his first bite. "We sure didn't have treats like this when you were gone."

"No, as much as the boys love cookies, they won't bake for themselves. I've even tried to teach a couple of them."

Nick chuckled. "I can only imagine how that went."

She laughed. "It was a real mess."

They fell silent for a moment while Nick popped a whole cookie in his mouth.

"They're a good bunch of guys. I'm sure

you've already figured that out." Elise leaned against the rail and looked out at the dock. "They're like an extended family to me. And most have been with us awhile. Tom is like a little brother. He once told me he never felt truly loved until coming to the *Mary Elise*. Isn't that an awful thing?"

"Indeed it is. It's a terrible thing not to know love."

"He's been on his own since around the age of six. Orphaned and living in the streets." She shook her head. "It breaks my heart to think of a little child roaming the streets to find food, trying to find somewhere safe to sleep and keep warm." Tears threatened to pour, so she changed the subject. "Of course, losing Joe is hard on Papa because they've been together for so many years. Joe was like an uncle to me. Each one of the men is like an uncle or a brother."

"I doubt you'll feel that way about the new man, Booker Duran. His nature is so selfish and self-assured. He doesn't even try to be nice. He feels it's completely acceptable to hurt other people. He insulted young Tom, and when the other men told him to stop, Duran said the boy was too soft and needed to learn how to be tough."

"He had many years to learn that lesson as an orphan on the streets," Elise said, already feeling some disdain for this Mr. Duran. "I hope the men set him straight."

"I think they tried, but Duran isn't the type to care."

The sound of men coming aboard ended their conversation. Elise even stepped away, as if they'd gotten caught doing something wrong. She might have laughed out loud, but she didn't want to draw attention to them.

She didn't need to. The seamen noticed the couple right away.

"Don't try to woo her, Nick," one of the men declared. "She's taken a vow never to wed."

The other man shook his index finger at Nick. "She's married to the *Mary Elise*."

Elise crossed her arms. "And to think I spent the evening baking you cookies."

"Cookies!" The men gave her a bow. "We'd best check those out."

"They're better than any I've ever had," Nick admitted.

"What kind?"

"Molasses," Elise answered before Nick could. "They're on the table."

The two men quickly headed off for the galley.

Elise suppressed a yawn. "I suppose I should get to bed. Dawn will be here before I know it."

"Thanks for the cookies. I appreciate the thoughtfulness of bringing them to me on watch."

Elise nodded, hating to leave his company. She wanted to explain what the men had said about her taking a vow never to wed. She wanted to know more about him. What he liked and disliked. What his life's goal might be.

"Well, ain't she the beauty," a strange voice called out.

Elise hadn't realized just how much Nick had consumed her thoughts. She looked across the deck and found a big man sauntering toward them. He was more than a little tipsy. "How about giving me some attention now? No doubt the first mate has had enough."

"There are cookies in the galley. That's all the attention you'll get from me. Who are you, anyway?"

"Booker Duran, at your service." He gave an exaggerated bow and nearly fell over.

"He's the new man," Nick added.

"Then he ought to know my father doesn't allow for drunkenness on the ship." She glared at Duran, remembering what had been said earlier.

"A man can't help having a few when he's back in port. No ship's captain can tell a man what to do while he's ashore."

"But you aren't ashore now." Elise kept her tone stern. "He might discharge you if he hears about this."

"Then maybe he shouldn't hear about it." Duran raised his brows and gave her a look that suggested she keep quiet.

Duran stepped closer, and Nick cupped Elise's elbow. "You should probably go," he whispered against her ear.

She nodded. She didn't usually let anyone boss her around except for her father, but something about this situation told her it was the better part of wisdom.

"No, she should stay. I want to convince her to keep my secret," Duran slurred.

Nick pushed her toward the deckhouse and put himself between Duran and Elise. "Get to your bunk and sleep this off. Otherwise, I'll have Elise go get her father right now to dismiss you."

Duran started to take a step toward him, then seemed to think better of it. "I didn't want any cookies anyway." He stumbled around and moved off toward the bow of the ship.

Elise headed to her cabin but gave Nick one last glance over her shoulder. He was still watching Duran. There was an air of danger in that man, and Elise was glad someone was keeping track of him.

Booker Duran had been told the captain
had a fetching daughter, but they had lied. She
wasn't just fetching, she was a great beauty.
The kind of woman a man might fight to the
death to keep by his side. Of course, Booker
had no desire to keep her by his side—but he
wouldn't mind having a little sport with her
now and then.

"You were right," he said, stumbling to
his berth in the forecastle.

The four men already in bed gave him
an odd look. "What are you talking about?"
Sam asked.

"Miss Wright. She's a beauty. Ain't never
seen a woman like that in all my years. I'd like
to get to know her better—if you know what
I mean." He laughed.

Sam rose up out of bed in one fluid motion. "You leave her alone, Duran. She ain't
for the likes of you."

"I'd say that's up to her. She just needs a
little coaxing."

"You bother her, and you'll answer not
only to her father but to every man on this
ship."

"Including that first mate? She seems
rather familiar with him."

"I don't even want to hear you talk about

her," Sam said. "Not to mention you're drunk. That isn't tolerated here. You had time off and could have drunk your fill early on so that you'd be sobered up by now. It's going to be reported, and you'll have to answer to the captain."

Duran surprised them all by grabbing hold of the old man. "You'll be keepin' your mouth shut if you know what's good for you. That's all I've got to say about it."

The last of the crew came to ready themselves for bed. The only exception was Ollie Johnson. He was putting a bag of horehound drops away in his locker in preparation for leaving. "I've got the watch, so sleep well, children."

"'Night, Ollie," a couple of men muttered.

The other men fell back in their beds, but Duran had yet to doff his boots and outer clothes. He ought to teach them all a lesson, but he was much too tired, and his watch would come in four hours.

He sat on his bunk and pulled off his boots while the men settled in for the night. He despised each and every one of them and would happily have killed them in their sleep, but with the law already on his heels, it was best to leave well enough alone.

Booker eased back in his bunk without undressing. He was too tired. Besides, it wouldn't be the first time he'd slept in his clothes. Most of the men kept some or all of their clothes on when out on the lakes, but in port, the men usually got a bath and clean clothes and slept as unencumbered as possible. Not Duran. He never knew when he'd have to be on the run again. He wasn't going to drop his guard and get caught. He'd done all he could to see to that—changing his name and getting away from his hometown, where he'd killed a man in front of a dozen witnesses. It wasn't as if he hadn't killed before, but this time he let his emotions get the best of him, and instead of planning it out for a dark alley or a midnight visit to his victim's house, Duran had pulled a knife at a gaming table and ripped away at the cheating player to his left. He could still see the look of surprise on the man's face when the knife sank deep into his heart.

It made Duran smile as he faded off to sleep.

Chapter 7

After breakfast, the tug deposited the *Mary Elise* in Lake Ontario, and they put Oswego behind them. Elise was grateful to get back to her routine. There was a certain comfort in keeping to the same schedule she'd followed for twenty-five years. Of course, there had been changes from when she was a child and worked part of the day at schoolwork. She now filled those hours with laundry, sewing, and occasionally a little reading.

"Elise, I want you to take the wheel while I speak to all the men at lunch," her father declared. He grabbed a cup of coffee and tossed it back, not even bothering to see how hot it might be.

"All right. I'll be glad to." Her father often had her take the wheel when he wanted to

116

speak to the entire crew. It was pretty much standard procedure while in open water.

"By the way, did you see Mr. Duran drunk and disorderly last night?" he asked.

She hadn't intended to say anything. She figured if it needed to be told, Nick would report it, as any first mate should. Still, she wasn't going to lie. "I did."

Her father nodded. "And was he out of line with you?"

"Well, not exactly. He called me a beauty and said he'd like me to give him some attention. Nick put him in his place before he could say or do much more."

Papa poured himself another cup of coffee. This time he only took a sip. His expression said he was pondering a problem. Elise had seen him like this many times.

She put her hand on his arm. She would never tell him what he should or shouldn't do about one of his men. She didn't like Duran, but she didn't wish to be the cause of him being given the boot. "It's probably hard for a new man to find his place. I don't much care for Mr. Duran, but I wasn't harmed by him."

Her father looked down at her. "Thank you for your honesty. There's something about him that makes me want to give him a chance. I was like him before I met your mother and Jesus. Hard and unyielding. Foul and unfit. I was unwilling to surrender myself to any authority. I thought my own authority was all I needed. Your mama changed all that in me." His eyes grew damp. "I sometimes fear I'll go back to being what I was without her."

"No, because you still have Jesus. He's the one who made the real change."

"I know that's true," he admitted, "but sometimes it seems that it was her who brought it about. She had a way of calming me and helping me take another look at a situation. She taught me patience and kindness . . . concern for others."

"She may have taught it, Papa, but Jesus was its originator, and Mama herself would have told you that."

He rubbed his graying beard. "Yes, she did exactly that. You're so much like her." He drew a long drink from the mug and set it on the table. "All right. I will reprimand without condemning. Take the wheel from Nick once you get lunch on the table and Tom rings the bell."

Elise smiled. "Will do."

The huge pork roast was tender when Elise sliced into it. She'd long ago learned to slice up meat before putting it on the ship's table. Men left to their own hand would take huge chunks and leave their fellow seamen to fill up on vegetables and bread. Sometimes even now they were tempted to take more than one portion, but Papa would usually remind them of allowing everyone to have a share and then worry about having more after that.

Once the meat was ready, Elise checked the stovetop with its railed ridge to keep pots from sliding off. The potatoes and green beans were ready, as were the cabbage and ham hocks. Elise salted everything one last time. She didn't bother to put the food in pretty bowls as they had done in Uncle James's house. Her mother usually served everything in the big pots due to the way some of the men handled things. It saved much wear and tear on her dishes. She placed the pots in the center of the table. What they didn't eat for lunch they'd get for supper, with the exception of the meat. She knew there wouldn't be a bit of that left and had already started roasting four chickens for the supper meal.

With everything prepared for lunch, Elise pulled off her apron and headed to the wheel just as eight bells rang to announce it was noon. Outside, the wind was strong and pulled at her carefully pinned hair. She stepped back just inside the door, reached into the pocket of her skirt, and pulled out a scarf. She deftly secured it on her head before trying again to reach the wheel.

"I'm here to take the helm," she told Nick.

"The wind is moving us right along. Are you sure you're strong enough to handle things?" She gave him a look with a raised brow that caused Nick's eyes to widen. "All right, then. I see that you are."

She laughed. "I've been doing this a long time. If there's trouble, I know my father is just ten feet away."

"I'll be there too."

"Yes, but I can count on my father." She hadn't really thought through her words before replying and hoped Nick wouldn't take insult.

"I hope you know you can count on me too." His voice was soft and his expression almost tender.

She met his gaze even as the men started filing past to head into the galley. "I think I do know that." She smiled and took hold of the wheel.

"Keep her headed due west," Nick said, grinning.

Elise glanced at the binnacle, which held the ship's compass. "Aye, aye."

He chuckled and made his way into the galley. Elise couldn't help but like him. He was charming and gentle, not at all condemning of her participation on the ship.

"Well, we meet again, pretty lady," Duran said, pausing at the door of the deckhouse.

"How about you have a drink with me tonight after my watch is through? We can get to know each other better."

She looked the big, burly man over. "There's no drinking allowed on the *Mary Elise*, Mr. Duran."

"Ah, I know the rules, but rules were made to be broken." His lips twitched behind his reddish-brown beard. "And I can think of quite a few I'd like to break with you."

The deckhouse door opened, and Elise's father appeared. His gaze fell on Duran. "You're holding things up, Duran. Next time you won't eat."

Duran's eyes narrowed. Elise didn't like the way he looked at her father. She took a step back, putting the wheel between herself and the men. If Duran decided to take a swing, she didn't want to encumber her father in any way.

"Sorry, Cap'n." There was no sincerity in Duran's voice. He brushed past her father and down the deckhouse steps.

Elise's father looked her way. "Are you all right?"

"I'm just fine, Papa. Go have your lunch and meeting."

"Well then, hold the course." He hesitated only a moment, then followed Duran.

Elise shuddered. She liked Duran a little

less every time she encountered him. Mama would say just to take it in stride—that some men had known a worse existence than others. She'd admitted that their behavior could be quite foul, but that answering hatred with kindness was important in order to change hearts.

"I suppose I'm not doing a very good job at this, Lord. Help me be more like my mother. She always seemed to understand the right thing to say and do. I feel like a poor substitute."

She looked off to the side of the ship. It was nearly impossible to see what was coming with the deckhouse blocking her view. She would steer the open waters based mostly on the compass, but at times she moved to the side to get a look across the expanse, just in case another ship should cross her path. In this case it wasn't likely, but Elise never took her job for granted. The very lives of the men on board were in her hands. She wasn't about to risk them, nor let her father down.

Poor Papa. He was so weary and sad these days that she didn't want to do anything to add to his misery.

"Help me, Lord." She heaved a deep sigh.

"Losin' Joe was a hard blow," the captain began as they ate their lunch. "However, I've no doubt Nick will do us a fine job."

"If he doesn't sink the *Mary Elise* like he did the *Polaris*," Duran muttered.

"I believe I have the floor for now, Mr. Duran. If you wish to speak to the men later, that can be arranged."

Duran glared at Nick. "Everyone already knows the truth."

Nick had no doubt they did. If not from the stories passed around in port, then for certain Duran had made it known.

"And no one cares," the captain said, making his position clear. "I've damaged and even lost a ship myself, just as many other captains have. You can't always predict what will happen, and sometimes our choices aren't the best. From our mistakes . . . we learn. If any man here at the table can say he's made none, I'll put him off at the next stop because he'll be a liar. Mistakes I can tolerate when a man learns and makes amends. Liars get no tolerance from me whatsoever. Now, is there anything more you wish to address, Mr. Duran?"

Duran shook his head and focused on his food. Nick felt strangely unburdened by the encounter. The captain continued to his next topic of order, and before long and without

the interjections of Duran, the meeting concluded and so did lunch.

Nick made his way out to see that the men
got back to work. The captain wanted the
inside bow of the ship scraped and painted.
There was plenty of work to keep the men
busy, and the sailing was fair.

Tom was busy cleaning the deck when
Nick passed by. "How goes it, Tom?"

The boy paused in his work. "It goes
well enough. Can I ask you something, Mr.
Clark?"

Nick smiled. "Of course."

"Well, I heard Mr. Duran talkin' about
the *Polaris*. He said you deliberately ran her
on the rocks. I just wondered what really happened."

"I suppose I'm guilty as charged. The
ship was breaking up, and I tried to get us to
safety so as to save the lives of my men."

Tom nodded. "I figured it must have
been that way." He turned away and resumed
scrubbing the deck.

Nick started to go, then called back to the
boy, "You're doing a mighty fine job, Tom."

The captain had a good crew in the men
who worked for him. Nick had been impressed with their loyalty and the gentle way
they acted around Elise. For all intents and
purposes, the men treated her like a little

sister. They were protective, seeing to it that neither Nick nor Duran got out of line where she was concerned. As the newest men on board, Nick supposed it would be that way for some time. At least until Nick could earn their trust. Only time and working together would see that come about. Trust wasn't easily given by seamen.

When Nick signed on to his first ocean schooner ten years ago, the second mate had been put in charge of him. The man had been in his late forties and had nearly as many years' experience working on board ships. He had shown Nick the way of things, teaching with great patience and swift reprimand for repeated mistakes. He quickly became like a father to Nick, which had eased the loss of his family and the anger he held toward his own father.

That ship ran regular trips from Boston to Barbados with other stops along the way. But when it was announced that they were soon striking out for California, Nick resigned his position, not wishing to put that much distance between him and his family. Even if his father had disowned him, he didn't want to be that far from home. The second mate suggested he get a job on a Great Lakes ship, and Nick had put it to prayer and done just that. It had been a wise decision.

He went to check in with Captain Wright and found him thoughtful at the helm. The older man didn't seem to notice Nick for some time, and then he began to speak as if they'd been talking all along.

"Some days pass so slow, and others speed by."

"That's true enough," Nick replied. "I just thought I'd let you know that it's clear ahead as far as the eye can see."

"Those wisps of clouds are suggesting a weather change. Won't be long before autumn is here. In six weeks or so, it'll be September."

Nick glanced at the skies. "Aye. And a few months after that, the winter freeze."

Captain Wright's voice became distant. "When I was a boy, I hated autumn. I knew that meant school, and soon the water would freeze over. My father was a fisherman, so the water has always been my life." He pulled himself out of his daydreaming. "What about you? Where'd you grow up?"

"Boston. My father was in the textile mill industry." Nick shook his head. "I could never get interested in it. I suppose one of the biggest reasons was that it was confining. I wanted to be outdoors and free. If you've never been inside a textile mill, you should know it is as far from the outdoors and free-dom as anything can be."

"I've never been in a mill," Wright admitted.

"Hot, humid, and dangerous. They have to keep the place humid for the sake of the threads, so they nail the windows shut so the workers can't raise them for air. It's unbearably hot. I worked there one summer when I was sixteen. My father was certain I would develop a love for the industry, but it wasn't to be."

After a moment of silence, the captain nodded. "I couldn't live like that either. I suppose that didn't sit well with your father."

"No. He disowned me. He wasn't even willing to send me to college for an education. Just told me to leave—that if I wasn't going to follow with family tradition, then I was no longer part of the family."

"That seems harsh."

Nick remembered the sound of his father's voice and the look on his face as if it were yesterday. "It was. I think he honestly thought I would change my mind. I might have, too, if he'd been less cruel in his attitude."

"So you ran away and joined a ship?"

"It wasn't exactly like that. He put me from the house with nothing but the clothes on my back and the money in my pockets. I was eighteen and sure I knew everything." Nick smiled and shook his head. "I learned very quickly just how ignorant I was."

"I can imagine. My bad attitude brought me to that place. God interceded, however, just as I'm sure He did with you. He has a way of doing that." The captain smiled. "Thank God He does."

Elise and her father sat at the galley table with their Bibles in hand. Each evening, if possible, they took time after supper to share a moment of Bible reading and prayer. They had done this as a family when Mother and Caroline were still with them, and Elise insisted they continue.

"Where are we reading from tonight?" Elise opened her Bible and looked at her father.

"Philippians chapter two." He opened his Bible to the marker he'd put in. "I was studying this recently and thought it very good."

"Shall I read, or will you?"

"Go ahead. Start with verse fourteen."

Elise followed the words with her index finger. "'Do all things without murmurings and disputings: That ye may be blameless and harmless, the sons of God, without rebuke, in the midst of a crooked and perverse nation, among whom ye shine as lights in the world,'" she read, then stopped. "How hard that is. I complain all the time."

"When? I never hear you," her father said with a hint of amusement. "You rarely ever complain or grumble."

"Perhaps I do it in the silence of my mind, but it's there. These verses suggest that as a child of God I should do all things without such an attitude, otherwise I'm no different from the rest of the world and cannot be a beacon of light for God."

"It's hard not to grumble and complain, especially when things go wrong." Her father shook his head. "Your mother always had a way of keeping me in good spirits. When I'd start in on how bad we had it, she'd make me stop and think about the good things first."

Elise smiled. "Yes. She did that with me as well. 'Count your blessings before listing what's wrong,' she used to say. I was always frustrated by that when I was younger because it felt like she didn't care, but now that I'm older, I understand. I would give this long list of blessings, and then she'd tell me to go ahead and tell her what was wrong. I might have been frustrated with Caroline for something, but having listed my sister as a blessing, it was hard to bring up my complaint against her."

"Your mother had a way of making sense and simplicity out of difficult matters. Not that these verses are difficult. They're pretty straightforward. The world spends all its time in conflict and complaint. Nothing is ever large enough or small enough or busy enough or restful enough. People get sick and complain, yet do the same when they're healthy. They fight wars and complain, then seem out of sorts during times of peace and loudly issue their opinions."

"I wonder what my life would be like if I truly did all things without murmurings and disputing?" Elise considered the problems of the day and could name a half dozen times she'd complained. "I pledge to try harder. I am confessing my sin and ask you to help hold me accountable, Papa."

He smiled. "I accept the job, for I believe it will be an easy one."

"I think you'll be surprised."

Chapter 8

It was said that a three-masted schooner needed a crew of only five. The captain, the cook, and one man for each mast. Nick was glad Captain Wright saw it differently. The *Mary Elise* had a crew of eight regularly and sometimes as many as ten. Bill Wright was unlike any man he'd ever met. Nick supposed it might have been his Christian faith, but he'd known other men of faith who were captains. It might have been his deep love of family that made him extend that same attitude to his crew. Whatever it was, Nick felt that the older man genuinely cared about each and every man in a way that ran deeper than mere employer to employee. He was even generous in patience with Booker Duran, who was quickly losing the respect of every other man on board.

"Stop playing that cursed thing," Duran demanded across the deck.

Nick frowned. He knew Duran hated young Tom's harmonica playing. The boy was pretty good, however, and the rest of the men enjoyed it and even asked for it in their personal time.

"Pay him no mind, Tom. Play." This came from the second mate, who had stood up to Duran on more than one occasion.

There was momentary silence, and then Tom started up again, this time playing a jaunty jig. Nick appreciated the boy's resilience and willingness to continue. Duran could make a person feel nervous, even threatened, just by his large size.

Nick glanced at his pocket watch. The second mate would soon take the helm, and Nick would inspect the work being done at the bow. Without warning, however, Tom's music stopped, and a commotion began. The men were shouting, and there was the sound of a scuffle. Nick hurried to where Duran and Russ Davis, a wiry, all-muscle man in his forties, were rolling around on the deck. The other men were doing what they could to clear the area of paint and brushes.

Motioning to Sam, Nick wondered if young Tom's harmonica playing was at the bottom of this.

"Aye, Mr. Clark," Sam said, coming to his side.

"Go take the wheel." Sam nodded and

hurried away. Nick turned back to the rest of the men. "Stop this now!" He'd never had reason to bellow in such a way before.

"What's going on here?" roared Captain Wright. It rather surprised the men, and everyone came to attention except for the two on the deck who were still fighting. Nick wasn't surprised the altercation had drawn the attention of the captain. The captain nudged him. "Take hold of Russ. I'll get Duran."

It was a risk to jump into the fracas, but Nick did as instructed and pulled Russ backward. The seaman fought against him.

"Let me go. You didn't see what he did." Russ tried to squirm away from Nick, but Nick pulled him farther away from Duran.

Duran raised his fist to Captain Wright, then seemed to realize who held him and lowered his arm. He went still as the captain fixed him with a stern stare.

"Stop this now," the captain ordered. "And somebody tell me why we have fighting on my deck."

Russ calmed as he became aware of what was going on. Nick let go his hold, and Russ stepped forward. "I'll tell you, Cap'n."

"Very well, go ahead." Wright still had a grip on Duran's collar.

"Duran threw Tom's harmonica over the side."

Wright let go of Duran. His stoic gaze turned into a frown as his eyes narrowed. "Is this true, Duran?"

"What if it is? I hate that sound. It was givin' me a headache. I asked him to stop."

"You demanded it, don't you mean?" said Ollie Johnson.

"No matter. He wouldn't stop, and you all just encouraged him to continue."

Nick glanced at Tom, who stood beside Ollie. The scrawny kid's face was red in anger and maybe embarrassment at being the center of attention.

The captain shook his head. "Duran, I don't tolerate such behavior on my ship. I'm putting you off at the next town."

Duran seemed to consider this a moment, then shook his head. "I didn't mean to lose my temper, Captain. I'm askin' for another chance. I have a powerful headache, and it made me lose my reason for a moment."

This turn of events surprised Nick. Duran didn't seem the type to beg anyone for a second chance.

Captain Wright looked to Tom. "What do you say, Tom? Do you think Duran should get a second chance?"

Tom glanced from left to right. "I guess so."

"He's caused more than his share of trouble," Ollie added.

The captain shook his head. "I didn't ask for your opinion, Johnson. This is Tom's call."

Duran looked at the boy. "I'll give you money to buy another harmonica."

"Well, Tom?" the captain asked.

"Let him stay. I guess I'd want the same consideration if I made a mistake."

"Weren't a mistake," Russ muttered under his breath.

"Good," the captain declared. "It's settled, then. There will be no more fighting. We have a deadline to get this coal to Duluth, but I won't hesitate to do what needs to be done. Even if it means stopping. Is that understood?"

"Aye, Captain!" the men said in unison, with the exception of Duran. He seemed in agreement, but he watched everyone around him with the eyes of a hungry tiger. Nick didn't trust him at all. He always seemed to be up to something.

"Duran, I want you to apologize to Tom," the captain added.

Nick held his breath. Duran wasn't the type to apologize to anyone. All of the men turned to Duran, awaiting what he would do. To everyone's surprise, Duran didn't try to get out of it.

"Sorry there, Tom. Like I said, I had a headache, and sometimes that makes me lose control."

The words were sincere enough, but Nick

didn't believe them. There was a look in Duran's eyes that suggested next time it would be the boy going overboard instead of the harmonica. Nick vowed then and there to keep a close watch on the big man.

"Nick, come have a cup of coffee with me," the captain said once the matter was concluded.

They walked in silence to the deckhouse. Captain Wright noted Sam at the helm and gave him a nod. They made their way to the galley, where Elise was busy rolling out pie dough.

She beamed at her father. "Hello, Papa." She stopped long enough to give him a big kiss on the cheek. "How's my favorite man?"

"Not too bad. We had to break up a fight."

"A fight? On the *Mary Elise*?"

Nick could tell by her tone that this was a most unusual event. Her father grabbed a mug and gave one to Nick. "Aye. The new man threw young Tom's harmonica overboard. Russ didn't care for that, and the fight was on."

"Well, I guess so," Elise declared. "I wouldn't have tolerated that either. How dare Mr. Duran do such a thing? How heartless."

"He said he had a bad headache," her father replied. "It was a mistake and he apologized, although how sincerely remains to be seen. He said he'd buy Tom a new harmonica."

"And well he should, but what if that

harmonica had been a gift or an heirloom?" Elise shook her head. "There'd be no replacing that."

Nick poured himself a cup of coffee. "I just don't trust him."

The captain came and filled his cup as well. Nick caught Elise's compassionate gaze as she watched her father. "Some men have a hard time finding peace within themselves."

Her father nodded and took a seat at the far end of the table. "That's for certain."

Nick sat and sampled the coffee. Elise certainly had a way with making it. It always seemed to taste fresh and strong but without the bitterness that often came in the stoutness of the brew.

"Well, I'll get back to my work, or we'll have no pie for dessert tomorrow." She left them to their discussion.

Nick smiled and watched her walk away. He found her intriguing.

"She's a fine woman," her father declared as if knowing full well where Nick's thoughts had taken him.

"She is. I'm surprised she can keep such a softness to her spirit." He looked at the captain, not even trying to hide his feelings. "She's unlike any woman I've ever known . . . save maybe my mother."

"Her death must have been hard for you."

"It was, but even harder on my two younger sisters. I was fourteen, but they were only twelve and nine."

The captain nodded with the cup halfway to his mouth. "That's a time girls need their mother, to be sure."

"My father had little patience for the tears and questions. He ended up sending us all to boarding school in Virginia. He said it had already been planned, but I know Mother would never have allowed it. I once confronted him about it when I was eighteen. He admitted he had lied and then asked me what purpose it served for me to have him admit it."

"And what did you reply?"

Nick remembered the moment as if it were yesterday. "I was angry at him and myself. I wasn't sure exactly why I'd asked the question, since I already knew the answer. I told him I really didn't know. Maybe I was hoping to embarrass him. Make him accountable. Maybe even force him to issue an apology. He told me I was a fool to concern myself with it when there were so many more important issues between us. It taught me something about forcing people to admit their lies."

"What was that?"

Nick met the captain's eyes. "A true liar doesn't care about getting caught. He'll have some excuse for you because he's already validated it for himself. Satan is the father of lies, and the lie itself never matters to him. He's after the finished result."

"That's true enough. Rather like our Mr. Duran. He doesn't mind giving a false apology. The end result is all that matters to him." Captain Wright tossed back the rest of his coffee. "I wanted to give him a chance to change. God gave me a chance and a good woman, and I did come to my senses. He could do the same for Duran."

"He could."

"But you aren't overly hopeful of that happening, are you?"

"No." Nick glanced at the end of the room where Elise hummed and sliced up apples. "I think he's dangerous and deceptive. Furthermore, I think he enjoys causing an uproar. He loves the chaos. He'll play the men against one another at the first opportunity."

"And that's where we differ. I always tried to avoid people and conflict. I wanted no part of them or their troubles. I would have been content to just manage my own affairs and have nothing more to do with people."

"That, I understand. When I left home at eighteen, I was bitter and angry at my father's actions. He disowned me and demanded I leave the house, and I did. Not even saying good-bye. When I signed on to my first ocean schooner, I had no idea what I was doing or how hard the work would be. The first week my hands bled and swelled. I never had enough sleep and swore I'd never adjust to the schedule. The second week was hardly any better, but after a while, the routine became normal, and there was something healing in the ocean air and rhythm of the ship in full sail. As time went by, the men around me became family, and thoughts of home were replaced." He stopped and cradled his cup. "Sorry. I didn't mean to go on."

"Don't apologize. I like knowing my men. A captain needs to know his men, wouldn't you agree?"

"I would." Nick stared at the coffee in his mug. "He needs to know them as well as he knows the ship—because they are the ship."

Elise finished her duties by placing a large platter of cookies in the center of the galley table. After baking the pies, she had baked several dozen cookies in between washing up dishes and pots. She had a regular routine for everything, and when things went just as she planned, it was as if the world was in perfect order.

She put away her cleaning supplies, then locked the pantry. She trusted the men for the most part to leave the pantry foods alone, but there was no need to make it a temptation or challenge. Duran came to mind, and as if thinking of him could make him materialize, he walked down the stairs and gave her a smile.

"And there's our pretty little cook. Seems we never get any time alone. God must have heard my prayers."

"Oh really, Mr. Duran. You pray?" Elise asked after securing the lock. She turned to face him. "There are cookies on the table and coffee on the stove."

"I was thinking something more hearty would do the job. Maybe a sandwich or two."

"You know there are some leftovers on the shelf and other foods that you're allowed to eat."

"But I don't see any of that ham we had for supper. I think that would make the perfect sandwich."

"That ham has been designated for another dish we're having tomorrow."

She tried to sweep past him, but he took hold of her and pulled her into his arms. "Maybe I'll just nibble on you instead." He leaned down as if to kiss her.

Elise stomped down on his booted foot and pulled away.

Duran just laughed. "You don't weigh enough to make a dent in my boot." He tightened his hold and bent her backward. "I've been looking forward to this."

She saw that his intent was to kiss her lips and turned away with a scream. Duran shifted his hold and put his hand over her mouth, but thankfully her single call for help was enough. Several of the men showed up en masse, making it hard for them to pour into the galley at once. Seeing the problem, they were shocked into inactivity, except for Nick and her father.

"Unhand her," Nick said, pushing Duran aside.

He released Elise so fast that she didn't have time to get her footing and started to fall. Nick easily caught her and pulled her away from Duran.

Elise watched as her father stood nearly nose to nose with Duran despite Papa being a couple of inches shorter.

"My daughter is not to be handled. Do you understand me?"

"We were just engaging in a little fun." He winked at Elise. "I came for a midnight snack."

"Well, seeing as how it's not even close to midnight, I'd suggest you get back to whatever it is you're supposed to be doing. Or I can find something for you."

Duran was unmoved by the underlying threat. "Beggin' your pardon, but it's my own time, Captain."

"Then it doesn't include my daughter." Papa continued to stare the man down. "If we're going to have continuous trouble with you, Duran, then I'm going to have to put you off the ship. This is your final warning. Do you understand?"

Duran's jaw clenched, and his eyes narrowed. It was easy to see the hate in his eyes. Elise wished her father would just get rid of him once and for all.

She felt Nick's hand tighten on her upper arm and glanced up at him. He appeared as angry as Duran. He looked down at her as if to ask what she wanted, and she smiled. "Your hold is steady but tight," she whispered.

He seemed to realize all at once what he was doing. "I'm so sorry." He let her go.

The other men began to file out of the deckhouse, seeing that Elise was all right. Papa, however, wasn't finished with Duran. Once everyone but Elise and Nick had gone, he pointed his index finger at the seaman.

"You had better understand me. My daughter is off limits to you, and you will leave the other men alone, as well. Keep to yourself if you can't keep your hands off of folks."

Duran looked as if he was barely restraining himself. "Aye, aye . . . Captain." Every syllable was punctuated.

"Good. Now get out of here. The deck-house will be locked tonight, so be so kind as to put the plate of cookies by the wheel for the men."

Elise wondered if Duran would obey the order. After a long moment he walked to the table and picked up the dish. He walked from the galley without another word. Elise shivered at the ugly scowl on his face. She had a feeling that none of this was over.

"Are you all right, daughter?" her father asked, a look of concern replacing his rage.

"I'm all right, thanks to all of you." She smiled and gave her father a kiss on the cheek, and he bent down to hug her. "I recently commented on never having been attacked by a man at sea. I guess I can no longer say that." She sobered. "I'm going to my cabin. My door will be locked." She glanced at Nick and pulled away from her father. "Thank you both. Thank the men for me. Hopefully, Mr. Duran has learned that I have protectors."

"If he hasn't learned yet, he definitely will," her father replied. "I hope he can swim." His lips curled into a smile.

Elise knew her father would never throw anyone overboard, but the thought of it made her grin. "If not, it might serve him well to learn."

Chapter 9

With their trip to Duluth nearly done, Nick tossed and turned as he tried to sleep. The winds had been stiff that day, and Nick couldn't help but remember the storm that had claimed the *Polaris*. His sleep was filled with nightmares of the ship breaking apart and men slipping into the sea even as he reached for them. He woke in a cold sweat to the sound of other men snoring peacefully. How he wished he could put it all behind him.

He dressed and made his way up on deck. It was still dark—probably another hour before dawn. He pulled his coat close and made his way to the deckhouse. He wasn't surprised to find Elise already busy at her work.

"Good morning." Nick glanced around to see if her father was also present. He wasn't.

"Good morning. You're up early. Coming off of watch?" Elise asked, mixing some concoction in a bowl.

"No. Couldn't sleep."

She smiled and nodded. "It happens to everyone. Why don't you sit down? The coffee will be ready soon."

Nick did as she suggested but said nothing. She fascinated him, and though he tried not to be overly interested in her, Elise completely held his attention.

"I hear we're due to dock later this afternoon in Duluth." She set the big bowl on the counter and added several teaspoons of white powder. She went back to her stirring. "Duluth is definitely an interesting town."

He nodded and watched her work. "What are you making?"

"Hot cakes. We'll have these and sausages, and of course plenty of maple syrup. Papa got a large supply of Canadian syrup, and it's quite tasty."

"Sounds good."

"It sticks to the ribs."

She poured batter into the large cast iron skillet, then checked the coffee. Nick watched as she took up a mug and poured him a cup. She was so poised and perfect. Her black hair was plaited down her back, and her blue eyes seemed to sparkle. There was no sign that she'd had anything less than a perfect night's sleep.

"Thanks." He took the cup from her and held it for a moment. He watched as she went back to the stove, minding her steps as the ship's rocking increased.

"The winds are picking up again," she said, turning the cakes. "I hope there's no storm on the horizon."

"There weren't any signs of such. I think we'll be all right." He sampled the coffee. "This is good. Thank you again."

"Of course." She smiled, causing his heart to do a flip.

"So you've been on the lakes all of your life, is that right?" he asked.

"Pretty much so. I've stayed a few weeks here and there on land, and of course in the winter the lakes freeze over, so we stay in Duluth."

"Why there? Why not in Oswego with your uncle?"

"For that very reason—my uncle is there. He and my aunt would expect us to stay with them. Papa and even Mama always maintained they didn't want to spend their winters pretending to be someone they weren't, and they didn't want Caroline and me to take on airs. Of course, Caroline did anyway." Elise frowned and pulled the hot cakes from the pan. She quickly put them aside and poured more batter into the skillet.

"Are you and your sister close?"

"At one time we were." Elise met his gaze. "We have so little in common now that I don't feel that closeness. When Mama died, I thought maybe we'd be drawn together again, but Caroline says I'm seeking to fill our mother's shoes by bossing her around." She paused, looking thoughtful. "I don't feel that's what I was doing, but I could see her taking it that way. I do feel it's right for me to take my mother's place on the ship and to take care of Papa. Maybe I included Caroline in that plan."

"Why do you feel it's your job to take your mother's place?" Nick hoped she didn't mind such a personal question.

She flipped the hot cakes. "We've always been very close, my parents and I. When Mama fell ill, I promised her I wouldn't leave Papa alone, that I'd take care of him and the men on the ship." She shrugged. "I've always known it was what I'd do. I've never had any intention of leaving life on the lakes. I figure I'll always be a cook and seamstress for the *Mary Elise*."

"The men said you plan to never marry."

Elise blushed and gave another shrug. "I made a promise to take care of Papa, and my own desires do not outweigh the need to remain faithful to it."

"So you aren't averse to marriage."

"Of course not." She put her attention on the cakes, and once she had quite a few on a cookie sheet, she opened the warming receptacle and put them inside. "But he'd have to be a seaman, and he'd have to pledge to stay on the *Mary Elise* until my father got too old to sail or died." She gave a little laugh. "That's why it's easier to tell the men I'm married to the *Mary Elise*."

Nick started to say something to that fact, but Elise changed the subject.

"Do you mind my asking you a question?"

"Not at all."

She checked the clock and went to get another skillet from the counter. It already held several rows of sausage links. She put it on one of the burners, then went to the woodbin for more fuel. "Why didn't you want to work in your family business with your father?" She fed the wood into the stove, then moved it around with the poker.

"My father and I were never close. He was so consumed by the textile factory he had very little time for me. I was kept upstairs with a nanny until I was twelve, then allowed to come to the family dinner table unless my parents had company. I was to be silent and refrain from any childish behavior. I was never to offer my opinion unless asked for it, nor to suggest topics for conversation. Frankly, it was more fun in the nursery with my sisters."

"It sounds horrible, but in fact, I've had some experience with that. As children, Caroline and I ate in the nursery when we stayed with Uncle James. It wasn't much fun, however. The nurse wouldn't allow us to speak or play. We were to sit up straight, napkins in our laps, and learn how to be little adults."

He gave her a sad nod. "Yes. That's it exactly. And it's not that I don't understand the importance of order at the table. I guess it just would have been nice to talk to my folks and other family members. As I grew older, I mentioned this to my father. He said as children we had nothing to offer adult conversation. Our presence at the table was merely tolerated."

"How sad. My folks always asked Caroline and me what we thought, what we had done that day, what we had learned. They knew full well what we had done, since we lived very tight aboard a schooner." She put more cakes into the warmer, then went back to add more lard in the skillet. "I loved that Papa would tell us what was going on with the ship. Caroline hated learning about it, but I didn't. I enjoyed setting sails and helping with the ship's upkeep. As I saw it, it was the duty of each of us to make the ship ready at all times. It was our home, after all."

"I'll bet you make a good hand."

"I am just as able as most men. I get out there and help hoist the anchor alongside the others, and I'm pretty strong."

He grinned. "I don't doubt it."

He heard a door open behind him. Nick turned and found Captain Wright gazing across the room at his daughter. "Morning, Elise. How goes it with you?"

"The waves are rocking the boat pretty good, so I'm fighting for balance, but other than that, I'm doing well, Papa." She went to kiss him, still holding the spatula in hand. "Hot cakes and sausages in fifteen minutes." She glanced at the clock. "Make that fourteen."

"Sounds delicious. I'll be there." He looked at Nick. "Ready for a new day and port?"

"I am. I've only sailed up this way a time or two. They didn't have their new canal in Duluth yet last time I was here, so I came in by way of Superior, Wisconsin."

"The new canal makes it very nice. It hasn't come about without issues, to be sure.

152

The rivalry between those two towns goes way back and probably won't ever be set aside. Everyone wants to see their own city succeed and the other fail. I say there's plenty of land and sea for everyone." The captain pulled on his billed cap. "I'll be checking a few things out, Elise, and then I'll be back in . . . twelve minutes."

She laughed. "See to it. When the bells ring, don't be late, or I'm afraid Nick might very well eat your share."

Her father chuckled as he headed out. "That will be the day."

Duluth Harbor welcomed the *Mary Elise* as it did all ships—grateful for the product she brought and happy to have trade increased. Elise secured her kitchen and found Sam. As second mate, he was responsible for the ship's inventory and shopping unless otherwise informed, as she had done in Oswego.

"Sam, here's my list. Papa said it will be morning before we'll head out with the grain shipment. You might talk to him to see what time we'll set sail. Could be you can wait to secure these things until tomorrow."

"Thanks, Miss Elise. I'll talk to him. Do you have anything else you wanted me to pick up?"

She shook her head. "I have need of some sewing supplies, but I'll fetch those. I know exactly where to find them and what I need." She smiled. "But thanks for asking."

She headed for the gangplank and heard her father talking to Nick. "Come on to the house later, if you like. I'm sure Elise won't mind one more for supper."

"That's all right. I'm happy to stay aboard the *Mary Elise*."

"Tired of my cooking already?" Elise asked.

Nick looked horrified. "Not at all. I . . . well, I don't want to intrude on your time alone. I know your father is very important to you."

She laughed. "It's all right, Nick. I wasn't serious. But Papa's right, you are very welcome to eat with us."

"I have watch tonight, so I'll have to decline. But maybe another time."

Elise found herself wanting to push back the lock of brown hair that had fallen across his left eye. Instead, she continued to the docks. "I'll see you at the house, Papa."

Duluth appeared no different from when she'd been here in early June. The trip took twelve to fifteen days, depending on the weather and other issues, to get from Oswego to Duluth, so with the return trip, it was nearly a month. They could usually count on eight to ten round trips each year, but this came at the mercy of the weather and the lake herself.

Elise made her way to the small cottage her father had purchased for their family. She saw her neighbor Mina Osbourne hanging clothes on a clothesline and waved.

"Welcome back," Mina declared, fighting against the wind to pin up her wet sheets.

Elise put down her bag and came to the rescue. "Here, let me help."

"Thanks so much. I love to hang the laundry out when it's this windy because by the time I put up the last piece, the first one is dry." Mina laughed and finished pinning the sheet to the line. "How about some coffee?"

"Let me set my things in the house, and I'll come join you for a cup. Thanks."

Elise hurried to their cottage next door and slipped the key into the lock. Everything was as it had been well over a month ago. She put her bag in her bedroom, then came out to the kitchen stove and began the process of starting a fire. Once she had plenty of fuel and a good blaze going, Elise headed next door.

"It seems like you've been gone for so long," Mina declared.

"Well, I was. We went to my sister's wedding, and then an accident caused me further delay."

"I want to hear everything. It just isn't as exciting with you gone."

Elise smiled. "Well, the wedding was everything Caroline hoped it to be. She wore a lovely gown of lace and satin. There was ruching on the bodice and sleeves. Oh, and it had a very long train and veil. She looked beautiful."

"And the groom?" Mina handed Elise a cup of coffee and nodded to a small pitcher of cream and the sugar bowl. "Was he dashing?"

"I suppose he was handsome enough. We really know very little about him. He's wealthy and manages several of his father's factories that make tools. Although I seriously doubt he knows anything about the manufacturing aspect. Caroline says he has a college education and is very well off due to his grandfather leaving him his fortune. Or, at least, the fortune was to come to him upon his marriage to Caroline."

"So, was it a love match, then?" Mina asked.

"It seemed to be. Caroline was quite content, and Nelson—that's her husband's name, Nelson Worthington—seemed equally happy." Elise poured a little cream in her coffee.

"I thought maybe your uncle had arranged it."

"Well, he did bring them together, with Aunt Martha's help. I'm sure Aunt Martha had planned it out for some time. She tried to marry me off while I was there."

Mina giggled. She was five years Elise's senior but acted more like a teenager. "And was there someone you fancied?"

Elise immediately thought of Nick. "Not that Aunt Martha introduced, but I did meet an intriguing young man when he saved my life."

"What?" Mina came to the table with a plate of cookies and sat down. "I must have you tell me everything. What happened?"

"A freight wagon got away from its owner and careened into my uncle's carriage. I was sitting outside of our first mate's house when it happened. Father was inside visiting Joe, and out of nowhere this wagon appeared, and the next thing I know, I'm waking up in the street. When I looked up, I found the most beautiful blue eyes gazing down at me."

"Do tell."

Elise sampled the coffee and added a bit more cream. Mina's coffee was always strong and bitter. "There isn't too much to tell about the accident. I had a slight concussion and thought at first I'd broken my back. The doctor looked me over and ordered me to stay in bed for two weeks. I recovered much more quickly, however."

"And the gentleman who saved you?"

"Nicodemus Clark. Father learned he had been a ship's captain and hired him on as first mate."

"How lucky for him that Mr. Clark came along."

Elise grinned. "I thought it rather lucky for all of us."

Mina giggled again. "What does he look like?"

Elise thought for a moment. Nick's image was never far from her thoughts. "He has brown hair that looks sun-kissed. His eyes are blue, and his lips are full. He often offers the sweetest smile. He's muscular and tall, with broad shoulders."

"Sounds very much like my Carter," Mina declared. "Did he take to life on the *Mary Elise*?"

"Very much so. He's a good leader, and the men like him. He's a godly man with an even temper and certain devotion to the people in his care."

"And were you one of those people?" Mina raised her eyebrows. "Have you kissed him?"

Elise nearly choked on her coffee. "Certainly not. I hardly know him."

Mina leaned back in her chair. "I thought it sounded like you knew him very well."

"No." Elise paused a moment, then offered Mina a sly smile. "But I would like to know him better."

"Well, maybe the accident was God's way of bringing the two of you together."

Elise shook her head. "I'd like to think God could have brought us together in a less painful way, but nevertheless Nick has been well received on the *Mary Elise* and knows the job well." She figured it was best to get back to her sister's wedding. "Speaking of my sister, Caroline had a lovely reception in my uncle and aunt's garden."

"We weren't talking about your sister, but that's all right. I want to hear about everything." Mina laughed. "Were there lots of flowers?"

"There were flowers everywhere, and the guests seemed quite pleased. What the garden didn't grow, the staff rounded up and wove into the scene. I tell you no lie, they actually bound additional flowers to the rosebushes to make them look three times as full."

"Oh my. Can you imagine the expense?"

Elise laughed and then sobered almost

as quickly. "Before we left, I was in the garden picking herbs to take with me on the ship. One of my cousin's friends thought I was a housemaid and accosted me. Can you imagine? He had his hands all over me. I was appalled. In all my years among the seamen and rowdies on the dock, I've never been attacked."

Mina looked properly shocked. "What happened?"

Elise laughed and grabbed a cookie. "I did that flip Papa taught me. The poor man looked absolutely dumbfounded. I had screamed in surprise when the man grabbed me, and Nick heard me screaming and came to my aid. I think he was surprised to see I could take care of myself so well."

"What was Nick doing at your uncle's house?"

"He'd come with Papa. He needed to write a letter home, and Aunt Martha helped him out with stationery, then invited him to stay for dinner."

"He was refined enough for your aunt's requirements?"

"Yes, he grew up in Boston in a well-off family. They were textile people, and Nick found he didn't care for such factory work." Elise imagined him as a young man longing for the sea.

Mina chuckled. "I think this Nick is someone to be observed. Seems to me he comes up in conversation often."

Elise hadn't meant to refocus their discussion on Nick, but he was quite prevalent in her thoughts. She nibbled the cookie, wondering what, if anything, that meant.

Chapter 10

Elise finished making supper and called her father to join her at the table. He waited for her to take her chair before taking his own. He looked tired.

"Are you going to get some extra rest— maybe sleep late tomorrow—since you found out they can't load the grain until later in the day?" she asked.

"I might. Sleeping in sounds good, although I don't know if this old body of mine will let me. It seems my clock is set to chime at four each morning." He smiled. "There was talk of even further delays, so we might not get out of here tomorrow."

"Well, I think the rest would do you good. The men could do any work on the *Mary Elise* that you need, or you could just give everyone an extra day off. They'd love you for that."

He chuckled. "Everyone loves you when you're givin' what they want. Let me offer grace, and we can eat." He bowed his head and said a simple prayer. Even his voice betrayed his weariness.

"Amen," he concluded.

"Amen." Elise looked up. "I hope you enjoy it."

"I always enjoy your food. You cook just like your mother." He dug into the casserole of homemade egg noodles and chicken in cream sauce.

Elise passed him hot bread she'd just taken out of the oven. "Mina gave us some fresh butter. I thought it'd be perfect for the bread. Plus, there's plum jam that she canned."

"The Osbournes are good neighbors. We need to do something special for them."

"Maybe I can bake them a pie or a cake." Elise slathered butter on a chunk of bread and popped a piece in her mouth. It was wonderful.

"I think you ought to take Nick a big portion of this for his supper. He's got the evening watch, and I don't know if he had time to arrange something for his dinner."

"I'll do it as soon as we're finished. I'll even let the dishes keep." She smiled. "I think you did well in hiring him, Papa. I like him."

"I've noticed. He likes you too."

She laughed. "It's nothing. He's just the friendly sort. He's also very intelligent."

"He is. I like him very much, just as you do."

Elise decided to press the matter. "You could give him more responsibility. I'm concerned about your health, Papa. You haven't been the same since losing Mama, and I'm worried about you."

"It's hard to go on without her. I thought maybe time would ease the pain, but, if anything, it feels more acute. I keep expecting her to walk through the door, and when she doesn't . . . it feels like losing her all over again."

"You two had such a wonderful love. I envied it, and I pray I can find one like it someday."

"You would be blessed if you found a love even half as deep," her father replied. He stared past her as if seeing something else.

Elise wondered if he would ever feel whole again without her mother. She couldn't help but worry about him. He wasn't that old, yet he'd aged so much in the last year. No matter how much she tried to cheer him up, his sorrow kept a tight grip. Having never been married, much less in love, Elise knew she couldn't begin to comprehend what he felt. She was smart enough to know, however, that a child couldn't take the place of a beloved spouse.

After supper she grabbed a plate and heaped a large helping of the casserole onto it. She added a piece of buttered bread, as well as another plate of apple cobbler. It was a favorite of Papa's, but he'd hardly touched it. After putting both plates on a tray, Elise covered them with a dish towel.

"I'm going to clean up when I get back," she told Papa.

He looked up and smiled. "Sounds good. I'll walk you partway to the *Mary Elise* and then come back and get ready for bed. You wait at the ship until Nick's off his watch and ask him to walk you home. I don't want to worry about you encountering any rowdies. Especially not that Duran."

Elise appreciated his concern for her well-being and happily agreed.

While the afternoon in Duluth had been warm, the evening air was a bit chilly, so she pulled on her jacket. The moon was beautiful, and she knew her father would much rather be on the lake. Hopefully the delays would be short and they'd get back on the water tomorrow.

"It's such a beautiful evening," Elise murmured as they walked. The winds had calmed, and the reflection of the moonlight on Lake

Superior was romantic. She wondered if Nick had noticed and appreciated the scene.

"Well, I think I'll go check in with a couple of the other captains and see what's being said about the grain loading," her father declared halfway to the harbor. "Then I'll head home and see you there." He kissed the top of her head. "It's early, so I figure most of the boys are still enjoying their evening. Hopefully you won't be bothered."

"I never have been before." Elise didn't mention that a lot of first-time problems had occurred over the last few weeks. Still, she wasn't afraid.

She continued along the docks toward the *Mary Elise* at the far end and had nearly reached it when Booker Duran appeared out of the shadows.

"Well, well." He smiled. "Imagine meeting like this under the moonlight."

"Good evening, Mr. Duran."

He frowned. "Oh, come now. You aren't still mad at me, are you?"

"I have no feelings for you one way or the other, Mr. Duran. And furthermore, I really have no time to stop and talk." She started past him, but Duran caught her arm.

She gave him a hard stare. "You won't have a job tomorrow if you touch me again. Now, let me go."

He dropped his hold, his eyes narrowing as he took a step back. "I just want to get to know you better. I don't mean any harm."

"Forcing yourself upon a woman is no way to get to know her better."

"I'll admit my manners do suffer. My mother died when I was just a boy. I've had no one to teach me properly. Surely you won't hold that against me. I think you're quite charming, and I think having a conversation with you would be pleasant."

Elise felt her resolve soften. That he would share such an intimate detail of his life touched her. Still, she had no desire to encourage him. "I'm busy right now. If you'll excuse me, I need to take Nick his dinner."

"You should forget about that one," Duran declared. "He's cursed. Everybody knows it. He knows it himself."

"Cursed?" She shook her head, amused. "I don't believe Christians can be cursed, Mr. Duran. Nick is a man of deep faith and therefore cannot be cursed. Jesus already took on all of that for him. Read your Bible, Mr. Duran. Particularly Galatians, chapter three." She paused and forced a smile. "I never thought to ask. Do you have a relationship with God, Mr. Duran?"

He laughed. "Hardly. I've never seen any sense in it. I keep my own rules and order."

"And has that blessed you with a quality life?" She fixed him with a questioning look. "Has it comforted you in times of trial and trouble?"

"As much as any pretense at the existence of God would. I'm a contented man, Miss Elise. I think you'd enjoy my company."

She studied him a moment longer, then shook her head. "I'm afraid that would never work, Mr. Duran. Now, as I said, I'm busy. Good evening." Elise hurried away before he could suggest she do otherwise.

Once on board the *Mary Elise*, she called out, "Mr. Clark, permission to come aboard." She smiled, knowing it would amuse him.

"Well, this is a pleasant surprise." Nick came from the bow of the ship. "What have you got there?" He nodded toward the covered tray.

"Your supper. Papa and I weren't sure you had time to eat before your watch, so I wanted to make sure you got a hot meal. Although, I was delayed in getting here, so I'm not sure how hot it will be."

"No problem—permission is definitely granted." Nick took the tray from her. "Can you stay a bit?"

"I can." She glanced across the deck of the boat. "All seems well."

"Yes. It's a quiet and lovely night. Most

of the crews have gone off to drink or find entertainment. One of the pastors came by to say there was a harvest party at the church and the men were invited. I think Tom was particularly excited."

Elise smiled. "He's a good man, our young Tom. I've always enjoyed his company, although when he first showed up, he had a lot of anger."

"Well, I'm sure he wasn't happy about being forced to work for the *Mary Elise* or go to prison. A fella likes to choose his own way."

"He was given a choice," Elise replied.

"True, but you must admit it was very limited."

She turned toward the deckhouse. "Why don't you let me take the tray below? I'll put it in the stove's warming receptacle."

Nick chuckled and held fast to the tray. "The stove has gone cold, so it won't do any good."

"I hadn't thought of that. It's probably just as well. Papa said there's some sort of delay and we might not get out of here tomorrow."

"Well, if that's the case, maybe you'd show me around Duluth."

Elise thought for only a moment before replying. "I would be happy to do that. Meanwhile, why don't you eat, and I'll wait so I can take back the tray and dishes."

Nick squatted on the deck and set down the tray. "Will you join me?" He sat as if having a picnic and pulled the towel from the tray. "It looks wonderful."

Elise knelt. "I'd be happy to keep you company. Maybe you can tell me more about your life."

"Not if my mouth is full. I think you should tell me about your life."

She shrugged and tried to think of something she could share. "I don't know what to say that you don't already know. I grew up on ships. My father has been a captain for as long as I can remember. He worked his way up, but by the time I came along, he was already captain. He worked for several companies until Uncle James decided there was good money in shipping. About then, Papa had saved almost enough to buy the *Mary Elise*—a brand-new schooner. She's his pride and joy."

"I can see why. She's a worthy vessel, tried and true. I worked my way up as well. The *Polaris* was my first ship to command. The company I worked for was out of Chicago, and they were impressed with my work history and willing to let me take charge. I did them proud—until the accident, of course."

"What happened? To cause the accident? I've only heard bits and pieces."

Nick frowned. "I'd really rather not talk about it, if you don't mind. One day I promise to tell you all about it."

"Of course." She saw the sorrow in his eyes. He had lost men on his first command. How awful it must have been.

"Tell me more about you." He smiled, then put a forkful of food in his mouth. His expression clearly showed his approval of the casserole.

"I love to read." She smiled and decided to sit on the deck as Nick was already doing. She swept her skirt around her and relaxed in the moonlight. "Especially the Bible. Papa and I try to do that every evening. I enjoy his thoughts about what we've read, and if we don't have a clear understanding of a passage, I note it. I write down our thoughts and questions, and then, when we're in town, I'll go consult the pastor. He usually has an answer, and if not, he makes a promise to do more research. When we return, he always stands ready with an explanation and understanding."

"That's a smart way to do it. You don't just leave it and wonder what it means."

"No. We do our best to search it out. I've learned a lot that way. Especially regarding the culture and language of the times. It's all quite fascinating, and Pastor Johnson is so good to help. He went to Harvard and learned a great deal, including Greek and Latin. Then he made friends with a local rabbi and was trained in Hebrew. He's brilliant."

"That's amazing. I had no idea. Johnson was the one who came to invite the men to the party."

Elise nodded. "That doesn't surprise me. He often comes to the ships with invitations. He also prays every morning with those who are going out on the water. Even the toughest and least God-fearing captain has come to enjoy the good pastor and readily accept his prayers."

They fell silent for a moment as Nick dug into the apple dessert.

"Mmm, this is delicious. But then, I've never had any complaints with your cooking. I have to laugh when I think of us cooking for ourselves while you were in Oswego. It doesn't compare, to be sure. I'm glad you weren't here to see how miserably we failed."

"It's nice to be appreciated. My mother taught me. She believed hardworking men needed a good meal to keep them content. She once told me that more problems are made by hungry men than for any other reason. Do you suppose that's true?"

"I can see it happening." He finished the dessert and leaned back on his arms. He stretched his feet out in front of him and gazed up into the night skies. "Hunger or love. Both cause a man to set aside his dignity."

His comment gave her a little shiver. Falling in love with Nick might well cause her to act rather undignified. She shook away the thought. "Well, it's nearly eight, and I should get back. Papa won't stay up late, and I certainly don't need him locking me out."

She knew he never would, but her nerves had gotten the best of her. Only after she stood did she remember her father's desire that Nick walk her home. She started to ask Nick, but he spoke first.

"Wait a couple of minutes. My watch is over at eight. Ah, there's Sam now. Let me go speak to him, and then I'll walk you home." He jumped up and started across the deck.

Elise felt relieved that if she ran into Booker Duran again, at least she'd have Nick by her side. She picked up the tray and waited only a minute or so before Nick returned.

He took the tray from her arms. "Ready?"

"Yes."

She looked up at him in the moonlight and felt something change inside her heart when he smiled down at her. Was this love? Wasn't it much too soon? She didn't really even know Nick. Yet the feelings were so strong that she was almost certain he could read them on her face.

With the tray balanced against his side, Nick put his hand on her elbow as they made their way down the ramp to the dock. Once on solid ground again, he let go, and Elise immediately felt the loss.

"It's a beautiful night," he said as they made their way back to her house.

"It is. And the walk isn't far."

"If I'm not mistaken, this is Minnesota Point."

"Yes. You're right. Our cottage is right on the water. Papa can never be far from the lakes. He says lake water flows through his veins instead of blood. He and Mama both loved the water more than land. We even buried Mama in the water. She wanted it that way, and Papa will someday follow. Although I pray it will be a long while yet."

"And what will you do then?"

She shrugged. "Probably find another ship to cook for. Or maybe I'll talk Uncle James into letting me captain the *Mary Elise*." She laughed at the very thought. "Wouldn't that be something?"

"And why not? You handled her quite well, as I recall."

"Yes, but that was in open water. I don't

know how well I'd handle her in tight situations or storms."

Nick paused mid-step and looked at her. "You'd learn. I'd teach you." As if realizing he'd suggested they would still be together, he changed the subject. "You'll have to lead the way. I have no idea where your cottage is except that it looks out on the lake."

Elise felt another shiver go up her spine. Could it be that she and Nick might have a future together?

Booker Duran sat at the bar, drinking his fourth beer. His hopes for the evening were dwindling. He'd wanted nothing more than a hearty meal, a good woman, and some strong drink. Unfortunately, the food was unsavory compared to what he'd enjoyed on the *Mary Elise*, no woman seemed interested in his charms, and strong drink was only acceptable so long as he was sleeping somewhere other than the *Mary Elise* tonight.

Of course, it was hard to attract the attention of a woman without also attracting the attention of others around him. He was doing his best to blend in at the crowded bar rather than stand out, so a woman would most likely have to do all the pursuing. Something he wasn't used to. Still, he couldn't risk having anyone dwell on him. By now there were probably drawings of him out to the police. A wanted poster might not be posted on every street corner, but the authorities would certainly be notified, and though he could change his name, it didn't do a thing for identifying him by his face and description.

He tossed back the rest of his beer and got up to leave. There was no sense in remaining. The place was getting rowdier by the minute, and it wouldn't be long until a fight broke out and the police were called.

Duran left the tavern and kept to the shadows as he headed back to the ship. The smart thing to do would be to head out west or even sign on with an oceangoing vessel, rather than remain in the Great Lakes region. But the latter would confine him and leave him with little freedom to escape if necessary. Heading west was probably the better of the two ideas. Nobody knew him there. If he made it to the coast, maybe he could pan for gold. That idea had always appealed to him. The problem was, he had little money to his name. The *Mary Elise* paid monthly on the first. Here it was the middle of the month, and he was already broke again.

He shoved his hands deep in his pockets. If only he'd done things differently, he could still be making his living gambling. He wasn't sorry he'd killed that man, just sorry that it had been done where others had witnessed it. It truly had complicated his life.

Something caught his attention just ahead. A man struggled to stay on his feet. It was clear he was drunk and had little common sense left to him. He was alone in a dark alleyway and obviously incapacitated.

Booker smiled. This should take very little effort, and he wouldn't even have to kill anyone.

Chapter 11

The *Mary Elise* had been offloaded of coal and the hold cleaned so they could take on grain. Just after the hold was swept clean, the crew was surprised with an inspection by the Board of Lake Underwriters. The *Mary Elise* easily passed with an A1 rating. Her hold was solid and showed no cause for concern. Elise was relieved, as she knew her father had some concerns about a particular area. One of the things he had planned to work on that winter was that area, which seemed likely to develop rot.

The grain loading was once again delayed, however. There was some sort of trouble at the grain elevator, but Elise had no idea what had happened. She was, however, glad for extra time to spend with Nick. When he was free later in the morning, they met for a long walk around Duluth.

She took pleasure in his company, as well as in showing him the places she knew. They took the short ferry ride from the Minnesota Point side of the canal, then continued the tour in Duluth.

After a bit of a walk, Elise pointed to a church building. "That's the church we attend during the winter months. Pastor Johnson and his wife have only been here for a couple of years, but already the congregation loves them. They're good people, and he teaches solidly from the Bible."

"That's a blessing. So many people have been led astray by pastors who don't preach the Bible."

"Yes, that's true." Elise led him to the train depot. "Mr. Cooke, a wealthy banker, was responsible for seeing that Duluth got the railroad." They continued to walk parallel to the train tracks. "That building over there—the big white one—is the Northern Pacific Immigrant House. There are hundreds of immigrants who were hired by the railroad. I've heard this building will hold over seven hundred men. They live there rent-free, so long as they are working for the railroad. There is another immigrant house on Sixth Avenue at Michigan Street. It's brand-new, in fact."

"You seem to know quite a bit about Duluth."

"I've lived here in the winters for over ten years. Caroline and I used to visit all the shops. Of course, there weren't very many then. Not like now. Things are really growing. Every time I come here, I'm surprised to find more people and stores. I heard from my friend Mina that there are now three jewelry stores. Who could ever need that much jewelry?"

They turned a corner, and she continued. "It's still not a very pretty town, but I have hope for it. Once they clear all those tree stumps and get more grass planted in the yards of those new houses on the hill, it'll look a whole lot better. I'm going to plant a bunch of flower bulbs when we get back next trip. The accident made me forget about my plans, but Aunt Martha promised me bulbs from her garden's abundance."

They slowed their pace a bit, and when a small restaurant came in sight, Nick pointed. "Why don't you let me buy you lunch?"

Elise glanced at the café. "All right. I am getting hungry."

They made their way inside Freda's. The café advertised the best fried fish in town. Elise decided to give it a try, along with an iced tea, as the day had warmed up considerably.

Nick did the same, then gave Elise a smile that caused her to lose herself in his gaze for a moment. He grinned as if knowing the effect he had on her.

Desperate not to betray her growing feelings for him, she asked the first question that came to mind. "Do you really believe yourself cursed?"

His smile faded, and his brows knit together in a look between worried and dismayed. "Who said that?"

"Booker Duran. Last night as I was bringing you your supper, I ran into him. He told me you believed yourself to be cursed."

Nick leaned back in his chair as the waitress delivered their teas. He took a sip and put the glass down before answering. "I don't know. I sometimes feel that I might be. My father abandoned me, my mother died. My siblings care very little for me, and of course, there's what happened on the *Polaris*."

When he didn't elaborate, Elise considered asking for details again but remembered his promise to tell her when he was ready. Instead, she said, "I don't believe Christians can be cursed."

"No, I suppose I don't either, not when I really consider that I belong to God—that He directs my steps and forgives my sins."

"How did you come to the Lord?"

The waitress approached with two white plates steaming with food. The fried fish smelled heavenly and was served with peas.

"Shall we say grace?" Nick asked.

"Of course. Please do." Elise bowed her head, wondering what kind of prayer Nick might offer.

"Father, thank you for a safe journey and for this food to nourish our bodies. Amen."

She looked up and smiled, meeting his blue eyes. "Amen."

They each sampled the fish. Elise nodded. "It is very good."

"I'll bet yours is better," he teased.

"I use different seasoning, but I can't fault this meal." They continued eating as other customers filled the restaurant.

"I learned about God at my mother's knee," Nick said after a few moments of quiet.

Elise was glad he'd remembered her question and was willing to answer it. Sometimes people didn't like to talk about their personal experiences with God. For her, it was something precious and worthy of discussing, but for others, she'd learned it was often difficult.

"My mother was a God-fearing woman, while my father was more focused on business. We attended church, of course, as most of our society did. It was expected, and my father wasn't a man to do something that might harm his acceptability in society. But Mother was devout and believed the Bible was the only truth. I was reading it before I knew what the words meant." He grinned. "How about you?"

"My mother led me to God as well. She helped Papa find his way too. They fell in love, but Mama told him she couldn't be unequally yoked, nor could she marry a man who got right with God only because he wanted to marry her."

"What happened?"

"They didn't marry for two years after falling in love. Mama prayed for strength, and Papa prayed for wisdom and knowledge in the Lord. When he finally felt he had a solid relationship with God, he came back to her, and they married. It's a beautiful story. Their wisdom on the issue of faith was what Uncle James said convinced him of their love. What two people so in love with each other would ever wait to marry unless it was a truly convicting reason of greatest importance?"

"Faith in God has become the very core of who I am," Nick said, toying with his fork. He didn't look up but grew very thoughtful. "I have thought on many occasions, when dangers were everywhere, that perhaps it would be my last moment in life, but there was always such a peace. I know whom I have believed."

"Second Timothy one, verse twelve. I love the part after that. 'I know whom I have believed, and am persuaded that He is able to keep that which I have committed unto Him against that day.'"

This time their gazes met. They nodded in unison, and for Elise, it was a moment like no other. Their spirits were in one accord with God. There was no unequally yoked aspect to their relationship.

After lunch, they continued their walk. Elise loved having Nick at her side.

"That's where the old theater stood. Most called it the Opera House or the Pine Shed," Elise said, pointing to a building under construction. "A man named William Branch purchased it this year and plans to make a three-story opera house."

"That's quite the endeavor." Nick walked over to the building across the street and pointed to a posted notice. "Look here, there's going to be a fair in October."

Elise smiled. "The county fair is very popular."

"I think we should make a pact to attend if we're in town," Nick said, giving her a sweeping bow. "Would you do me the honor of letting me escort you to the fair?"

Elise giggled and felt like a young girl being courted. "I would be honored."

"Then it's settled. You won't attend the fair with anyone else but me." He grinned and took hold of her arm.

The church bell chimed three o'clock, and Elise knew it was best she went home and checked on her roast. "I need to get home."

Nick didn't protest. "Thank you for a lovely day."

She hated the thought of ending their time together. "Would you like to come for dinner tonight? I happen to know you have the evening free, and Papa would enjoy your company . . . as would I."

His grin broadened into a full smile. "I would be happy to join you and your father for dinner. What time should I come?"

"Six would be fine."

They began walking toward the ferry landing. Elise couldn't help but smile. It had been a perfectly wonderful day, and for the first time in her life, she was experiencing feelings that could only be one thing.

It must be love.

Bill Wright sat at the table with the ship's log, invoices, and financial journal. He'd been doing his best to focus on what needed to be paid and what needed to be collected. Sam had done a good job posting entries, but things seemed confusing in light of the fact that his wife had always taken care of this job.

How could she be gone?

He leaned his elbows on the table and planted his hands in his thick graying hair. "Mary, I'd give anything if you were here again, safe and sound."

A warmth spread over him at the mere speaking of her name. She'd been his pride and joy—the reason he awoke happy each day. How could he not be happy with her at his side? Mary made life better. Her cheery countenance and joy in the Lord never faltered. Oh, she had moments when something troubled her, but her first move was always to take it to the Lord in prayer. He wished he were more like that. His faith in God had grown strong, to be sure, as had his prayer life, but with Mary it seemed to come naturally, while his still took some effort.

A chill soon robbed him of the warmth Mary's memory had brought. It seemed he was always chilled, even when the days were warm, which this one had been. Bill moved to the fireplace and loaded it with wood. He maneuvered the logs and embers with the poker, and soon the fire came to life, but his heart did not. How could it, without the love of his life there to share the hours?

He went back to the table, then remembered he'd promised Elise he would keep the oven fires going. Opening the stove, Bill could see he'd failed. There was a nice bed of embers but little more. He quickly went to work repairing that neglect. Satisfied he'd made amends, he went again to the table. This time he sat down and stared at the books and papers.

Sam had offered to take over this task for him. He knew his second mate was trustworthy. He'd been with Bill for over five years, and he had proven himself more than once.

So why not just give it over to Sam? Or even Elise?

Bill drew a deep breath. "Because it was hers to do. The last bit."

Elise had taken over the cooking, laundry, and mending. She even came into his cabin and cleaned up after him. Those were all Mary's duties, and she'd done them with skill and love. Elise offered the same, but it was different. She knew she was appreciated, but she felt her mother's loss just as well.

The door opened, and Elise stepped inside. "Hello, Papa. I'm back from my walk about town with Nick." She pulled off her bonnet. "I see you've made it quite warm in here. Were you chilled?"

"Just a bit, but don't go worrying that I've caught some horrible sickness. I'm just getting old."

She gave a good-natured laugh. "You shall never be old, Papa." She made her way to the oven.

"I just put the fire in order," he said, hoping he hadn't ruined anything. "I'm sorry to say it got away from me. The stove too, but I just added wood to both."

She turned before reaching the oven and came to kiss the top of his head. "I'm sure it'll be fine. Oh, I invited Nick to come to dinner. I hope that's all right."

"It is. It'll be good to go over a few things with him before we head out tomorrow."

"So they were finally able to load the *Mary Elise*?"

"They're doing it tonight. There are a couple of other ships ahead of us."

She quickly pulled on her apron. "I'll finish up the laundry, then. I have some ironing to do." She checked the food in the oven. "It looks perfect."

"Elise . . ." He paused and shook his head.

"What is it?"

"Nothing." He forced a smile. "Thanks for your hard work."

She came and gave him a hug. "I love taking care of you, Papa."

"Your mother always said that she took great joy in serving me." His eyes dampened. "I wish I'd served her more."

"But you always served her! Mama said as much. She said she never once felt unloved or forgotten. You made her feel safe and protected and loved. What better service could you offer?" Elise stood back, and he looked up. She frowned, no doubt because of his tears.

"She helped me be more than I was without her. Now I fear I'm a lesser man."

"Nonsense. I'm a better woman for what she gave to me, and I will always have that. Just as you will always have her mark on your heart and life. No one can take that from you."

"I miss her greatly."

"I know, and I do too." Elise sat down beside him. "But I keep thinking of how unhappy she'd be to imagine we'd given up on life or let her passing rob us of our joy. What a dishonor to her to spend all our time mourning her loss. Mama was a woman of life and love. She wouldn't want to be the cause of such grief and sorrow. She would tell us, 'Rejoice in the Lord always,' just as the Bible says."

Bill considered this and knew his daughter was right. Mary would have admonished him to take hold of the joy God gave, to focus on all that was yet to come from His blessings rather than dwell on what could never be.

"I can hear her saying those very words." He gave Elise a sad smile. "I will endeavor to take hold of the joy and love God offers me."

He felt the warmth again. It was time to put aside his mantle of mourning. He knew there would still be sorrow on occasion. He would still know loneliness most of the time. But he would also seek God's joy, no longer waiting on love when he already had it in abundance from his daughter and friends.

The image of his sweet wife came to mind once again as if to give her approval. *"No big job is done all at once, Bill. Slow and steady will see you through with God's help."* She had often said that when tasks seemed daunting. Even during the darkest storms, she had often reminded him that each step forward was still a movement of progress.

He smiled to himself and sighed. He didn't have to completely miss her. She was always there with him in his thoughts and memories.

Chapter 12

Nick knocked on the cottage door and waited patiently for someone to answer. When Elise appeared at the door, he presented the small bouquet of flowers he'd purchased shortly after delivering her to her home earlier.

"I thought you might enjoy these. I know we'll be leaving tomorrow, but maybe you can enjoy them tonight."

Elise drew them to her face and breathed in deep. "I'll take them with me on the ship. They won't require that much room. Thank you for your thoughtfulness. No one has ever brought me flowers before."

Nick started to say that he would see to it that she always had flowers, but he hesitated. He knew she enjoyed his company, but that might be a bit too presumptuous.

"Come on in, Nick," her father called from the living room.

"Good evening, Captain." Nick entered the house and took off his cap.

Elise reached for it. "Here, I can take that and your jacket, if you like. We keep the house warm so Papa can thaw his bones from the weeks on the lake."

"But at the same time, we're rather informal here," the captain added. "No dinner coats or fancy trimmings like at my brother-in-law's house."

Nick doffed his coat and handed it to her. "Which is such a blessing. I used to overheat something fierce when we had important dinners in the summer. Boston temperatures can be overbearing at times."

Captain Wright stretched out his legs. "You'll have to tell us more about that fair city. I've never been."

"I've read a little of its history and about the fighting that took place near there for our independence from Great Britain," Elise said, hanging his coat and hat on a peg by the door. Soon she rejoined them with just the bouquet in hand.

"What pretty flowers," her father declared.

"Nick brought them for me. Wasn't that thoughtful?"

She smiled at Nick, making him wish he could sweep her into his arms and kiss her. He reined in his thoughts. They were a long way from that kind of behavior, and it did no good to dwell on it before its time had come. He pushed the thoughts aside, but they continued to come back to the forefront of his mind. He'd never felt like this about anyone.

"It was very thoughtful. Have a seat, Nick. I think Elise said it would be a few more minutes."

"Yes. I'll put these flowers in water and then slice the roast." She headed to the kitchen.

Nick took a seat on one of three empty chairs. The one he chose happened to be cushioned and covered in leather. He offered his captain a smile and picked up their conversation about Boston.

"I'd be happy to share about my hometown. It is quite the place."

"We'd best wait for Elise. I wouldn't want her to miss out. For now, I want to say how much I appreciate the job you've been doing. The men are pleased to work with you. Even Duran has stopped bringing up the sinking of the *Polaris*."

"I'm grateful for that, to be sure." Nick had already revealed all of the facts regarding the shipwreck to the captain, but even so, the topic made him uncomfortable.

"My point is that I believe your period of probation has been met and you have passed with flying colors. I want you to consider the

Mary Elise your home, and I want you to know you'll be given greater responsibility . . . as well as pay."

"Thank you, sir. I'm grateful for the opportunity to restore my reputation."

"Well, I'm certain any reasonable person would understand you can hardly judge a man by one mistake."

"Dinner is served," Elise announced from the doorway.

The captain rose quickly. "I feel half starved. Make haste, Mr. Clark. Pot roast awaits us."

"Aye aye, Captain." Nick grinned and rose to follow Captain Wright into the kitchen.

"I hope you don't mind that we are without a dining room. The kitchen is large enough to fit a table and chairs, so we eat here," the older man said.

"I don't mind at all. I rather like the coziness of it. It's very personal."

"*Personal* is another way of saying *tiny*," Captain Wright replied, grinning. "We didn't want a big house, however. The land never called to us like the lakes did. Like they continue to do."

"I know exactly what you mean." Nick wished his own father could have understood that feeling.

Elise put bread and butter on the table and

then took the chair her father had pulled out. "Please sit. We don't want the food to get cold."

The captain offered grace, speaking of his trust that God would redirect him to joy of spirit and peace of mind. Nick had no idea what was going on but figured he could ask Elise later.

"Amen," Elise whispered after her father blessed the food. She reached for a large porcelain bowl and handed it to Nick. It was full of creamed corn. Next came the platter of roast beef cooked with a mixture of onions, carrots, and potatoes. Last of all was a gravy boat of beef broth. Nick found his mouth watering for the feast. By the time the bread and butter made its way around, he was more than ready to dive into the fare.

"Elise, this looks amazing," Nick said, cutting into the tender meat.

"The girl can cook, there's no mistakin' that," her father said.

"Caroline learned how to cook as well, but I doubt she'll have any cause to use it now. I was told her house has twenty servants." Elise took a sip of the fresh apple cider Mina had given them.

"With a four-story house and five acres of ground, I would think they'd need at least that many," Captain Wright said matter-of-factly. "I wonder if she's yet had time to explore it all."

"I doubt it, since they boarded a ship for New York the day they wed. I do admit I would love to see Europe," Elise said as she put butter on her bread. "But probably not for the reasons Caroline wants to go. She plans to buy a new wardrobe in Paris, and Nelson has promised her more jewelry."

"So why would you want to go?" Nick asked.

She stopped what she was doing. "For the history, of course. The history and art and architecture. Mother used to talk about how grand it was when she visited as a girl. The palaces and churches, the great houses. Her descriptions were so lively and brilliant, I almost felt as if I could see them through her eyes. Do you remember, Papa, when she described the tulip fields in Holland?"

Her father chuckled. "I do, indeed. Your mother certainly had seen it all, and yet she preferred her life on the *Mary Elise*."

"I believe I would feel the same," Elise admitted, "but I would like to see it."

Nick wanted to promise that if he had anything to say about it, she would. He had gone on a grand tour at the age of sixteen. His interests had fallen in line with those of Elise. His father had even hired an architect to take Nick around and show him various places and discuss the details of how a particular building had come to be. Of course, there had also been tours of textile mills.

"But what about Boston, Nick? Tell us about your town."

Nick shook his head. "It's hardly mine. I left at eighteen, and with only a few exceptions of port call, I've not returned. That's been over ten years."

"And you've not seen your family in all that time?" Elise asked.

"No. My father turned me out, and my sisters felt it their duty to side with him. I think I mentioned that I write to my friend Mrs. Schmitt. She has been the head housekeeper for as long as I can remember. She keeps me aware of the family's health and activities. I doubt my father knows about it, however. I'm sure he'd soon put an end to it."

"How sad." Elise frowned. "I can't imagine Papa not wanting to see me."

"That's because it will never happen," the captain said. "Sometimes a man makes decisions he regrets. Your father may one day decide he was wrong—or perhaps he already has. It's good that you maintain some sort of connection to your family."

"I agree," Elise said, picking up the small piece of bread she'd buttered. "I think you should make it very well known that you are eager to mend your fences."

But was he? Nick considered that for a moment. He wasn't at all sure he wanted to go back to Boston and attempt reconciliation. After all, he would never take over the textile industry his father had built. Wouldn't it just reopen old wounds to go back and state this fact once again?

"What did you love most about living there?" the captain asked, seeming to understand Nick's thoughts were warring.

"The parks, the water, the architecture. There are some wonderful old buildings with such detail that you could study them all day and never tire. I used to stroll along the walks and be mesmerized by the detail. And the music! There's always a concert somewhere or an organ recital. There are great pipe organs in the churches that play with the most amazing sound." He touched his napkin to his lips. "There is always something different to study. I learned small boat sailing there and signed onto my first ocean schooner out of Boston Harbor. But I admit that I prefer the lakes."

"I've never known the difference, but I agree with you all the same, lad."

Elise smiled at her father. "I made your favorite custard pie. I hope you saved room for it."

Captain Wright reached over to pat her hand. "Of course I did. I saw you with the cream and eggs and knew what you were up to."

Elise scooted back from the table. "Then I'll go retrieve it now." She made her way to a small table on the other side of the stove. "I've sprinkled it with nutmeg, just as you like it."

"She's an amazing girl, my Elise. Always lookin' to please and most generally accomplishing that and more."

"I can well imagine," Nick said, watching her as she made her way back to the table. "Talented and beautiful."

She met his gaze and blushed. "You should stop that. I've already promised you pie. You don't have to charm me to earn your share."

"Even if there were no pie, I would sing your praises," Nick assured her.

"Robert Wayfair!" a burly, bearded man called to Booker Duran.

"I'm sorry, you've the wrong man." Booker kept his face down. Thankfully the tavern was noisy and full of strangers.

"Now, Bob, I'd be knowin' you anywhere. 'Tis you, or my name isn't Rummy Carlson."

Duran knew there'd be no shutting the man up unless he acknowledged him.

"For pity's sake, man, shut up." Booker glared up at Rummy with a look that would have stopped the devil himself. He yanked the man down into the chair beside him at a small corner table. In a whisper, Booker spoke his mind. "I don't go by that name anymore."

Rummy's eyes widened. "Well, why didn't you say so?"

"I just did," Booker growled. "The name is Booker Duran." He held his hand out as if to shake the other man's hand, but Rummy was still uncertain what was going on.

Booker refocused on his drink. "I've got some marital problems, so I changed my name. I don't want the old witch to find me."

"Oh," Rummy replied, nodding. He gave Booker a slap on the back and a grin. "We all know how that goes. I thought mebbe you had forgotten your old pal."

"Not at all. Let me buy you a beer. But you'll have to promise me your silence on my true identity."

"But that goes without saying," Rummy declared, motioning toward Booker with crossed fingers. "I promise. I can't have a good man such as yourself hounded and hunted down by a woman."

Booker raised his hand as the serving girl approached. "Another beer for me and one for my friend." He tossed her a coin.

"Sure thing." She gave him a promising smile, then made her way back to the bar.

"And the next one is on me," Rummy stated, putting his coins on the table. "I got paid today and am more than flush."

Duran perked up at this. Maybe his run-in with the old sailor would serve his purposes after all. If he could get Rummy drunk without spending too much, there just might be a nice payday coming Booker's way.

"What brought you to Duluth?" Rummy asked.

"The *Mary Elise*. I'm an able seaman on that schooner."

"I know it well. I once served on her. Captain Wright still commanding her?"

Booker hid his disdain by tossing back the remainder of his drink. He wiped his mouth before answering. "He is."

"Ah, a good man. A fair man. I hated leaving him, but I don't make much of a sailor. I'm better working with the trees. I signed on with a logging company up north. Good group of men. Everyone knows their duties. It won't be long before I rejoin them. We work mostly in the winter because of the boggy ground, don't you know."

"No, I can't say that I did."

"Well, I got me a job at the sawmill right now. So I've always got something to be workin' at. Keeps me fed and in plenty of drink."

The waitress returned with their beers.

"Let me know if you'll be needin' something else," she said, looking at Booker.

"I'm sure I'll be calling on you," he said.

"The *Mary Elise* was brand-new the year I went to work on her," Rummy continued. "We had a crew of only six, since she was in pristine order. Captain Wright was a good teacher, but I am a poor student. You'll have to be tellin' him hello from me. Maybe I'll just make my way over and tell him myself. That would be a grand thing, now, wouldn't it?"

"I don't think it would be wise. The old man's wife passed away, and he's not in good spirits."

"Now, that is a loss. Mrs. Wright was a kindly woman. Good cook too."

"Her daughter Elise takes care of those duties now." Duran wasn't sure why he mentioned that. Rummy Carlson presented a problem. He was a liability Booker couldn't afford. If he got it in his head to visit the captain and gave up Booker's real name, there would be trouble with the law before Duran could get away.

"Let's have another one," Rummy said after emptying his mug. He pushed his coins toward the edge of the table. "You're fallin' behind, Bob." He lowered his voice and chuckled. "I mean Booker."

Duran shook his head. "I can take care of my own. You probably don't have the funds."

"I have plenty. Been helping out at the lumber mill." He lowered his voice and glanced around. "Got paid today."

Booker decided it would be all too easy to take care of his problem. "All right, then, let's get to it." He slammed down the contents of his mug and placed it empty beside Rummy's. "This round is on you!"

~

"Good night, Nick," Elise said on the stoop outside the open cottage door. "I'm glad you could join us for supper. Thanks too for the flowers." Her heart seemed to race, and she took deep breaths, trying to calm it.

"It was my pleasure." He took her hand and placed a light kiss on her knuckles. He held her hand just a few seconds longer than necessary and rubbed the back of it with his thumb. "I've never met anyone quite like you."

She felt her cheeks grow warm. "Nor I you." For a moment she felt as if it would be impossible to move. Then Nick dropped his hold and turned to go.

"I'll see you in the morning."

She nodded and watched him saunter down the walkway and disappear around the side of the house. Looking out over the lake, Elise hugged her shawl around her arms and gazed up at the moon.

I've lost my heart to him, Lord. I've never felt so wonderful and yet so confused. I promised Mama I'd take care of Papa. I know Nick loves what he's doing, but he's not always going to be content to remain first mate. Not after having commanded his own ship.

She paused in her prayer. She hoped he might trust her soon with the details of what had happened on the *Polaris*. She knew he blamed himself. He said it was his misjudgment. But she knew little else.

Help us, Lord. If we are meant for each other, then he will have to agree to remain on the Mary Elise *and help Papa. He'll have to forget about being a captain on his own ship.*

She frowned. That wasn't likely. Papa had often told her there was a certain type of man meant to lead and command, while others were equally designed to follow. Nick was a leader, and being put in the position of answering to her father for the rest of his life would be difficult, if not impossible.

Hugging her arms to her body, Elise prayed on. "You could make it work, Lord. I know you could. If it be your will." The last few words seemed to echo back to her in the night skies.

If it be your will.

Chapter 13

Filled to capacity with Minnesota wheat, the *Mary Elise* was well on her way to the Soo Locks when Elise's father sighted the bank of clouds building to the west-southwest and moving in fast. He ordered them to head for the safety of Whitefish Bay.

"The wind is churning up the lake," he told Elise. "Ready the galley and stay put. I'm not sure how rough this is going to get."

Elise wished she could lend a hand. Carrying grain was always a concern when storms came up. The load shifted back and forth with the ship's rocking and often got out of balance and had to be trimmed. If not dealt with, the ship could capsize.

Elise knew the best thing she could do was stay out of the way. With the storm nearly upon them, she had let the stove go cold so as not to risk fire. She felt confident the storms would pass quickly. Papa had said nothing about expecting them to linger. He usually had an intuition for such things.

Earlier in the day, she had gathered the men's laundry. She figured she might as well put it to soak. She went through the pieces, looking for any particularly bad stains or tears. When she picked up one of Booker Duran's shirts, she was startled to find blood splattered all over the front of it. She frowned. Had he hurt himself? That much blood surely would have required a doctor's assistance. Then again, she recalled men receiving blows to the nose that caused an abundance of bleeding but needed no doctor. Booker seemed the perfect candidate to find himself in a fight.

She took the shirt to the table and wet it down, then smeared it with salt. Scrubbing salt against the stain would remove a good portion of the blood. She rinsed and repeated the action, even as the rocking of the ship increased. She wondered what kind of trouble Mr. Duran had gotten himself into. He always seemed to be looking for a fight.

The door opened, and a man pressed in with the wind at his back. "Miss Elise, your father says it's lookin' to be a bad one," Sam declared. He battled the wind before pulling the door closed, then hurried down the galley steps. "Are the fires out?"

"All but the lamp." Despite the lamps being secured, they took no chances on the *Mary Elise*. Sam put out the lamp in quick order while Elise left Duran's shirt to soak apart from the other laundry.

"I'll let the captain know the galley is secure," Sam said, then left as quickly as he'd arrived.

With very little light, Elise took herself to her cabin and decided it would serve her best to pray. She tried not to worry when the storms came upon them, but sometimes she couldn't help herself. Ships were damaged or lost with nearly every storm. Whenever a bad storm came when she was growing up, she and her sister would pile into Elise's narrow bunk and pull the covers over their heads. Mama always encouraged prayer, but Elise would often entertain her sister with stories from the Bible to keep her calm.

"Tell me about those men in the boat with Jesus," Caroline would ask. *"The one with the bad storm."*

It was something they could definitely relate to, and Elise loved the story. *"They were out on the water when the storm came up. Just like today. Jesus had decided to take a nap."*

"*Didn't he know about the danger?*" Caroline asked.

It was always the same question, and Elise would give the same answer. "*Jesus knew, but He wasn't afraid. He knew God would take care of everything.*"

Elise stretched out on her bed and smiled at the memory. Caroline was always afraid and worried about the situation.

"*But the men were afraid because the waves got to be really high . . . like now.*" Caroline's soft, frightened tone always melted Elise's heart.

"*Oh, these aren't really high waves today.*" Elise always said that, whether they were or not. "*The waves that day with Jesus were much higher, and the men were afraid they would capsize.*"

"*But they didn't, did they?*"

"*No. They got really afraid and woke Jesus up. They said, 'Master, carest thou not that we perish?'*"

"*They thought they were going to die.*" Caroline's voice was edged with fear.

"*Yes, but that was only because they didn't understand that Jesus was in control. Remember, He got up and told the storm—*"

"*Peace. Be still,*" Caroline interrupted as she always did.

Elise smiled at the memory. "Peace. Be still," she murmured.

Such thoughts easily led her to wonder how her sister might be. Was she enjoying her tour of Europe? Had she purchased her great wardrobe and received beautiful jewels from her husband?

The ship shifted to port, nearly dumping Elise out of her bed. At least there wasn't any thunder or lightning. Just the wind and rain, which was plenty bad enough.

She imagined her father in his oiled canvas coat, barking out orders, fighting the wind and the waves to get the *Mary Elise* to some safe cove. Gradually things calmed, and the terrible rocking ceased. She knew the worst of the storm had passed, but she could still hear the rain pummeling them. After another ten minutes, even that stopped, however. She rose from her bed and went to the galley. Everything was in good order. All had been secured prior to the storm and remained in its place. The boat, however, was listing to starboard.

Before long, Sam reappeared to light the lamps. "Captain says it's all clear, but the load must be trimmed. The boys are already at work on it."

"I'd best get back to my work," Elise admitted as if nothing had happened.

"We'll be headin' for the Soo Locks," Sam informed her.

Elise lit the stove to get it warming up.

"I'll put fresh coffee on. It'll take a while to get hot, but let the boys know. I'll have a snack for them too."

"Aye, Miss Elise."

She loaded wood into the stove and soon had it lighted. She put on the coffeepot before going back to her laundry. The baskets had fallen over, splaying clothes everywhere. Oh well, better now when they were dirty than later when they were clean. Elise put a big pot of water on the stove to heat up along with the coffee. Next, she started putting together ham sandwiches. The boys would have to work hard to put the ship right and deserved something heartier than cookies. After that was completed, she went back to the laundry and waited for the ship to be righted.

There was only a half hour of light left when they had their turn at the locks. Elise walked the deck, watching the entire process as they waited for the water to go down twenty-one feet so they could enter the St. Mary's River.

"You're looking mighty fine, Miss Elise," Booker Duran stated as he came toward her carrying a shovel.

She bristled at his comment but decided not to take offense. "Are we trim now, Mr. Duran?"

"Aye. Fit and trim." He grinned. "Just like yourself."

She eyed him for signs of injury, but there were none. "I thought maybe I'd find you in stitches, Mr. Duran."

He looked at her oddly. "Why would that be?"

"I'm doing laundry today. Your shirt was covered in blood."

He gave a hearty laugh. "You should see the other fella."

"You got into a fight?"

"The whole tavern was fighting. It was just a good time. No harm done."

She looked at his face. There wasn't even a bruise. "Well, you seemed to have come out of it without a mark."

"I always do. I'm taller than most, so they can't reach my beautiful face." He laughed again and threw the shovel over his shoulder. "I'm touched that you're worried about me."

"Well, when you see that much blood on a man's shirt, you figure the worst."

He leaned closer. "Never fear for me, Miss Elise. I'll be just fine. I'm good at taking care of myself and them that belong to me." He gave her a wink and moved on.

Elise felt rather fouled by his nearness and familiarity, but she drew a deep breath and pushed her ill feelings aside. At least he wasn't injured in a way that would interfere with his duties and cause problems for her father and the crew.

Supper waited that night until nearly eight. Meals were usually delayed when something like the locks passage was on the agenda. The men ate as if they were starving, and everyone seemed to grab for everything at the same time. Elise had made a huge pot of beef stew. She'd also baked biscuits and served them with honey. There wasn't so much as a scrap left of anything after she served the dessert of lemon cream cake.

After supper, the men on duty went to their jobs while the others went to bed. Elise washed dishes and put the kitchen in order, then resumed her time on deck. She loved it when the evening was quiet and the world seemed to slip by in the soft wash of the river.

She stared out over the rail and marveled at how long the light lasted. During the summer it stayed light well into the evening and left one with the feeling of eternal summer. But September was nearing, and each completed trip was a marker against time that seemed to be slipping by much too quickly.

"You seem reflective," Nick declared, coming to stand beside her. "You hardly said two words at supper."

"I guess I feel the approach of winter even

though summer is still with us. I can't help feeling that sense of ending, like a good book you've spent hours reading and know you're just a few pages from finishing."

Nick smiled and nodded. "I can understand that, but really, there's plenty of time left for sailing."

"I know, but maybe it isn't the sailing. Maybe something else in my life is ending. Or maybe something for someone else, like my father. I just don't know."

"Do you want to talk about it?"

She shook her head. "It would do little good. I can't even form a thought around these feelings. It might be foreboding, and if it is and it's from God, I know He will direct me in time."

Nick smiled and gave a nod. "I agree. Let's talk of more pleasant things. Will you see your uncle when we're back in Oswego?"

"No doubt I will. Even when we don't go to the house to see the family, my uncle will come to us and talk business with Papa. I will probably send Sam to buy groceries, but sometimes I like to arrange them myself."

"If you don't go shopping, what do you usually do?"

"Enjoy time to myself." She smiled and looked out toward the waning moon. "Sometimes I just like to sit and read."

"The book you're about to finish, eh?"

She laughed. "I suppose so. It'll soon be September. A few trips after that, and we'll be looking for the end of our shipping until next spring." Here they were, talking about her feelings. She hadn't intended it, but it just seemed the natural flow of conversation.

"Most of the men will join the logging companies unless Papa has asked them to stay on and help make repairs to the *Mary Elise*. I'm glad you'll be one of them staying on."

"Why is that?"

She shrugged. "I'm not entirely sure myself. I know your presence has been helpful to my father. I think he's truly enjoyed your company."

"I noticed that he seems a little less morose."

She had sensed the change as well. "We had a long talk about Mama. I think he's turned a corner on mourning her. He knows she would never want it. I've encouraged him as best I can, but God will have to do the rest. Papa has to find his will to go on without her."

"I can't imagine how hard that must be for him. To find the love of your life, make a family with her, and spend every day working together, only to lose her so soon." He shook his head. "It makes me rethink my own plans."

"For a family?"

He nodded. "I had never thought much of it. Of course, the right woman hadn't yet come along."

The way he spoke made her think that perhaps she had come along now. Was he suggesting that to Elise? Was he saying that his feelings for her were just as strong as hers were for him?

She wasn't sure she was ready to hear a declaration of love. Things were happening much too fast. "Tell me about your family. You told us so little at supper the other night."

Nick seemed happy to change the conversation topic. "My mother was a great beauty. I was told she was sought by suitors far and wide before she settled on my father. She had hair the color of spun gold and eyes as blue as a fair summer's sky. She was petite like you and could sing. She used to sing at various gatherings she and Father hosted. She would also sing to my sisters and me when she visited us in the nursery. Which was quite often. She loved being a mother. My father often chided her to leave nursery work to the governess, but Mother insisted she wanted to care for her own children. Whenever we were sick, she was there to wipe our brow and still our tears." His voice took on such a loving tone that it increased the ache in Elise's heart for her own mother. "She loved to read to us too. I remember her reading Aesop's Fables and Bible stories."

"I was just remembering one of the Bible stories our mother read to me and my sister. It came to mind during the storm. It's the story of the disciples being with Jesus on the Sea of Galilee when a storm comes up. I used to recount it to Caroline when bad storms came upon us and Mama was busy with something else."

"It's always been a favorite of mine," Nick replied. "I was always in awe of the power of our Lord to calm the wind and waves."

She nodded. "I've rarely felt afraid when storms come, because I think of how God holds me in His hand. My future days are His to number. If I'm to die in a storm at sea, I know even so that He has control."

"It's such a peace of mind."

She bit her lower lip, wondering if she dared ask the question on her mind. Finally, she cleared her throat. "Did you remember it when the *Polaris* sank?"

He nodded without hesitation. "I did. As everything fell apart around me, I remembered Jesus calming the sea. The sea didn't calm around us, but the storm inside me ceased for the moment. Later, when I was rethinking it all and dealing with my sorrow and guilt, the storm came back with a vengeance." He fell silent and looked out across the water and dimly lit landscape.

Elise didn't wish to press further. "You have two sisters?"

After a long pause, he answered. "Yes. Deborah and Miriam. They're two and five years younger than I am. There were two more sons, but they died. In fact, my mother died trying to give birth to the last one. He was stillborn, and I remember looking at him and thinking him a murderer, as foolish as that sounds. It took years to forgive him. He took the only person I felt ever truly loved me."

"How sad." Elise tried to imagine feeling such anger toward an infant who never even started his life beyond his mother's womb. "How terrible it must have felt. I'm so sorry."

Nick looked at her and smiled. "Our housekeeper, Mrs. Schmitt, understood. She was the only one who did. My sisters cried for weeks. At first, they cried for the loss of their mother and the baby, and then I believe they both faded into despair when our father took off on a trip and sent us to boarding school. Mrs. Schmitt said he had often wanted to send us away, but Mother wouldn't allow it. With her gone, he had no reason to keep us near."

Elise couldn't imagine the emptiness Nick

must have felt as a child. Her own loss as an adult was difficult, but the idea of losing a mother as a child was overwhelming. "I'm so sorry you had to endure that. It must have been devastating."

Nick nodded, then changed the focus of their discussion. "Mrs. Schmitt is a good and godly woman. She did her best to comfort us and offer what love she could. When we came home on holidays, it was to a new governess and later to a very strict tutor. Father didn't want us to fall behind in our studies while away from school. Mrs. Schmitt remained the only constant besides our father."

"He sounds like a man with no feelings." Elise clapped her hand to her mouth, then slowly lowered it. "I'm sorry. I should never have said that. It's not my place to criticize."

"It's nevertheless true. I never understood if Mother's death killed his ability to feel, or if he had always put such things to one side. Maybe he was taught that feelings were dangerous and avoided them. I have no idea. I never knew my grandparents. Perhaps they taught him to be that way."

"Maybe he didn't have the strength to deal with such feelings. Have you ever considered that? A moment ago I was harshly judgmental, but it comes to mind that perhaps he was heartbroken and had nothing left to give. How old was he when his own mother died?"

"Just a child, like me." Nick shrugged. "He always made such unfeeling demands on me that I gave little consideration to his feelings. Looking back now, I can see that was wrong. When he disowned me ten years ago, my immediate thought was, 'You did this years ago, and now it's just a formality.'"

"Oh, Nick. I am sorry. What a terrible thing to endure. I'm sure some fathers think they know better than anyone. They believe their children have no understanding of what's best for them, but rather than try to discuss it and help the child or young man understand, they just place their demands and edicts."

"That was definitely my father's way. He wanted me in the mill business and saw no other option. When I refused, he was so dumbfounded that he did the only thing he thought might change my mind: abandoned me."

Elise swallowed the lump in her throat. She might have wept for that young man but knew it wouldn't help the situation.

"Elise?" her father called from the stern.

"I need to go to him." She touched Nick's arm. She hoped he understood the tenderness she felt toward him. "Life is often painful and difficult. That's why love and kindness are so important. I'm glad you had Mrs. Schmitt."

He met her eyes. "I am too."

"I hope you know you have a friend in me . . . and my father. We'll be here for you no matter what."

It was as much of a pledge as she dared give him for the moment. She hurried to go to her father, knowing that if she stayed, she might say much more.

Chapter 14

Once again, they were safely in Oswego, emptying their load of grain. Next they would take on another load of coal and head back to Duluth. It was the routine of the *Mary Elise*, and only on rare occasion did it change or include an extra stop along the way. For Nick, it was a perfect job. He wasn't in charge, he was simply a crew member, and although he longed to command again, he felt that he owed the world some sort of penance for the eight men who died on his watch.

Sometimes those memories were more than he could bear. He relived the scene so often in his thoughts and dreams that he wondered if he'd ever be free. Working on the *Mary Elise*, however, had been healing, and except for Booker Duran, Nick found everyone there forgiving.

He made the short walk to the post office to collect his mail and found a letter from Mrs. Schmitt. Dear woman. She was so good to him. Her faithful correspondence had kept Nick from feeling too alone in the world.

He walked to the nearby park and took a seat on one of the benches. He opened the letter and read.

Dearest Nick,

I am glad to hear of your new job and of the young lady who has caught your attention. I have long prayed for you to find a mate—a woman of godly character who will stand faithfully beside you through the trials and storms of life. Elise sounds like a woman who might be my answer to prayer. I hope that you will be able to get to know each other better. Remember that honesty and respect are two of the most important things in a relationship. Never take each other for granted, and always pray for each other.

On the home front, there is news is of some concern. Your father hasn't been well. I believe it's his heart, although he refuses to see a doctor. He shows signs of constant weariness and is far less active

*than he used to be. He manages busi-
ness arrangements from home these days,
which, as you know, is very unlike him.
I tell you these things only to keep you
apprised. I know that you care about him
greatly.*

*Your sisters don't appear overly con-
cerned for him, so perhaps it's just my
propensity to worry. Deborah was here
to see him just yesterday and brought
the baby. He was oddly entertained
by this and even held the child, which
surprised us all. She commented that
he appeared quite well and suggested
he come to share dinner with them on
Friday night. He declined and told her
he was already committed elsewhere. I
knew this wasn't true, but of course I
said nothing. I suppose it is possible he
has something scheduled that I know
nothing about.*

The letter continued with tidbits of neighborhood intrigue. Mrs. Schmitt had talked
to the next-door neighbor's housekeeper,
who revealed that the estate was going to be
sold now that the old master had died. Mrs.
Schmitt was concerned about whether an es-
tablished family would move in. She feared
it might be a person of new wealth and was

unsure such people could be trusted. Nick smiled at this. Mrs. Schmitt could be very suspicious and prejudiced.

He finished the letter, rereading the portion regarding his father. Was he very ill? It was hard to tell. His father had always been a very private man, but especially in matters that concerned his own health. Paired with Mrs. Schmitt's penchant for worry, it was hard to know whether there was a real problem or not. Yet another thing to commit to prayer.

Nick tucked the letter in his pocket and leaned back against the bench. It was a beautiful day in Oswego, and people everywhere were taking advantage of the day.

Father wouldn't care if I worried or not. He wouldn't want me to come. He's disowned me. Severed all ties because I wouldn't go into the textile business. Showing up now would no doubt make any heart problems worse.

Nick knew it had to be a big disappointment for your only son to turn away from the empire you'd built. For a father to anticipate passing his knowledge and industry on to his son, only to have that ungrateful wretch refuse, had to be a tremendous disappointment. Nick had tried to explain, but Father wouldn't have it. Father had told him that his reasons were merely excuses. Later Nick tried talking to his sisters, but they were afraid of offending their father. Years later, they married the men Father had chosen and nodded approvingly as their husbands went to work for the family textile business without causing difficulties. They were the obedient sons. Nick was nothing more than an outcast—ungrateful, unfeeling.

But that wasn't how Nick felt. He'd wanted to know his father better and knew working at his side would make that possible. However, as he caught glimpses of his father's stoic, demanding nature, Nick didn't like what he saw. His father's lack of concern when a child lost a hand in one of the looms, his unreasonable insistence that the windows be nailed shut, and so many other coldhearted decisions had cut Nick to the quick. His father was cruel when it came to his business dealings, and Nick could not accept that behavior as humane.

"Cap'n Clark?"

Nick was pulled from his thoughts and glanced up from the park bench.

A man smiled down at him. "It is you. I thought so." The young man extended his hand. "Do you remember me? Jack Kilroy."

Nick felt as if he'd been gut-punched but maintained a smile. Jack was one of two men Nick had been able to get off the *Polaris* alive.

"Of course I remember you, Jack. How are you doing?"

"Well enough. I got a position helpin' load the ships. Pays well enough and puts my mum's thoughts at ease, what with me havin' a job on land."

"I'm sure it does. I'm glad you're doing so well." Nick could hardly look him in the eye.

"I wouldn't be if not for you havin' saved me. My mum says you're an angel sent from God."

Nick frowned. "She doesn't understand that my bad judgment put us in that position in the first place?"

Jack's eyes widened. "It weren't your fault, Cap'n Clark. Those storms change course in the blink of an eye. Every seaman knows the dangers. You did your best and saved two of us from drownin' with the others. No sir, it weren't your fault."

Nick wished he could see it the younger man's way. "Maybe not, but it was my responsibility, and so it remains my deepest regret. We lost eight good men that day."

"Aye. We did for sure. Mum says we three didn't die because God still has things for us to accomplish and not to take that lightly."

Nick narrowed his eyes as he considered that idea. Something about Jack's words touched him deep in his heart. "Your mum said that, did she?"

"Aye. She said God is the only one who can give life or claim it, even when we put ourselves in peril—we don't have the power over life and death."

"No, I . . . suppose not." Nick had never really stopped to think of it from that perspective.

"Mum says we must make the best of the time we have. Especially when we're given a second chance." He stuck out his hand. "I've got to be on my way. My time for lunch is nearly gone."

Nick shook the young man's hand. "Thank you for stopping to speak with me, Jack. You may have made a bigger difference than you know."

The younger man smiled. "Be glad for your life, Cap'n. Don't be dwellin' on the past." With that, Jack jogged up the road toward the docks.

Nick got to his feet and began walking back to the ship, still lost in thoughts of what Jack had said. He supposed it was possible he was leaving God completely out of the situation. If three people had been saved from the *Polaris*, there could have just as easily been eleven. God had other plans. Plans that certainly weren't Nick's.

He would have to ponder that for a time.

~⌒~

Elise was just as surprised as her father to learn that Mrs. Brett had taken her children and moved away to live with her brother. It was disappointing not to be able to see her and perhaps do something nice for them. Of course, small gestures of kindness weren't enough to keep her household fed and clothed. Elise figured the widow had no choice but to seek the help of family.

"I hope she's all right," Elise said as they walked back toward the ship.

"I do too. I knew she'd be hard-pressed to support herself and the children," her father replied with a frown. "I'm glad she has family. Joe said they were all quite close."

"It's the biggest blessing to know your loved ones are there for you." They walked the rest of the block in silence before Elise got an idea. "We should get your hair trimmed. Mother would be appalled at how long it's grown, and there's a barber just across the street."

Her father chuckled. "You still think you need to fill her shoes, eh?"

Elise grew solemn. "I could never fill her shoes. But I desire to try to fill in some of those empty places. I feel it's my duty, even if it weren't my desire. I promised Mama I would take care of you."

"And because of that, you won't allow yourself any pleasure."

"What do you mean?" She looked at him for a moment but continued walking.

"I mean that Mr. Clark seems quite enamored with you, and you with him. You should be spending this time with him rather than seeing to my hair." He gave her a smile. "I'm quite capable of taking care of it myself."

"I know, Papa." She paused, trying to think of how to explain. "It's just difficult sometimes to know what I should and shouldn't do. Like with Caroline. I'd like to be there for her as well, but she pushes me away."

"You aren't her mother, so stop trying to be. Go back to being her sister, and I'm sure she'll be happy to have you."

"You're right. I know that. She said as much. Maybe we should stop by Uncle James's place and see if she's written."

"We can certainly do that, but what of my haircut?"

Elise laughed. "What's another couple of weeks?"

Her father signaled a hired cab and waited for the driver to circle around to pick them up. He gave the address, then settled back in the carriage with Elise. "The weather's going to change. It's probably hardly noticeable to most, but my joints can always tell."

"Mama used to say you were better than any weather station."

"Probably a good thing for a ship's captain, but rather hard on my body."

"Papa, do you ever think about giving up the *Mary Elise*?"

"It might surprise you, but I have. Everything changed for me when I lost your mother. The joy is gone. We sailed together as a team. We were one, and now a part of me is gone."

Elise immediately felt a sense of guilt. She had failed miserably if he were considering giving up the ship.

"But you know, after our talk the other day, I began to consider this from another angle. Your mother is always with me in a sense. I have our memories, and I have you and your sister. In so many ways, she will always be near me. I need to focus on that. She'll never really be gone."

"But still, you might leave off sailing?"

"I don't know. For the time being, all is well, but there could come a day. My future isn't as fixed as I once thought it."

His reply left her feeling unbalanced. Elise had never considered the lakes not being a part of her daily life.

The carriage pulled up in front of the Monroe house. Her father helped Elise from the conveyance, then paid the driver.

"I hope we don't upset Mrs. Cavendish by showing up unannounced," Papa said in a teasing tone.

"I'm sure we will, but we are the black sheep of the family. It's to be expected." Elise grinned at the thought of the housekeeper huffing and puffing her displeasure.

Papa knocked on the door. "I guess we'll know soon enough."

Mrs. Cavendish opened the door. "We were expecting you. Please come in."

Elise looked at her father and shrugged.

Mrs. Cavendish took Papa's hat and Elise's gloves. "They're gathered in the music room. I'll go announce you."

"Thank you," Papa said. He returned Elise's shrug. "I don't know what that was all about."

They followed Mrs. Cavendish to the music room and waited for her introduction, even though it was completely unnecessary. Uncle James came to greet them.

"We were glad to hear the *Mary Elise* was in port. Come join us. We've actually been waiting for you. I sent my man Cobert for you some time ago, but it seems you'd already left the ship."

"Yes, we had a few things to tend to. You act as if something is wrong," Papa said, his expression turning worrisome.

"There is something wrong." Uncle James stepped back to reveal Caroline sitting at the piano.

"Caroline!" Elise couldn't help herself. She rushed across the room to embrace her sister. "How are you?"

Caroline looked from Elise to their father. Tears came to her eyes. "Terrible. I'm just terrible."

"What's happened?" This came from Papa before Elise could speak.

Caroline shook her head. "Everything is wrong. Positively everything." She began to cry in earnest and buried her face in her hands. Elise sat beside her on the piano bench and put her arms around her sister.

"What has happened?" Papa asked Uncle James.

Her uncle crossed his arms. "It would seem Caroline has left her husband."

Elise's mouth dropped open. "Whatever for? I thought you were in love."

Caroline sobbed. "He canceled our wedding trip because he said he had an emergency that obligated him to stay." She began to wail. "He's hideous and awful."

"I've tried to tell her that she must go back

to him. The poor man has been here several times, demanding to see her, and she won't even talk to him."

Papa's jaw was clenched tight. Elise had never seen him so angry. She wanted to pat his arm and reassure him that everything would be all right, but she could sense that it wouldn't be well received.

"Why did he cancel the trip, Caroline?"

"He wouldn't tell me," she said, looking away as she often did when she lied. Elise knew she was deliberately keeping the truth from them, but why?

"Jim, did you ask him why?" Papa asked Uncle James.

"I did, but he said it was personal and none of my concern."

All gazes went back to Caroline, who was now sobbing into her handkerchief. Elise knew they'd get nowhere with her. She had told what portion of the story she was willing to share. Despite Caroline's deception, Elise could sense something was very wrong.

It was late. Very late, and Booker was very drunk. He had made his way from one disreputable bar to another, hoping no one would recognize him or desire his company.

Oswego wasn't very far from Buffalo, where he was wanted by the law. And he had absolutely no doubt there were wanted posters up for his arrest. Thankfully his beard was coming in nice and thick.

He hadn't intended to stay on the *Mary Elise* for the return east, but then he'd killed Rummy Carlson in Duluth and knew he couldn't stay there. So he'd stayed on with the *Mary Elise*, thinking perhaps he could simply hide away on her while the others went to town, but the need for alcohol was much too strong.

He purposefully didn't come back to the ship early. He hoped by the time he returned that everyone but the watchman would be fast asleep. With any luck, he could slip into bed unnoticed. But luck had never been his ally.

"Who goes there?" the watch called out.

It sounded like young Tom. Booker straightened and smiled. "Duran."

Tom stepped out of the shadows. "Hey, you're back really late."

"Yes, well, the evening got away from me." Duran pushed down his anger at having to answer to this runt of a child. "I'm going to bed."

Tom said nothing, and Duran figured he'd gotten away with it by the time he reached the forecastle entrance. But unfortunately, Nick Clark stood there as if awaiting Duran's appearance.

"Duran, you've been warned about returning to the *Mary Elise* drunk."

"Who says I'm drunk?"

"I do. I watched you approach the ship and walk across the deck. You've clearly been drinking."

Duran struggled to focus. "Well, what if I am? You can't dictate what a fella can do when he's off the ship."

"No, you're right. I can't. But I can enforce the rules when on board. Captain Wright said there's to be no alcohol and no drunkenness. You'll be on extra cleanup duty this week, and this is your last warning. If you show up drunk again, you'll be fired once and for all."

"You think you're in charge now, is that it?"

"I'm the first mate. In the absence of the captain, I *am* in charge. Captain and Miss Elise sent word that they're staying with Mr. Monroe tonight. They won't be back until it's time for Miss Elise to start working on breakfast, which I believe will be about two hours from now."

"I'm going to bed."

"As long as you're back up when the bells

chime." Nick smiled. "As I said, I believe that's in just about two hours."

Duran had had enough. He turned and took a swing at Nick, but in his drunkenness, he telegraphed it so clearly that Nick had plenty of time to get out of the way.

"You're only adding to your punishment, Duran."

He hated Clark. Hated him more than he'd ever hated anyone. He swung again, and again Nick easily dodged the attack. But then, as Duran turned, Clark had the audacity to kick him in the backside. Duran fell to the deck.

"Two weeks of extra cleaning duty."

Duran stumbled to his feet. "You'll get yours one day. You're just as much a murderer as—" He realized he'd been about to implicate himself and backed off. "You didn't deserve to live. One of these days, the men of the *Polaris* will come and take you down to the depths."

He barely managed the steps down to the sleeping quarters. He sat on the edge of his bunk, listening to the snores of the other men. Duran fumbled with his boots and finally managed to get them off before falling back against his bed.

One of these days he was going to kill Nick Clark.

Nick saw Elise and her father walk up the gangplank just before the watchman sounded eight bells.

"Welcome back, Captain," Nick announced in greeting.

"Nick," the captain said with a nod. "Thanks for managing the loading. Any problems with the coal?"

"None at all, Captain."

Wright smiled. "Is there anything else to report?"

"Duran returned just two hours ago and drunk. He took two swings at me, and I kicked him in the backside, knocking him to the deck."

Elise giggled. "I suppose it isn't kind to laugh, but I would have liked to see Duran put in his place. But, for now, I'll leave you two to your discussion."

Nick smiled and watched as she made her way to the deckhouse.

"Is that all?" the captain asked.

"I assigned him two weeks of extra cleaning duty."

"Good." Captain Wright's manner was no-nonsense. "I'll speak to him after breakfast and make it clear that he'll be put off the ship if it happens again." He rubbed his eyes.

"Didn't you sleep well, Captain?"

"I'm afraid not. My daughter surprised us by being at her uncle's house. Apparently, something happened with her husband having to cancel their wedding trip. Now she's decided to end her marriage and makes no sense as to why. It's a good thing I have a tight schedule and a brother-in-law to help in my absence. Otherwise I'd probably be sobbing alongside her. At times like these I miss her mother all the more."

Nick frowned. "I am sorry to hear of your troubles. If you'd rather rest, I can take on your duties this morning. I've had a good sleep."

For a moment he thought the captain would take him up on his offer. After a brief hesitation, however, Wright shook his head. "No, it's best I stay busy and get us out of here as soon as possible. Have we finished all the paperwork?"

"Yes. We're ready to go."

"Thank you, Nick. I'm glad I can count on you."

Nick watched him go. It wasn't going to be an easy morning.

Chapter 15

August drifted into September, and the sailing was good. The routine of their trips gave consistency to the crew that helped keep the peace among the men. Even Booker had been less trouble.

In mid-September, they left Oswego behind once again and sailed west toward the Welland Canal. The series of locks would take them from the lower-lying Lake Ontario to the higher-sitting Lake Erie.

Elise paused in her work to watch for a moment as the *Mary Elise* was tied off to bollards as the lock gates closed behind her. Elise was enthralled with modern mechanisms of efficiency. Her sister had never been interested in the locks at Sault Sainte Marie nor those at Welland, while Elise had loved both. There were other places along the lengthy trip that always fascinated Elise as well. But the Welland Canal had been built so ships had a way to enter Lake Ontario without having to end their trip at Buffalo due to the Niagara Falls.

"It's a good thing they're rebuilding these locks. The *Mary Elise* is a snug fit on some of them."

Elise looked up to find Nick watching her. "Yes. Papa said the improvements are much needed. He said they're also arranging it so that the locks will raise the ship higher and reduce the number of locks needed. That will also be very nice and will get us through this daylong production in less time. Not that I mind completely. I've always been fascinated by the genius of those who figured this out."

"I definitely appreciate it myself. Especially when one sees the falls at Niagara."

"Oh, indeed. I stand in awe at the handiwork of God there. Papa took us there to see it when I was nearly fifteen. All I could think of was how mighty God truly was, and how awesome it was that He's given men minds to figure out an alternative way around obstacles."

They fell silent, and Elise watched as the water leveled out and they prepared to open the gates.

"I enjoyed lunch. It was wonderful, and I didn't get a chance to thank you."

"I'm glad you liked it. I wasn't even sure I would be on this trip."

"Why is that?"

She kept her gaze fixed on the lock gate. "My sister Caroline is in trouble, and she wanted me to stay in Oswego with her. I was torn but couldn't abandon all of you."

"What seems to be the trouble now?"

Elise sighed and turned to face him. "Oh, Nick. She truly wants to end her marriage. She still won't really say why, except that her husband allowed some emergency to cancel their wedding trip. I've never known her to be so shallow-minded and selfish. I mean, she's always been willful and liked nice things, but this was different. She's never been one to embarrass herself by causing a scandal. Scandal is something she's avoided at all costs."

"I am sorry." His frown deepened. "I think, however, it's best not to come between married folks."

"I agree, but I can't help worrying." Elise shook her head. "She's never been in a situation like this, and I couldn't help soothe her. I'm not a wife. I wish our mother was alive. She'd know best how to handle the matter."

"I'm sorry. You must be very grieved over her situation."

"I am. My father is angry because Nelson wouldn't even speak to him. Papa went to his house, but Nelson wouldn't receive him. Nor would he see my uncle and, well, Uncle James is the one who helped to make this match and paid a large dowry. He promised Papa he'd see that the problem was resolved, but I'm not sure I understand what that means. Caroline wouldn't even be honest about the problem. I know her well enough to know she's holding back the truth."

"Again, it's not good for others to insert themselves into problems between a husband and wife."

"Did your parents fight? Ours rarely even disagreed."

"They had their issues, to be sure. My father was too often away with work, and my mother longed for him to be at home. I never understood that, however, for I saw my father as mean and temperamental when he was with us. My mother endured a lot for the sake of her marriage and children."

Elise watched as the gate began to open. "Caroline's changed so much. I'm very concerned about her."

"Of course you are. You love her." Nick's words momentarily soothed her.

She continued to ponder her conversation with Caroline. "I feel responsible for her in so many ways since Mama is gone. I made promises to our mother that I would take care of her—that I'd always be there for her. But I can do nothing."

"Sometimes we make promises we have no right or calling to make. Sometimes you can only stand by and watch as life plays out."

Elise thought of his shipwreck. "Is that how it was on the *Polaris*?" she asked before considering how the question might make him feel.

Nick's brows rose, and he looked away. For a long moment he said nothing. Finally, he nodded. "Yes. It was exactly that way. It was like I was chained to the mast. I needed desperately to save the ship but couldn't. It was like everything had been taken out of my hands. I was nothing more than a puppet—controlled by someone else."

The ropes used to keep the *Mary Elise* from bouncing around in the lock were released from the bollards. The canal men used horses in this section to move the *Mary Elise* to the next lock not far away.

"Tell me what happened . . . please." Elise turned to face him. "I want to know for myself."

Nick seemed to consider for a moment. He seemed so apprehensive that Elise immediately regretted her request.

"You don't have to tell me if you don't want to."

"We were running late," he began. "I saw the storm building to the southwest, but it appeared to be heading northeast and away from us. I figured we might have a bumpy ride from higher waves, but I wasn't overly worried. We were carrying crated goods and wouldn't suffer from the load shifting much, so I thought there was little reason to fear. I dismissed the storm from my mind and got caught up with my bookwork. By the time I realized the storm had back-built and shifted directions, it was too late.

"I could see the storm approaching and thought I could outrun it, but of course I couldn't. I finally sought a place to ride it out, but the storm was too fierce and powerful. It slammed us from side to side and tried to drown us. When I knew we were breaking apart, I tried to get us near enough to shore, but the water was too powerful and threw us against the rocks. The boat fell apart beneath our feet, and even as I tried to rescue the men, they were swept away. I managed to save two, but the other eight were lost."

His face bore the look of a tormented man. "I still dream about them . . . about the storm. It torments me to know my pride caused their death. If I'd kept a better watch—if I hadn't thought I knew best—it might have been a different story."

"It seems to me you judged correctly, but things changed."

"A captain should always be aware of his surroundings. He should be constantly on watch for dangers, seen and unseen. I got caught up with my own agenda. I wanted to make up time, and instead I lost everything."

"But, Nick, you didn't intend for those men to die. You are one of hundreds, if not thousands, of captains who have been caught off guard and had no chance to get to safety. Even if you had . . . there's no telling what might have happened."

"There's no excuse for my lapse in judgment." He shook his head. "I took the news to each of the dead men's families. They were brokenhearted—devastated. I gave them my apology as well as a bonus in lieu of each man's life. It was my own money—not even the company's funds. I thought it the very least I could do. Later, as the story was passed around the community, some saw no fault in my choices and others did. Some forgave me and others hated me. I hated myself." He gazed off across the landscape beyond the locks. "I still do."

"I wish you didn't."

He looked back at her. His blue eyes bored into her heart. "Why? Why should it matter so much to you?"

She smiled. "Because you can't love with hate in your heart."

Caroline looked at her uncle in disbelief. "What are you saying?"

"Nelson doesn't want a divorce. He will not agree to grant you one. He wants you back at the house, fulfilling your role as wife."

"I won't go. I want nothing to do with him."

"He has assured me that he will never again speak harshly to you, nor will he fail to include you in his plans."

"Ha! He's a liar and a beast. Why should I believe him? I thought he loved me, but he clearly only loved the money you gave him. Had I known he demanded such a large dowry . . . well, I never would have agreed to marry him."

"But what's done is done. Oh, I do wish your sister had stayed here. Perhaps you would have talked to her . . . or better yet, listened to her. Your aunt is positively beside herself at the thought of scandal."

Caroline shook her head and rose to leave. "That's what concerns you?" No thought for the beating Nelson had given her on their wedding night. Of course, she hadn't told her aunt and uncle about Nelson's striking her. She had held back, uncertain what her father might have done had he known. Now she was beginning to regret not just telling them. Except for Etta, no one knew how black and blue she'd been when she first arrived here. Nelson only hit her where it wouldn't show.

"I am sorry that your marriage is less than ideal, but, Caroline, you must give the man a chance to make it right. After all, you are married in God's eyes, and . . . well, I assume that you have been together as man and wife."

She turned a bit too quickly and stared at him blankly. "Yes, unfortunately, we have been together as man and wife, but if I have anything to say about it, we never will again."

"Caroline, be reasonable—"

"I have been reasonable," she interjected. "Frankly, I'm done being reasonable."

She left the room and climbed the stairs to her old bedroom. She'd said nothing about the extent of her injuries nor of Nelson's indignities, but perhaps she should. Maybe it would give her uncle a reason to reconsider his push for her return to Nelson's prison.

"I'm going to lie down," she told Etta. "Help me rid myself of this gown . . . please."

It was odd how Elise's suggestion to show kindness had changed Caroline's relationship with the maid. The girl seemed to care about her rather than just go through the paces of her duties.

"Of course, madam." The maid went to work unfastening the buttons and hooks. After she'd helped Caroline step out of the dress, she reached for the corset ties.

"No, leave it. I'm sure I won't be able to rest for long."

The maid nodded. "Would you like the window opened a bit? It's quite pleasant outside."

Caroline nodded and pulled one of the lacy pillows into her arms to hug. "That would be very nice. Thank you."

Etta opened the window and then headed for the door. "Should I wake you in time to dress for dinner?"

"No, I'd prefer you bring me a tray tonight. I don't want to sit through another formal dinner with Uncle James interrogating me about my situation."

The maid nodded and exited the room, pulling the door closed behind her. Caroline sighed. None of them knew how great her pain was. She was humiliated amongst her peers, and all of society would look at her past and her upbringing and whisper about how expected it was that she should embarrass her aunt and uncle and husband in such a fashion. After all, she was just a ship captain's daughter.

She closed her eyes as tears began to fall.

She had stupidly chosen to fall in love in the wake of her mother's death. The pain of losing her had been more than Caroline could bear. More than she could admit to Elise, who had remained true to the family. When Caroline had learned of her mother's death, she hadn't even been able to cry. She'd been numb—unable to know what she was feeling. Uncertain that she was feeling anything at all. Nelson made her feel alive again. He was attentive in his courtship, which upon reflection, surprised her more and more. His game had only been about money, and hers had been about status. Her mother had left society and her privileged life because of love. Caroline thought she was getting it back for the sake of the same.

"I was such a selfish girl," she murmured as the hot tears fell. "And now I'm being punished. God must hate me."

The *Mary Elise* reached Duluth on the thirtieth of September. There had been more than one storm to contend with, but they'd come through in good order. Elise was glad her father had taken no chances with the *Mary Elise* and crew. He always made her feel safe and protected with his knowledge of the lakes and places where they could find shelter.

Elise headed to the cottage while her father instructed the men and took care of unloading the coal. Mina was glad to see her and greeted Elise with some news.

"We're going to have a baby," she declared after inviting Elise in for coffee.

"Oh, many congratulations. This is so exciting for you."

"Yes, our first. I'm so happy, I could shout and cry at the same time. We only just learned for certain yesterday. The doctor said we will be welcoming the baby to our family around February, so you'll be here—won't you?"

Elise chuckled. "Yes, I'll be here. God willing."

"I'm so glad. Carter is thrilled about the baby but very worried about me being alone during the days while he's working. He's taken work at the sawmill, and come winter it will require he go to the logging camps from time to time."

"I feel certain from things Papa has said that our last trip will be around Christmas, if not sooner. He said it'll depend on the schedule of things and how bad the weather is."

Mina poured her a mug of coffee. "I hope this isn't too strong."

"It will be fine," Elise assured her. "So, do you want a boy or a girl?"

"A boy. Carter wants a son. I'm praying

it will be so, but I'd love a daughter just as much."

"I can imagine I'd feel the same way." Elise put cream in the black liquid and then sampled it. It was strong, but the flavor was good.

"How was your trip?"

Elise shook her head. "We had a storm going out and then several small squalls coming back. The hardest part was our time in Oswego. My sister Caroline wanted me to stay with her."

"Is she already back from her wedding trip?"

"She never got to go. I thought I'd told you. Apparently, there was some emergency, and her husband canceled. That started some sort of calamity in her marriage." Elise held back telling her everything. "There are other difficulties I am not at liberty to discuss, but I wanted to ask you to please pray for her. You've always been so good to pray when things were difficult."

The young woman nodded. "I love to pray for people. It seems like such a gift of love."

"Yes, I agree. What better way to show the depth of our love?" Elise took another sip of coffee. She thought of Nick and the pain he bore from the loss of the *Polaris*. "Oh, and if you could, pray for a friend of mine as well.

He's struggling to forgive himself for things he misjudged."

Mina met her gaze. "Of course. You do know, however, that sometimes that's a really hard thing to do."

"I do," Elise replied, knowing Nick blamed himself for the deaths of his crew. "This is definitely one of those times."

"And you might pray that the authorities find the murderer they're looking for."

"A murderer?"

"Yes. There was a murder here some time ago. It was just around the time you left in July. The dates are uncertain. A man was killed and his body hidden in a woodpile. Someone used a knife and robbed him. It was brutal and quite shocking. The police have been searching everywhere for the man responsible."

"Do they know who did it?"

"No, but someone saw a man slip away from the scene and gave them a description. They said he was big."

Elise thought immediately of Booker Duran and his bloody shirt. Could he be the man they were looking for?

By the time her father came in, it was late. She wasn't sure why it had taken him so long to deal with the Customs House and unloading, but he wasn't in a good mood, so she decided to say nothing about her concerns regarding Booker Duran. She didn't know with any certainty that it was him.

"I have supper warming on the stove. I think I'll leave you to yourself and go take a bath. I was just getting ready to do that when you came in."

"Thank you. That's fine. I'm quite tired and would prefer just to eat and go to bed."

Elise gave him a nod. She wanted to ask what was bothering him but knew he'd say nothing.

She slipped into the room they'd set aside as a pantry and space for laundry and bathing. She locked the outside door and made certain to lock the inside one as well, just in case her father forgot or someone came calling. No sense in embarrassing someone, including herself.

Her blouse was dirty from a day's work, and her skirt hadn't fared much better. More laundry to do. The thought of laundry reminded her of Duran's bloody shirt. So much blood.

He said it had come from a fight at one of the bars. That everyone had been fighting. She wondered if there was any way to find out about that. She could hardly go around from tavern to tavern, asking about fights they'd had two months ago. Fights were common.

Maybe she shouldn't have made assumptions about Duran. He had a temper and a bad disposition, but that certainly didn't mean he'd killed someone. And yes, he'd been much too forward with her, but that also wasn't a reason to despise him. After all, her cousin's friend had also attacked her, and she'd never thought of him again until just now.

Elise sank into the copper tub of warm water, wishing it were hotter. She let down her hair and slipped as deep as she could. Once her hair was wet, she began to scrub it with the soap.

How could she find out what had really happened? Duran would surely never volunteer the information. Nick came to mind. Maybe she could find him and tell him what had happened. She hated to bother him on his evening off. She wasn't even sure where she could go to find him.

Maybe it was best to keep it to herself, and then, once they'd sailed, she could tell Nick what she knew, and he could check it out the next time they were in Duluth. After all, it might have happened when they weren't even in port, and the bloody shirt could be just what Duran had told her.

But what if it wasn't?

Chapter 16

Elise found her father in a worse mood the next morning. He was anxious to get the *Mary Elise* on her way and pushed for everyone to work double-time. The fact that it was October first made him keep to a very tight schedule. They were running out of time for shipping, and the worst storms of the season were due to come upon them in the few remaining weeks.

Knowing breakfast would be rushed, Elise didn't make a hot meal. Instead, she put out lots of hot coffee, fresh fruit, pickled herring, cold ham, and a variety of breads she'd picked up at a local bakery. With that done, she sat down to share their morning Bible reading and prayers.

"You seem preoccupied, Papa. What has you so concerned?"

"I didn't want to say anything to you last night, but Uncle James has another job for us before we return to Oswego."

"What does he want us to do?"

"Sail to Chicago and pick up some major parts. They're building a new mill, and apparently they've had no luck getting anyone to bring them up. I sent him a telegram back, telling him we were loaded with grain and ready to leave for Oswego, but this morning another telegram came, directing me where to deliver the grain in Chicago." He hit his fist against the table. "I don't like last-minute changes. He knows that."

"I'm sorry, Papa. I know that makes it hard on you. At least Nick is very familiar with that area. You'll have great help in getting there and back."

Her father's expression softened. "I suppose I should be counting my blessings."

Elise went to him and hugged him. "How can I help?"

"Just keep the galley for now. I'll let you know if I need something more."

Elise smiled up at her father. "You've got it. Coffee will be ready in another couple of minutes. We should probably get our reading done and pray."

"You're right again. Let's get to it."

The trip into Chicago had been complicated only by the length of time they'd needed to wait for a tugboat to help them navigate the Chicago River. With the grain quickly deposited and the load of sawmill machinery picked up, the *Mary Elise* was soon on its way back to Duluth, and the dreaded city was behind them.

The weather was so favorable on the return that to make top speed, Elise's father ordered every inch of canvas sail to be set. They even had a short race with the *Annie Peterson*, whose captain was known never to allow any challenge to go unmet. He was so sure of his ship's ability to best any other that he kept a broom perpetually tied to his main mast as a signal of challenge to any takers. Nick knew the captain personally and thought the *Mary Elise* could beat her, but alas, it wasn't to be. Nevertheless, the men enjoyed the challenge and cheered one another on as they went their separate ways.

The camaraderie between the men seemed to lift everyone's spirits, and by the time they were back in Duluth, it seemed the side trip had been more of a refreshing voyage than an extra duty.

Elise took the helm at lunchtime on the

day they left Duluth, once again bound for Oswego. Her father's mirth hadn't lasted, due to another telegram that awaited him—this time from Caroline.

"She insists that we come get her and bring her to live with us in Duluth," he told Elise as he traded places with her at the wheel.

"Why didn't you tell me before?"

"What good would it have done? I hardly know more than her determination to leave Oswego and her husband for good. I don't know what has happened to make it so critical that she leave now, but thank you for taking the helm. I need to speak to the men and let them know my plans for the day. The weather's due to change. I know this from the weather station as well as my knee joints." He smiled. "I'll send someone out to relieve you as soon as possible."

Elise didn't mind steering the ship. It was a wonderful time to contemplate and pray. She had often thought that if open sailing was all that was required of a captain, she might have sought out the job for herself. There were, after all, other women schooner captains. She'd heard of several who handled a ship as well as their husbands.

The wind picked up from time to time, but for the most part her job was uneventful. It was just the blue cloud-dotted sky, the endless water, and her. Elise could almost pretend she was alone. That was why it made such a great time for prayer.

"I never pray so much as when I'm at the wheel," she told her father when he came to relieve her. She gave him a kiss on his cheek, since no one was around to see.

"Me too," he admitted. "The men are nearly done eating. Good soup, by the way. Split pea and ham always sticks to the ribs."

"I'm glad you enjoyed it. There will be more of your favorites for supper."

She left him and hurried back into the deckhouse as the wind once again picked up. Depositing her coat and hat on a peg, she heard the men's various comments on the good lunch as they headed out the door. She'd barely reached the stove when a wave sent the nearly empty coffeepot sliding. Elise easily caught it, and Tom applauded.

"Looks like we're in for fun," he said, getting up from the table. "I'd best see if the captain needs me."

Nick was the last to go. He pulled on his knit cap and threw her a smile. "Lunch was wonderful. I feel I can face the dropping temperatures and gusting winds now."

She laughed and gave him a salute. "It's great to be appreciated. Which brings me to something I wanted to say to you. The way you handled things in Chicago really impressed me. Papa hates sailing into Chicago. He avoids it like the plague. You just did it with matter-of-fact grace."

Nick's face sobered. "I was plenty worried. Not having been there for six months makes a big difference. They've already rebuilt a lot from last year's fire. I was impressed by how much something could change in such a short time."

"Well, I thought it might have been hard sailing there again because of . . . well, what happened with the *Polaris*. I worried it might have caused you pain."

He nodded. "I didn't realize anyone else would even think of it. It was hard, but keeping busy and praying helped a great deal."

"I prayed for you too, but maybe next time you might talk to me." She smiled. "We all have our ghosts, Nick. Our regrets, our sorrows. I find they're handled easiest when sharing the burden with someone else."

He gave her a tender look. "Thank you. I'll remember that."

The moment tied her inexplicably to him. "Well, I was still impressed with the way you maneuvered Chicago ports. You made it look easy."

His smile returned, and the ghosts faded away. "It was all done just to impress you."

Elise chuckled and started making another pot of coffee. "Then you accomplished what you set out to do."

He gave a mock bow and headed out of the deckhouse. Elise couldn't help laughing all the more. He made her days better in every way.

That thought made her sober in an instant. Mama used to say that about Papa. The memory made her heart skip a beat.

A supper of pork roasts with onions and yams baked in the oven while Elise took on her mending. There was quite a bit of it. Four torn shirt sleeves, two frayed collars, a pair of pants with the backside ripped out, and Tom's good trousers that were in desperate need of the hem being let out. He was growing like a weed.

She settled down in her cabin to sew, mindful of the time. The stove would need to be loaded with wood from time to time in order for everything to cook through. Not only that, but she needed to keep an eye on the coffee and make sure there was plenty. Thankfully, the waters were fairly calm.

On deck, Elise could hear her father calling out commands. At one point the men were singing as they sometimes did, depending on the task at hand. Ollie said the music helped make the chores pass more quickly, while Booker Duran called it cater-wauling that was enough to make a grown man cry. It seemed there was very little that Duran liked.

Thinking of Duran brought back her previous concerns. What if they did have a murderer on board? She vowed to talk to her father when the first opportunity presented itself.

Mending sails was never a favorite job of Booker Duran. He always did whatever he could to get out of it—even volunteering to do extra cleaning duty. Unfortunately, he'd had enough of that as well.

The night before, he'd started to go for a drink in Duluth but then had seen the signs posted all over with descriptions of Rummy Carlson's killer. The height and weight listed was too closely a match for his own. It was enough to send him back to the *Mary Elise* to rethink his plans. The witness hadn't been close enough to get a real look at him. Not like the witnesses in Buffalo, who had described Duran right down to the scar on his chin. Yet another reason for his full beard and mustache. It had totally changed his appearance. He barely recognized himself in the mirror and felt certain the beard would keep the law from singling him out. But a fella couldn't change his height. Thankfully, Duluth was full of big-shouldered Dutchmen and Swedes. He wasn't the only large man around these parts.

He wasn't all that worried about either murder except for the fact that Elise Wright knew about his bloody shirt. He'd given her a good enough excuse. Men got in fights all the time, and weeks had gone by. As for the murder in Buffalo, even more time had passed for that matter to have died down. The dead man was a nobody—just a cardplayer who'd gotten out of hand. They'd both had knives, and the other man had threatened him. It shouldn't matter that Duran had pulled his knife first. The man brandished a weapon, and Duran had to take care of himself or the fella would have killed him.

"You done with that jib?" the captain questioned.

Duran got to his feet. "Just about, Captain. I was never very good at repairing sails."

For several long moments, Captain Wright just stared at him. "What are you good at?"

This sobered Duran. He felt his temper rise. "I'm good at a lot of things, Captain, and strong as an ox. You know full well I can trim a load in no time at all."

"That's true enough. It just seems you have no interest in much of anything on the *Mary Elise*. You're still bickering with the men, although you did purchase Tom another harmonica."

Booker grimaced. He had hated having to spend his hard-earned money on that boy's enjoyment, but leave it to Nick Clark to remind him. "I was happy to do it. It weren't right that I lost my temper with the boy."

"No, it wasn't. Most of the men have made complaints about you and the way you've treated them. Not a one of them trusts you."

"That's hardly fair, Captain. They don't know me."

"They say you cheat at cards, slack off on your work, and sleep on night watch. A complete disregard for your duties. I can't abide that in a man, much less one who works for me."

Duran's anger was barely under the boiling point. He'd never tolerated a man insulting him—not even someone in the position of being his boss. "Look, I've done nothing wrong. Those men are just jealous. I don't have to cheat to beat them. I can't help it if they aren't able to hold their own in a game of cards, but I'll just stop playing with them. It'll give me more time to sleep—when I'm not on watch," he said, his sarcasm thick enough to spread.

"I used to be just like you, Duran."

"I doubt that, Captain. You don't strike me as the kind of man who's been kicked around like I have."

Captain Wright squared his shoulders. "You'd be surprised. Before I made my peace with God, I was in quite a few jails for beating men half to death. My temper always got the best of me."

Duran could see the truth of it in the captain's eyes. "Why are you telling me this? I have to finish this jib."

For a moment the captain stared hard at him. Duran didn't like the sense of the man's disdain. He'd read it on the faces of others every day of his life. People didn't like him. He didn't fit in their world, and they despised him for it. Well, one of these days he'd see that they learned to accept him, and if not that, then they'd tolerate him with respect . . . or die.

"Booker, like you, I used to fight my way through everything. I did it so no one could claim a hold on me or the right to control me. I even became a captain because I wanted no man telling me what to do. What I didn't realize was that having all the authority meant I'd also have all the responsibility. While you're on the *Mary Elise*, you answer to me, and that in turn makes me responsible for you—just like all the others. I want . . . *need* my men to get along. I'm suggesting you find a way to make that happen."

"Aye, Captain." Duran refused to look him in the eye. He hated the captain almost as much as he hated his first mate. The day was coming when he'd show them both that neither of them had command over him. Booker Duran—Robert Wayfair—was his own boss, and no one else would ever take that from him.

Elise finished rearranging the room and stood back. This was how it used to be when she and Caroline shared a cabin. It had bunk beds that Caroline would no doubt hate even though she was raised in them. Elise had already decided she would take the upper bunk. As the youngest of the two, Caroline would have slept there when they were children, but her years of being a socially perfect lady would never allow her to climb up to bed, so Elise had resigned herself to the position. She wanted Caroline to be as comfortable as possible.

With this job complete and still another

week to reach Oswego, Elise felt anxiety course through her. She'd tried to keep herself busy, but there was so much going on that she couldn't figure out how to tell her father her concerns about Duran. She had started to on more than one occasion, but the conversation always led back to Caroline's situation and the coming winter. Father was very glad things had happened when they did so that Caroline wouldn't be forced to remain in Oswego. He couldn't imagine her wanting to leave her uncle's care, but since she did, he feared things had developed into an even more critical situation. It appeared to Elise that he was barely able to keep his mind on sailing.

After supper, the men took up their various instruments and played a little serenade for the captain and Elise. Mother had been the one to encourage them to form a small band. Two of the men played guitar, and of course there was Tom's harmonica. Ollie could handle a squeezebox well enough to charm them all, and Sam managed the fiddle. It was quite the merry band.

Duran seemed unhappy with the affairs of the evening and went to bed early. Elise found herself glad for his absence. She had never known such a dislike for anyone, but more than that, she feared what he could do to the rest of the crew. He always seemed ready for a fight or insult.

She walked to the rail to look out on the black water. The boys broke into their own rendition of "Cottage by the Sea." Those not playing an instrument joined in by singing. Elise thought it all quite lovely. The lake . . . the music . . . the night.

"You look so contented here that I hate to impose myself," Nick said, joining her. "But I've given something a lot of thought and would like your opinion on the matter."

Elise smiled up at him in the soft glow of lantern light. "I would be happy to hear your thoughts on most anything."

"Good. That makes this easier."

She waited for him to continue. Even though he said it was easier, he looked nervous. He glanced out at the water as if trying to find the right words, then finally straightened and looked her in the eye.

"Elise . . . I . . . well, I have feelings for you."

She smiled. "I have feelings for you, as well."

He let go a sigh and seemed greatly relieved. "I've never felt this way, so I can't say for sure exactly what the depth of those feelings are . . . but they seem very deep."

She chuckled. "I've wrestled with the same thing, but I believe it must be love."

She surprised herself by speaking so frankly and hurried to apologize in case she'd said too much. "I hope that doesn't offend you."

It was his turn to laugh, and for the first time since joining her, he relaxed. "You haven't offended me at all. In fact, just the opposite. I wasn't sure I could use that word without offending you."

Elise leaned back against the rail and gazed at Nick. "I've never known anyone like you. I've always avoided getting to know any man very well for fear of falling in love, because you know of my pledge to care for my father. Yet you like my father and sailing, so I see the possibilities of us all being able to remain on the *Mary Elise* . . . together."

Nick nodded. "I'm not trying to push for something at this point. I just wanted to share my feelings and see if there was a chance you might feel the same way."

"I think we both knew we were feeling the same thing. Sometimes I see it in your eyes, and I know you can see it in mine. I think in important matters it's best just to be forthcoming."

"I'm glad you feel that way."

"You two seem mighty talkative over here," Elise's father said, coming to join them.

"We've just declared that we have feelings for each other." Elise's tone was serious.

"Well, it's about time." Papa turned to go. "I won't be the cause of interrupting talk of love."

"But we can speak more of that later." Elise caught her father's arm, and he turned back to face her. "Papa, I've needed to tell you something since we were in Duluth, but it always seems something else comes up. The weather . . . my sister . . . something with the ship. Or Booker Duran is around, and I cannot speak."

"Why not?" her father asked.

"Because it's about him." Elise frowned. "You know there was a murder in Duluth when we were in port sometime around July or so?"

"Aye. Are you thinking the man responsible was Duran? The description did fit, but he isn't the only tall, broad-shouldered man in Duluth. There are a lot of Dutchmen and Scandies who match that description."

"I know, but he had a bloody shirt. Just after we left Duluth, it showed up in the laundry. I asked him what had happened. He told me it was just a tavern brawl, but it seemed an awful lot of blood."

Nick shook his head. "Why didn't you show the shirt to one of us and let us deal with him?"

"I didn't think of it. I was doing laundry and had already started the process of getting the blood out before I even asked Duran about it. Since he had a quick and ready answer, and I knew nothing about the murder . . . I simply dismissed any further thought. It was only when Mina told me there had been a murder that I thought of it again."

"Perhaps I can ask the other men. It's been a long while, but if he came back to ship with a bloody shirt, someone must have seen him."

"I hadn't thought of that, Papa. It wouldn't surprise me if one of the men had even been drinking with Mr. Duran. Maybe they saw the whole thing." She relaxed a bit. "I don't want to be quick to judge him just because he makes me uncomfortable. In fact, I've chided myself more than once about even making note of the matter."

"Nick and I will see to it. You leave it to us now and worry no more." Papa kissed her on the head. "Do you understand? If he is a murderer, I certainly don't want you having any chance to be harmed by him."

She nodded and hugged her father's waist. "I understand and will leave it with the two of you."

"And I'll leave the two of you to discuss your interests in each other." He gave a big smile. "If it matters to either of you, I approve."

Elise glanced at Nick, who seemed a little embarrassed. "Thank you, Papa."

She waited until her father left them, then took a few steps backward, pulling Nick with her farther into the darkness and away from prying eyes.

"What's all this about?" Nick asked in a teasing tone.

"I don't want anyone to see us. I'm glad you and Papa are going to check further into Mr. Duran's dealings, but if there is something I can do to help, let me know. I don't want to worry Papa, but I think this is a very worrisome situation."

He drew closer. "Is that the only reason you pulled me into the darkness?"

She smiled but doubted he could see her face very well. "No. I thought you might be encouraged to kiss me."

He gave a soft chuckle. "I need no encouragement." He wrapped her in his arms and pulled her close. "I can't tell you how many times I've wanted to do this."

"Probably as many times as I've wanted you to." She sighed as she turned her head up to meet his lips.

Chapter 17

"No, I won't go back to him," Caroline told her uncle. "I don't care what he has promised or threatened."

"He hasn't threatened anything. He knows what he did was wrong. He said the strain of all that happened on his wedding day was what brought on his poor behavior."

Caroline rolled her gaze toward the ceiling. "I'm sure he was filled with all sorts of remorse. He should be, but I will not go back. You don't know half the truth about him, and neither did I. I probably still don't, but I know enough to say he's not a fit human being."

"Gracious, child. I could hear you on the porch outside."

She looked toward the entryway and saw her father and Elise. "Oh, I'm so glad you've finally come! Maybe you can explain to Uncle

James why I will not stay married to Nelson Worthington."

"Perhaps if I understood the reason, I could," her father replied.

"You have us at a disadvantage," Elise added. "We don't know what all has happened or why you have telegraphed saying you wish to sail to Duluth on the *Mary Elise*."

"You what?" Uncle James asked, shaking his head. "You can't be serious."

Caroline turned and met his look of disbelief. "I believe that's better than remaining in a marriage where I will forever come in second to Nelson's mistress."

"What's this?" her father asked, his brow furrowing as he frowned.

"That was the emergency on my wedding day. That was why we canceled our wedding trip. His mistress tried to kill herself because Nelson had married."

There. She had finally revealed the ugly truth. Well, at least part of it.

"I threatened to tell his father and mother about the entire matter once I learned about it." She sat down on the chintz-covered settee. "That's partially why he beat me . . . the first time."

"I knew nothing about this," Uncle James said, staggering to the nearest chair. "I swear."

"No, no one did. I told no one of the beatings, and Nelson is a superb liar and quite cunning when it comes to hiding his mistress from public scrutiny. She knew about me but thought that since it was an arranged marriage, it would mean nothing. She figured me for a homely creature who had to pay in order to get a husband."

"Why did her opinion change on your wedding day?" Elise asked.

"She was at the wedding. I had no idea, of course. She snuck in with a group of invited guests. She wore appropriate clothing, so no one thought anything of it. She saw us take our vows and saw how beautiful I was and how happy we both looked, and realized this wasn't a marriage in name only, as she'd thought it to be."

"I'm mortified that she was allowed into the church," Uncle James said, shaking his head.

"Be that as it may, how did you learn of her attempt to end her life?"

Caroline looked at her father. "She sent a letter to say good-bye. We had barely arrived at our new home to allow Nelson to change for our trip when the butler met him with the letter in hand.

"Nelson raced out of the house, telling his valet to cancel our trip and see that I was installed in the house. I was stunned. I thought surely something must have happened to his mother or father, but since we'd left them at the reception, I couldn't imagine what it could be. It wasn't until the next morning that Nelson returned. He was haggard and clearly hadn't slept. I demanded to know what was going on. He didn't want to talk to me and went to his bedroom."

Caroline drew a deep breath. "You know me. I wasn't satisfied with his refusal to speak. I followed him upstairs and let myself into his room unbidden. He was angry but grew angrier still when I demanded to know why he had abandoned me on our wedding night. I told him that if he didn't tell me everything, I would go to his parents. That was the first time he hit me."

She could see her father's jaw clench. Elise's eyes narrowed.

"I think at first he was shocked by his own actions. He told me he was sorry that my pressing to know had forced him to react in such a violent way." She gave a bitter laugh. "He made it clear that it was my fault that he hit me."

"Nonsense," her father declared. "His lack of restraint was his fault and the reason for your despair. Go on."

"We argued. I reminded him again that we had just been wed and I felt I had a right to know what was going on. He finally told me. He said his mistress had been so distraught over our marriage that she had tried to take her life. Had she died, he said it would have been my fault. That was when he struck me again. I fell to the floor, and he kicked me several times. I begged him to stop. I kept reminding him that I was his wife." She felt the tears come and tried to sniff them back and control her emotions.

"That only served to irritate him all the more. He yanked me up from the floor and threw me on the bed—" She shook her head. "I can't go on."

She didn't have to. She could see by her father's expression that she didn't need to.

"Why didn't you tell me this when we first found out you'd left him?" Papa asked, his voice barely audible.

"I was still in such shock myself, and besides that, I feared you would kill him if you knew. I thought, too, that he'd be reasonable about ending the marriage. Instead, he locked me in my room and would not let me go. He said there would be no divorce. When I finally managed to get away and come here, I did so with little more than the clothes on my back."

Her father said nothing, which frightened Caroline all the more. She could see that Elise, too, was disturbed by his silence.

Her uncle spoke up. "I swear this is the first I'm hearing of anything about the physical abuse. As you know, I took Caroline in when she arrived. I thought it was just a lover's spat that would be easily resolved. Nelson came to me to talk, I suppose to see if he could figure out just how much Caroline had said. He's been here several times since, demanding she return to her home. He told me his father will not abide even a hint of scandal, much less a divorce. He told Nelson to do whatever it took to see this marriage remained intact or he would disinherit him. Furthermore, I learned that the inheritance he received from his grandfather was conditioned on his being married."

Uncle James looked so haggard that Elise couldn't help feeling sorry for him.

"I am not going back to him," Caroline insisted. "I am not with child, so there is no issue there. I will even lie and tell the court the marriage was never consummated. I want my divorce or annulment or whatever I can get that forever divides me from being Mrs. Worthington. Then he can marry his pregnant mistress."

"Pregnant? His mistress is with child?" Uncle James asked.

Caroline shrugged. "So she says. That was in her letter the day we were to leave for

Europe. She said she was going to bear him a child, but since he had done this horrible thing—marrying me—she knew they'd have no place in his life and so had decided to end both lives."

Caroline watched as her father got to his feet. He didn't look at anyone. "Caroline, you may come with us to Duluth. Pack your things and have them ready in an hour. I'll send some of the boys to get them."

"She can't go. Don't you see? We must not come between them. It's bad enough that she's taken refuge here in my house," Uncle James declared. "A judge will see that as us alienating the relationship."

Their father turned and fixed James Monroe with a hard look. "She's coming with us whether the court likes it or not."

***

"I'm sorry I didn't know," Elise told her sister after getting her settled in their cabin on board the *Mary Elise*. It would soon be suppertime, but thankfully the crew would be eating in town. Uncle James had promised his servants would bring something for them so Elise didn't have to cook. It was a welcome break from their schedule.

"I know it's bothersome, but would you brush my hair?" Caroline asked. "Mama used to do that when I was upset, and it helps so much."

Elise was happy to comply just for the chance to be closer to Caroline.

Her sister began to speak as the brush glided through her hair. "I never planned to tell anyone about the beatings, you know. I thought it was something I'd forever keep hidden, but as Nelson became more demanding of my return, I knew I had to tell the truth." She took a long pause, then added, "Even about his forcing himself on me."

"It's just too terrible. I am so sorry you had to endure such horror. How could a man be so heartless?"

"Apparently there are a lot of things that go on behind closed doors that we girls never hear about until it's too late."

"People should discuss such things instead of hiding them away like secrets. Such behavior should never be allowed." Elise drew the brush through her sister's brown-black hair. "Keeping them secret just encourages bullies like Nelson Worthington to act as they will."

"Yes, but it is very embarrassing. The woman always seems to be blamed for encouraging the attack. The man is never at fault. Aunt Martha even hinted at this while we were packing. You had gone downstairs for another trunk, and she came to my room and begged me not to do this. She said Uncle James would surely be able to make some sort of deal with Nelson. Imagine that. Paying someone not to strike his wife."

"Money has always been the solution to problems where Uncle James and Aunt Martha are concerned."

"And I bought into it." Caroline pulled away and turned in her seat. "I'm so sorry for what I did. Abandoning all of you for wealth and comfort. My circumstances have given me a lot of time to think, and I can see how truly blind I was. Mama and Papa would have given their lives for both of us. That was a love worth far more than material things."

Elise sat on the edge of her bunk. "You were young, and it wasn't unusual that you should desire nice things. There were times when I wanted them as well." She smiled. "I just wanted them here."

Caroline shook her head. "I broke Mama's heart. It's probably my fault that she's dead."

"No. A fever claimed her life. You know how strong our mother was. She wouldn't give up on you, nor let the separation cause her heart to break. She was eternally hopeful, and she knew she could see you each time we came to Oswego."

"But I treated you all so badly, and I'm sorry. I don't know why you even speak to me, Elise."

"You're my sister and I love you. I won't ever stop."

Caroline leaned forward and embraced Elise tightly. "I owe you an apology for so much."

"I owe you one too for my anger at your leaving and for trying to take over Mama's place in your life after she died." Elise hugged her sister close. "We've both made mistakes."

"But mine have been so much worse, and the consequences are far reaching." Caroline released Elise and began to cry. "I lied."

"About what?"

"I'm going to have a baby."

Elise felt the blood drain from her face. "What?"

"That's why I have to get out of town. I'm carrying Nelson's child, and he must never know."

Booker Duran stood outside the open window of Elise's cabin. He'd just overheard her entire conversation with her sister and felt as if he'd been given the answer to his circumstances. He would tell Elise what he'd overheard and threaten her sister with exposure if Elise said anything about his bloody shirt. Furthermore, he could force her to cozy up to him—be more affectionate. It was clear she loved her sister and was willing to sacrifice a great deal for her.

He grinned. It sounded like this Nelson Worthington was a wealthy man, and wealthy men and their families never wanted any scandal attached to their names. The situation was perfect. He could go to Caroline's husband and broker a deal—something that would give him the money he needed to really get away and head west—maybe California.

Knowing Elise was given to taking an evening stroll on the deck, even when in port, Booker waited for his opportunity, all the while running through the various things he might be able to accomplish with this knowledge. He felt powerful after so long living in fear and concern that someone might recognize him as Robert Wayfair.

When he spied Elise, he made a beeline for her. He grabbed her arm and dragged her out of sight of the gangplank and deckhouse. She started to protest, but he put his hand over her mouth.

"Shut up and listen or you'll regret it, because I know all about your little sister's condition." Elise went still, and Booker released his hold. "I thought that would get your attention."

"What are you talking about?" she asked in a hushed whisper.

"I stood outside your window earlier. I heard everything you two discussed. I know her condition and the situation of her marriage and the fact that her husband, Nelson Worthington, must never know about the baby." He grinned. "Seems to me that's valuable information. Information that can help me along my way."

"What do you want?" She glared at him in such a way that he could almost feel her fear. It didn't dissuade him in the least; rather, it excited him. He loved having power over people.

"I want you to keep your mouth shut about my bloodied shirt. I don't need to be accused of murdering that man in Duluth."

"Did you?"

He chuckled, keeping his laugh low, lest someone overhear. "Does it matter? You've already decided I'm guilty."

"Well, you're too late. I've already mentioned it to my father and Nick. They're going to check it out."

He squeezed her arm. "Then you'd best talk to them again and tell them you were wrong. Tell them you thought it through and realized your timing was off."

"Even if I did, don't you think they're smart enough to still check into the matter? If you aren't guilty, you'll have nothing to hide."

"I won't have anything to hide because you'll tell everyone we were together that night." The thought came to him so quickly as a solution that he accidentally raised his voice. He stopped the second he realized it and glanced around to see if anyone had overheard him. Thankfully, most everyone was still in town, leaving him to the evening watch.

"You're hurting me," Elise said, trying to twist away. "Let go of me, or I'll scream."

"You do, and I'll throw you overboard."

She settled immediately.

He loosened his hold slightly. "I can be easy to get along with so long as you do what I say."

She said nothing. Booker couldn't help himself. He reached up to touch her face. He'd wanted to do that for a long time. "You and me are going to get to know each other a whole lot better."

"I won't do anything with you."

"You will, or that sweet little sister of yours is going to pay the price. I know where her husband is and that he'd pay good money to get her back. You'll cooperate . . . or I'll telegraph him and let him know where to find his wife." He grinned and let her go. "Or maybe I should just go find him now."

"If you overheard everything, then you know how difficult this has been on her. Have you no consideration for anyone but yourself?"

"Not the least bit. I'm the only one looking out for me, so that pretty much takes up my time."

"My father was foolish to think he could help you."

Booker grinned. "Aye, he was. I don't need help."

"You need it to get out of being accused of murder," Elise replied, crossing her arms against her chest. "Which I'm beginning to think you must have done, or you wouldn't be so worried about having an alibi."

Her reasoning irritated him, and he leaned in closer. "The matter is settled. You'll do things my way or you'll regret it . . . along with your little sister. Think it over."

He could see the growing fear in her eyes, and it thrilled him. He wanted nothing more than to force a kiss upon those trembling lips, but he held back. Give her time to think, and she'd come willingly enough. He was certain of that. Certain enough that he'd stake his life on it.

~~~

Elise couldn't stop shaking. She knew if she moved, her knees would buckle. Why had she been so foolish as to leave that window open? It had been stuffy, and she'd opened the window to air out the room.

She gripped the rail, and tears began to fall. She'd ruined everything for her sister. All she had wanted to do was help her. She'd had no way of knowing Caroline was with child. She'd had no way of knowing Booker Duran was listening. Now she found herself in an impossible situation.

Oh, Father in heaven, what am I to do?

Chapter 18

Nick reread the letter from Mrs. Schmitt, torn as to what he should do. His father was quite ill. Mrs. Schmitt felt certain he was dying. A part of Nick wanted to race to Boston to see him one last time. But he wasn't sure he'd even be admitted to the house. His father had made it clear that he would never be welcomed back, but Mrs. Schmitt felt otherwise. In fact, she urged Nick to come home immediately. She pled for him to put aside the past and see his father before it was too late.

He glanced at the top of the letter. It was dated a week prior. It might already be too late. His father might be dead by now. He considered sending a telegram, but Mrs. Schmitt probably wouldn't have the money to send a reply without asking for help from Father.

"I must go to Boston." He shook his head. There was no other choice.

"I was hoping you'd be back from town," the captain declared, walking toward him across the deck. "I've got some problems."

"So do I." Nick glanced up apologetically. "And I'm sure they're about to add to yours."

Captain Wright sobered. "Let's talk in my cabin." He opened the door to the small but ample room and ushered Nick inside. "What's going on?"

"My father is dying. The housekeeper begs me to come for a final visit."

"My problems are simple in comparison. My brother-in-law is sending me to Toronto for a special shipment. It'll only tie us up for a few days, but it's enough." The captain smiled. "You must go to your father."

Nick had never tried to hide his circumstances from the captain or his daughter. "I don't know that he wants me there, sir. He did disown me and put me from the house."

"Ten years ago. That's a long time to rethink a decision. I wouldn't be surprised at all if your father is hoping to make things right before he dies." The captain gave a sigh. "And even if he doesn't, it might ease your mind."

"You talk like you know how this goes."

Captain Wright looked up and nodded.

"I do. When I was young, I used to fish with my father. We had the best of times. I always thought I'd grow up to be a fisherman like him, but I fell in with the wrong people. I did a lot that I'm not proud of, and my father told me I would have to part company with my friends or sever ties with the family. I was young and insolent and didn't want to be told what to do by my father, so I severed the family ties. The years passed, and I learned soon enough that my father only desired to protect me. I saw the true ambitions of my friends and put distance between us. I thought several times of going home to apologize."

"But you didn't?"

"No. I let the time get away from me, and then word came one day that my father had died. I hated myself all the more and gave up on trying to be a good man. I convinced myself that I must be rotten to the core and again chose friends who were just as mean and coarse as I was. Despair can be a crippling affair."

"Yes." Nick folded the letter and put it in his pocket. "If I go, can I . . . would you . . ."

"Take you back as my first mate?" The older man smiled. "I would. After all, you are a bit more than that to me—are you not?"

It was Nick's turn to sigh. "I hope to be. Thank you, sir. I think you know that it means a lot to me. I care deeply for your daughter, and I know she won't be parted from you and this ship."

"It does my heart good to know you care for her, Nicodemus. You are a man of God, and I know you wouldn't try to lead her astray. She is worldly-wise in many ways, yet naïve and easily misinformed in others. Both of my daughters are precious to me, and I would hate to see them mistreated. Caroline is to sail with us to Duluth when the time comes. For now, she'll join us on this short run to Toronto. She's desperate to be out of her husband's clutches, and given all that he's done to her, I'm just as anxious to have her gone."

"I'm sorry there are problems in her life that have sent her back to you, but I know you are glad to have her."

"Her husband beat her. I certainly can't leave her to be a victim of his abuse." Captain Wright's expression grew sad. "My wife and I worked hard to teach our girls the meaning of marriage and the commitment a couple make not only to each other but to God when they wed. Yet here I am, taking her away from her husband. I never should have let her leave to live with her uncle. I should never have let her marry a man I knew nothing about. I only wanted to give her what she wanted—to show her how much I loved her."

"Sir, I don't know exactly what the problem might be, but I believe children become adults and make their own choices."

"That's true enough, but if I could go back, I would do things differently. I don't know about the road traveled by you and your father, but I can honestly say I would do it all differently if I could. Since none of us can, I am encouraging you to go home and make things right, at the very least. Who knows, you might even find the need to remain there. I wouldn't fault you if you did."

Nick shook his head. "I could never leave Elise. Not for long."

"You should tell her what you're going to do. She's in her cabin with her sister."

"Thank you. I'll see if she might walk with me in town, if that meets with your approval. She can go with me to get a train ticket."

"Keep your faith, Nick. God isn't through with you yet."

Nick nodded and stepped into the galley. He was glad no one had come for snacks or coffee. Not that there were any to be had. He walked to Elise's cabin and knocked on the door. When she opened it and gave him a smile, Nick felt as if everything would be all right.

"I have to tell you something and wondered if you'd go with me for a walk."

"Of course. Let me get my hat and coat. The air's turned chilly."

He waited while she gathered her things, and they walked through the ship together.

"Where are we going?" Elise asked as they made their way down the gangplank.

"First to the train station. Then I thought I might buy you dinner . . . if you'd like."

"I'd like that very much, but why are we going to the train station?" Her expression was worried.

Nick hesitated to tell her the reason, knowing she would be upset. "I . . . I need to go home. To Boston. My father is dying."

"Oh, Nick, I'm so sorry. How terrible for you." She gripped his arm with her hand. "Have you spoken to Papa?"

"Yes. He convinced me to go, in fact."

She nodded. "He would. He was estranged from his own father once."

"Yes. He told me about it."

"He did?" She looked surprised. "He never speaks of it to anyone outside of the family."

"Maybe he's starting to think of me as family." Nick stopped short of asking for her hand. It was too rushed and definitely the wrong time.

They reached the train station just as the ticket office was closing. Nick quickly asked for a ticket on the next train to Boston.

"The trip will take over twenty hours. There's a layover in Albany," the station-master told him. He handed him the tickets. "You'll board at four thirty a.m."

"Thank you." Nick handed him the money and took the tickets.

Elise watched him, her expression questioning. "You didn't get a roundtrip ticket."

He heard the veiled sadness in her voice. "No. I don't know what I'll find when I reach Boston. The letter sent to me by Mrs. Schmitt was already over a week old. He may be gone by now."

She nodded and again put her hand on his arm. "I will pray for you both."

Elise didn't feel much like conversation as they sat and shared a meal. She hated that Nick was leaving and she had no way of knowing when—or if—she would see him again.

"I hate that I have to go. I don't want to be parted from you," he said.

She looked up from a plate of untouched noodles and sauce. "I know. I don't wish to be parted from you either. I know it's the right thing to do, however. I won't make you feel regret for that. I've long prayed that the walls might come down between you and your father."

"You have?" Nick looked at her oddly. "Why?"

She shrugged and toyed with her noodles. "I know there won't be any peace in your heart until the issues between you and your father are resolved. You love him, despite everything."

"I do." He sat back and seemed to be considering her comment.

"It is the right thing to do, then." She forced herself to eat a bit of the food.

They ate without talking for several minutes, and to Elise it felt as if a monumental weight had been placed on her shoulders. How was she going to keep Booker Duran under control?

"Is my departure all that's bothering you tonight?"

Her head snapped up. "Why would you ask that?"

Nick smiled. "I talked with your father. I know your sister is leaving Oswego to escape an abusive husband. I can't imagine you are bearing that well."

"No." Elise forced herself to relax. "She's so upset, and I cannot make it right for her any more than I can for you." She smiled.

"My mother always had a talent for making bad situations better. I had hoped to inherit some of that skill from her, but it seems I only make things worse."

"That's not true." His voice was full of compassion. "You have made my evening quite a bit better. Your sister will heal in time."

"It isn't that easy. I feel terrible for her. Marriage to a man of high social status was all she wanted. She thought he was in love with her, but it turns out he only married her for her large dowry. He already had a mistress who was with child."

Nick's eyes fired with anger. "He's a cad, and she is better off without him. Although I know it's hard on your father to think of coming between a couple God joined together."

"Did he say that?"

"Yes. Not in those exact words, but it was definitely implied. Still, what can he do? He can hardly leave her to be abused by that man. I don't believe that is the will of God."

"Nor do I. I hate that it is even an issue for Papa to deal with. He's so broken over this entire matter."

"He's got a good head on his shoulders. He'll do what's best."

"The anger in me wants someone to pummel Nelson as he did my sister." Elise was surprised by her own response. She had worked hard to be forgiving but certainly hadn't come to a place where she felt she could forgive Nelson Worthington. Especially since he didn't think he was in the wrong. He saw no need for anyone's forgiveness.

Nick paid for dinner, and they began their walk back to the ship. The skies had long turned dark and the breeze cold. Elise pulled her coat close.

"I'm sorry it's so gloomy tonight," he said.

"It fits what is happening in our life right now."

"I hope not. Not everything going on between us is gloomy. Is it?"

She shook her head. "No. My feelings for you are hardly that."

"Nor mine for you. Still, I wouldn't be offended if you were put off the idea of marriage and romance, given what your sister has gone through."

Elise was glad for his hold on her elbow as she took a misstep. He held fast and straightened her just as they reached the docks.

"Are you all right?"

"I am. Thanks to you." She stopped. "You've been a support to me in so many ways." She considered what he'd said. "I'm not against the idea of marriage and romance to the right man. A man of God who clearly knows what it is to love is certainly worthy of such things."

"I won't feel that I'm worthy until I attempt to resolve matters with my father," Nick said, moving her to face him. "But you know my feelings for you are growing ever stronger."

"Yes. As are mine for you." She saw no reason to pretend otherwise, even though she didn't want her feelings to make his leaving even harder.

"I've never known a woman like you, nor the feelings that you have stirred to life." He gave her such a look of tenderness as they stood beneath the gaslight. "Will you wait for me, Elise?"

She almost burst into tears, but instead she forced them back and gave a nod. "I will. I will wait for you no matter how long it takes."

He pulled her into his arms and brushed back the wisps of hair that had escaped her bonnet. "I promise I'll return as soon as I can." He pressed his lips to hers.

Elise was lost in the moment. She easily let go of her fears of Booker Duran and the worries she held for her sister and father as she put her arms around Nick's neck. She knew they must be a rather wanton display, but she didn't care about that either. She loved this man, and he loved her.

She was no longer waiting on love. It had arrived, and it was glorious.

Chapter 19

Nick embraced the old housekeeper. "It's so good to see you again, Mrs. Schmitt."

She pulled away, her eyes teary. "I wondered if I would ever see you again on earth. Just look at you. You've grown so handsome and rugged. I almost don't recognize you."

"Well, I recognize you, dear woman. You are a steadfast part of my life. Perhaps the only one. Now, tell me everything."

"I don't think your father has much time."

"Then he's still alive?" Nick felt a wash of relief.

"I think he's been holding on in hopes of you coming." She dabbed her eyes with the hem of her apron. "You need to go straight to him. There will be time for us to talk later."

Nick nodded and let go of the housekeeper.

He unbuttoned his coat, and Mrs. Schmitt helped him out of it, then took his hat.

"I'll have your bags delivered to your old room. He's hardly in a position to refuse you staying here." She met Nick's gaze. "I don't think he would anyway. He's different now that he's dying. He's been kinder since his heart attacked him."

Nick nodded and headed for the stairs. Taking them two at a time, he was soon bounding down the long hall to his father's bedroom. Glancing around him, Nick could see that nothing had changed in ten years. In fact, it hadn't changed since his mother died. Why hadn't he realized that before?

When he reached his father's bedroom, he paused. He suddenly felt like a child again. A lost and broken child who wanted only to find that his wrongdoings had been forgiven. The wreck of the *Polaris* and the eight men he'd lost came unexpectedly to his thoughts. They were good men, men he'd worked with on other ships and had stolen away for his own. They might be alive today except for their loyalty to Nick—their friendship.

"And I killed them."

He looked at his father's door, wondering if he had the strength to go through with this. Why had he come here? Why, after all this time, had he come?

Nick had no answer. He supposed it was to do his duty, but he knew he also wanted his father's forgiveness. Didn't all children long for the approval of their father, heavenly or earthly?

Lord, please let him be willing to receive me. Let him forgive me. Nick felt the muscles in his chest tighten. *Let me not be too late.*

He opened the door without knocking. "Father?"

He moved into the dimly lit room. A fire burned in the hearth, and a single wall lamp was lit. The flame was set low.

"Father, it's Nicodemus." There was a chair beside the bed, and Nick stood behind it for a moment, using the back for support.

The man in the bed looked small and fragile, perhaps even dead.

Nick called to him again. "Father."

This time the old man opened his eyes. He studied Nick for a moment, then held up his hand for just a second. "Is it . . . really you?"

Nick smiled. "It is. I heard you were sick and came to see you." He moved from behind the chair to take his father's hand. He had no way of knowing whether the old man would despise him for the act of tenderness or cherish it, but it seemed worth the risk. If for no other reason than that Nick needed to feel that connection.

"The letters," his father murmured.

Nick shook his head. "What letters?"

"The ones . . . you sent Mrs. Schmitt." His father seemed a little more alert as the stupor of sleep lifted.

"What about them?"

"I read them."

Nick was surprised by this and tried to remember everything he'd ever said. "Why? I thought you never wanted to see me again or know anything about my life." He regretted his words. He'd not meant to sound accusing.

"I know. I was . . . wrong."

Nick had never known his father to apologize or admit wrongdoing. He couldn't keep the surprise from his face.

"It's true. I know it comes as an unexpected . . . confession."

His father struggled for breath, and Nick wondered if he should do something. "Can I help you sit up? Would that be better for your breathing?"

Father shook his head. "No. Nothing . . . will help."

Nick could hardly bear watching his father struggle. He fought to focus on something less difficult. "If you read the letters, you pretty much know everything about me and the years between us."

The older man's breathing was raspy but

returned to an evenness that suggested calm. "I do. You're . . . a ship's captain."

"I was. I'm working as a first mate right now. I'm on the *Mary Elise*. I've met the woman I intend to marry."

"Elise," his father whispered.

"Yes." Nick smiled at the mere mention of her. "I think you'd like her." He never would have said this to the man he knew as Father ten years ago.

"She sounds strong . . . and smart." His father closed his eyes for a moment. "Like your mother."

In all of his years, Nick had never heard his father regard Nick's mother as either strong or smart. He ignored the old feelings of bitterness. There was no good purpose served by holding on to them.

"Yes. Like Mother."

"I'll see her soon. Much . . . to apologize for. To you . . . as well." Father reopened his eyes. "I am sorry."

The words were almost as powerful as a blow. Those three words left Nick with no doubt that his father was dying.

"About what, Father?" He lowered into the chair, feeling almost weak.

"Everything. I wish I'd been better . . . a better father. It wasn't until you'd gone . . . that I could . . . see what I'd done."

Nick didn't know what to say. The room seemed to close in on him. He'd come here not even knowing if his father was still alive. Now his father offered an apology for the past. It was completely unexpected. Especially since Nick had been the one to come seeking forgiveness.

"I know you are . . . surprised."

"I am. I wasn't even sure I'd be allowed in the house, and now you tell me you were wrong."

"I suppose . . . knowing death is near . . . makes me remember. I don't . . . like some of the memories."

Nick took his hand again. "Father, all is forgiven on my part. I came here seeking *your* forgiveness. I hope you will forgive me for the pain I caused you."

"No pain. You made me . . . proud. You were strong. I was the . . . weak one. Didn't want you to leave me . . . like your mother. I was deep . . . in sadness."

Nick had never considered that. His father had never once let Nick see him mourning. Nick hadn't been sure his mother had meant anything to the old man.

"I'm sorry. I never knew if you really loved her."

His father struggled to breathe and began to cough. It lasted only a moment, however, as if his body had no energy for anything more. "I loved her . . . so much. Now . . . I'll see her again." He gave a hint of a smile.

Nick dared a question. "Did she know—that you loved her?"

His father nodded. "She did. I might have . . . left you with questions . . . but she knew."

It made Nick glad to know this. His mother had never spoken a word against his father, but Nick had always thought that was just her way of being an obedient wife.

"So it is well between us?" Nick asked, giving his father's hand a squeeze. "You forgive me the mistakes—the disappointments?"

"I do. Do you . . . forgive me?"

"Yes." Nick's word was barely murmured, but the impact was monumental.

"When I thought . . . how I might have lost you . . . on the *Polaris* . . ." Father paused for a moment, then began again. "It made me . . . mindful. I felt . . . such regret."

Nick thought back to that moment. "There was much regret to be had."

"I . . . hired a man. Wanted him . . . to investigate the wreck."

Nick stared at his father. "You hired an investigator to check into the wreck of the *Polaris*?"

"Yes. Wanted to make sure . . . you were treated fairly."

"I was." Nick had never known or even suspected that his father had sought to investigate the wreck. Nick remembered a man who'd come to talk to him and take notes, but he'd assumed the man was from the insurance company.

"You weren't to blame. The storm . . . shifted. Caught . . . two dozen ships unaware."

"I'm to blame because it happened on my command. I was responsible for the ship and those men. Midwest storms can be tricky things. Then you add in the lake, and it only adds to the situation." Nick shook his head. "I wanted so much to prove myself to you."

His father smiled. "You did, son. The investigator . . . told me how . . . you risked your life . . . trying to save your men."

Nick remembered it as if it were yesterday. He'd tried to save them all, but there hadn't been time. Just as now, there was no time to spend with his father. No time to renew their relationship. No time.

"You're a . . . good man, Nicodemus. I am . . . proud of you."

Nick was overwhelmed and didn't know what to say. It was all that he'd wanted to hear from his father. That, and to know his father loved him.

"Was afraid I'd never . . . see you again."

His father closed his eyes. His voice was much weaker. "So . . . glad you came."

Nick could see that his father was exhausted and got to his feet. "Why don't you rest? I'll come back in a little while, and we can talk more."

His father nodded. "Must say this . . . first." He paused, and his eyes widened as if to see Nick more clearly. "I hold . . . abiding love for you . . . my son."

Nick bent down and kissed his father for the very first time in his life. "And I for you, Father."

After he'd settled in his room, Nick decided to stretch out on the bed for a few minutes. The twenty-some hours of travel and layovers had taken all of his energy, and even though it was breakfast time and he was starved, sleep appealed more. A short nap would refresh him.

When he woke and found the sun setting, Nick couldn't believe he'd slept so long. Someone had thoughtfully lit a lamp and turned it down low, and covered him with a heavy quilt. No doubt that had been Mrs. Schmitt. There was also a pitcher of water sitting in a beautiful porcelain basin of matching design. A towel was folded neatly beside it.

Nick washed off some of the travel grime. He went to the wardrobe, wondering what he might find there. To his surprise, the clothes from his duffel had been pressed and hung up. He pulled out a clean shirt and donned it before heading downstairs to speak to Mrs. Schmitt before visiting his father again.

He found her in the dining room. She must have heard him stirring, because she was setting a plate of food on the table.

"I knew you'd probably be hungry," she said as he entered the room.

He glanced around the elaborate dining room. His mother had ordered the walls papered in a beautiful gold and mauve. The rug had been specially woven to the precise measurements of the room, and the enormous mahogany table could seat forty when all of its leaves were in place. For now, it was better suited to no more than a dozen. In the ornate marble-framed fireplace, someone had built an ample fire to warm the room. It reminded him of days before his mother died. She had loved to have dinner parties, and even though the children weren't invited, Nick had often seen the servants putting the room together for such events.

"I'm hardly dressed for dinner," he said.

"No one here dresses for dinner anymore," Mrs. Schmitt declared. "Since your father fell ill, no one has even used this room."

"Perhaps I should just eat in the kitchen."

"That would hardly be appropriate. You'll soon enough be master of the house."

Nick had just pulled out the chair by the plate of food and stopped. "I was disowned."

"You were reinstated," Mrs. Schmitt said, smiling. "Three weeks ago, Mr. Clark called the lawyers and had a meeting. It was the last time he was out of bed, but he was most assuredly in his right mind. Your sisters and their husbands were present, as was I. I think he wanted me to be there so I would write to you about it, but then he fell so gravely ill that I forgot."

"My sisters know I've been reinstated in our father's estate? How did they receive the news?"

Mrs. Schmitt looked at him rather oddly. "They were happy. Deborah wept. I think Miriam did as well, but she's so private with her feelings."

Nick was deeply touched. He'd never known how his sisters felt about any of this, because he'd never written to them to ask. Mrs. Schmitt had told him of their affairs, but Nick never asked her to relay any of his actions to them.

"Will you join me?" he asked, looking at the abundance of food.

She smiled. "I will." She gathered another place setting and then took the chair to his right.

Nick prayed a blessing, and then they began to eat and talk about all the years that had separated them. All the while, Nick was aware of the man dying upstairs. How amazing that God could bring them together again. Had he not come home, he might never have had the chance to make things right.

"What caused Father's change of heart?"

Mrs. Schmitt shook her head. "I can't really say. I personally think it was staring death in the face. He talked very little of you after you left. One day I received a letter from you. I accidentally left it on the mantel. When I remembered and went to retrieve it, I found your father reading it. I thought he might throw it in the fire afterwards, but instead he refolded it and placed it back on the fireplace ledge. I was so surprised, but he seemed quite content. So the next time you wrote, I left the letter there again. It wasn't long before he found it and read it."

"He said he read them all. I suppose I'm glad he did."

"I think he needed to. You spoke of your sorrow in disappointing him, as well as your love of sailing. I think with their blend of homesick moments and self-doubt, as well as the pride in your accomplishments and interesting adventures, he looked forward to them just as much as I did. I think they also helped him better know you as a son."

"I'm sure you're right. I just never imagined I would come home to his welcome. I didn't even dare pray for it."

Mrs. Schmitt smiled. "Well, I did."

After supper, Nick went to his father's room with his Bible in hand. His father was awake, as if he were waiting for Nick. He seemed stronger, more like his old self, but a kinder version.

"I thought maybe I had just dreamed you were here, but Perkins, my valet, assured me you had really come."

"Perkins. A new valet?"

"Yes. Halsberg retired to go live with his daughter."

It was remarkable how much better his father was breathing. Nick silently thanked God for the improvement.

"I read my Bible on the long journey here from Oswego. That was where I left my ship and caught the train to Boston." Nick held up his Bible. "I brought it now in case you wanted me to read to you." He had no idea what his father's standing with God was, but it was weighing on Nick's heart.

"I'm glad you did, for I have a question. That minister who preaches at the church your mother and I once attended told me I had but to believe in Jesus as Lord and I would be saved. That seems much too simple, since the Bible says that even demons believe and tremble."

"Romans ten, verse nine tells us, 'That if thou shalt confess with thy mouth the Lord Jesus, and shalt believe in thine heart that God hath raised him from the dead, thou shalt be saved.' The demons may well believe in His existence, but they do not confess him as Lord. They have no honor for Him whatsoever. They mock and despise our Savior."

"As I once did," his father said in a tone that revealed his sorrow.

"But you no longer feel that way, do you?"

His father met his gaze. "No. I want to be saved by the Lord. I won't lie. Dying is a fearful and lonely process. I dread this journey without God."

"As well we should." Nick smiled. "But confess Him with your mouth and believe that He has overcome death, and through Him you will also overcome eternal death."

"I profess that here and now. He is Lord

and my Savior." Nick's father sat up a little straighter against the pillows. He looked at Nick in confidence. "I seek His forgiveness . . . and yours." He eased back, eyes closed, and for several seconds neither spoke. Finally, his father nodded. "I am at peace. The fear has left me."

Tears came to Nick's eyes. "There is no fear in His perfect love."

"It seems I remember a verse about no condemnation."

Nick nodded and opened his Bible to Romans, chapter eight. "'There is therefore now no condemnation to them which are in Christ Jesus, who walk not after the flesh, but after the Spirit.'"

"No condemnation," his father repeated.

"No condemnation," Nick said again, and then it struck him. The *Polaris*. The men he'd lost. There was no condemnation. Tears came to his eyes as he looked at his father. Father was watching him, as if waiting for him to understand. He gave a nod. "No condemnation."

Frederick Clark passed away peacefully later that night. When Nick was told the next morning of his father's death, he wept for his own loss and rejoiced for God's gain. He also thanked God for the mercy of reconciliation that had set his own heart free from the terrible burden he had borne for over ten years. Not to mention the guilt associated with the *Polaris*. For the first time, he felt he could finally lay those souls to rest.

Mrs. Schmitt found him on his knees beside his father's bed, offering praise and thanksgiving for the things God had done. She joined him on knees that were much too old to kneel, but she did so in love for her Savior.

They took turns praying aloud, and when they finally finished, one of the maids gave a soft knock on the door.

"Sir, your sisters and their husbands have come."

Chapter 20

The day after the funeral, Nick sat down with his father's lawyer, who'd invited Nick and his sisters to a brief meeting that their father had set up prior to his death. Nick sat across from his sisters, each with her husband at her side. He had little interest in the reading of his father's will. It delighted him merely to know that they had been reconciled. If the lawyer would only hurry, Nick could catch a train to Oswego that afternoon and hopefully meet up with the *Mary Elise* back from Toronto.

"The will is fairly simple," the lawyer began. "There are provisions left for each of Mr. Frederick Clark's children, with the bulk of his estate going to his son, Nicodemus Clark. Each of you were provided with details of what your inheritance is to be. Are there any questions?" He looked to each one of them.

Nick cleared his throat. "I don't have questions, but I do have directions. You and I talked in some length about this directly after the funeral. I want my sisters each to receive one of my father's textile mills. Their husbands are already managing these, and it seems only fitting that they become the owners." He had already told his sisters, so there was no surprise here, just a desire to make it legal.

"I've taken care of the transfer of deed, and you have but to sign these papers," the lawyer said, holding up two stacks of documents.

"We've also discussed the house and wish it to be sold, with the revenues being split three ways."

The lawyer nodded. "I will see to it."

"You're more than generous with us, Nick," Deborah declared. "Thank you for being so kind."

"It's only right. I think our father knew your husbands were successful enough to keep you in good order, but I see nothing wrong with settling this on you. You remained faithful to our father when I did not. I want no bad blood ever to rise between us."

"Of course not." Deborah looked to her husband, and he nodded with a smile.

Miriam, only two years Nick's junior, took her husband's hand. "We are grateful for your gift, and you are always welcome in our home."

"I appreciate that. You two have always been precious to me." Nick smiled at each of his sisters. "I'm sorry for having failed you so miserably. I think I'm only now realizing how selfish I was."

"All is forgiven," Miriam said, glancing at her sister. "We're just glad to have you back."

"But I'm not remaining," Nick told them. He hadn't yet had a chance to explain his plans. "I'm heading back to Oswego this afternoon. I intend to continue working on the *Mary Elise*."

"But why? You have enough money to buy your own ship now or do nothing at all." Miriam's voice sounded almost alarmed. "I thought you might stay."

"I will visit from time to time, but this is no longer my home. There is a young woman who holds my heart, as you well know." He smiled. "Now, let us finish this and be done with it once and for all." He reached for a pen and signed all of the papers the lawyer presented.

That accomplished, he turned to the older man. "Is there anything else I have to oversee?"

"Just this," he said, handing Nick a deed. Nick smiled. "I will deliver this myself."

He got to his feet. "I must be about my business, or I'll never make my train." He kissed Deborah first, since she sat nearest him, then went to Miriam.

"Try not to worry, sister. I know you fear what I'm doing, but should I die, it will be while doing what I love. Put me in God's hands, I pray, and leave me there." He kissed her cheek and offered her a big smile. "And I will expect letters regarding your growing families and how things are with your various interests. Write to me in care of Captain William Wright on Minnesota Point in Duluth, for I expect he will always know of my whereabouts, since I intend to marry his daughter."

He shook hands with his brothers-in-law, then tucked the deed in his inside coat pocket and headed out.

Nick snugged his hat down tight, as the day had grown windy. Winter would soon be upon them, and he had many memories of icy-cold Boston days. He smiled and signaled for a cab. Now Boston no longer held regrets. One day he'd bring Elise here and show her where he'd grown up and where he'd fallen in love with sailing.

It was a long ride to the new neighborhood where Nick had installed Mrs. Schmitt. She had told him where her cousin and elder sister lived, and he had purchased her a house nearby. Although she didn't yet know that the house was hers.

They arrived at the address, and the driver opened the carriage door to assist Nick.

"Please wait here. I'll need you to take me back to the city," Nick said.

The driver nodded.

Nick admired the small two-story house. It had been newly painted white, and the windows were trimmed in blue shutters. There was a brand-new picket fence surrounding the property because Nick recalled Mrs. Schmitt mentioning that she had always longed for a home with a white picket fence. The cobblestone walkway that only two days ago had been in a rather bad condition was now smoothed out and refashioned to be less dangerous. It had taken a hefty amount of money to get everything done in just a few days, but Nick wanted Mrs. Schmitt to be settled before he left.

The older woman opened the front door to bid him welcome before Nick could even knock. She looked so happy that it blessed Nick deep in his soul.

"So, is there anything else we need to change before I head back to Oswego?" he asked as she ushered him into the house.

"Goodness, no. It's quite perfect. Just look at it."

He did, noticing how homey it was with its small fireplace blazing and the mantel set with her own framed tintypes.

"I think you've done quite nicely with the place."

"Well, it didn't hurt that you sent over some of the household people to help me set it to rights."

Nick chuckled. "I'm glad I could help." He reached in his pocket. "I have one last thing to give you." He handed her the deed.

She looked at it for a moment and shook her head. "I don't understand. What is this?"

"The deed to your home. You'll see it's free and clear and in your name. It's my gift to you for all that you've done for me and our family over the years."

Tears came to her eyes as she slipped into the nearest chair. "Oh my. Oh my." Her hands trembled as she looked it over. "My father would be so proud. We've never been property owners. He always dreamed of it but could never get enough money put aside and was forced to rent."

"Well, I'm glad I could help a little of his dream come true. His daughter is a property owner. I know he'd be proud of you, Mrs. Schmitt."

She nodded. "The entire family will be. We will have to have a party."

"You do that. Meanwhile, I'm heading back to Oswego and Elise."

Mrs. Schmitt rose and came to him. "Oh, I so hope she will marry you soon. You need a good wife to care for you."

"I hope so too." He leaned down and kissed her weathered cheek. "Write and tell me all of the news, and should you need anything at all, you will let me know."

"I won't have any needs. You already set me up with a bank account and more money than I'll ever know what to do with."

He smiled, thinking of the modest account. "I hope you'll treat yourself to something lovely from time to time."

He made his way outside and to the carriage. He glanced back and found the woman who had been like a mother to him waving good-bye. Tears streamed down her weathered cheeks, but she was smiling.

He gave a wave, then climbed into the carriage with a great sense of satisfaction. Now he could go back to Elise with a clear conscience and a much lighter spirit.

"Take me to the train station."

Nick settled back to think of how his fortunes had changed. He was a fairly rich man. Of course, he might have been extremely rich had he held on to the textile mills, but they were of no interest to him. It wasn't as if they were long in the family. His father had bought them when a friend decided them no longer as profitable as he'd hoped. Father had been very young, and the deal had been quite good. He had done everything possible to bring them to their current success.

Nick wondered how Elise would take the news of his newfound wealth. He doubted she would care. Her world was the *Mary Elise* and sailing the lakes. Just as his was. They were in complete agreement on that, and he couldn't help but wonder at their future. He had been so driven to prove to his father that he was worthy of respect, and now that Nick had it, what was yet to be accomplished?

He hadn't thought much past settling his father's estate and making certain that Mrs. Schmitt was cared for. He had given the other servants good letters of reference based on Mrs. Schmitt's suggestion, as well as two weeks' pay. They would stay at the estate and ready it for sale. They didn't need to leave before the house was sold, giving them even more time to secure their living arrangements. He felt good about handling things in a generous manner. It made him feel that he was pleasing God.

They arrived at the busy station amidst chaos and what seemed to be hundreds of people either coming or going. They waited their turn so the driver could drop Nick closer to the entrance. Nick was grateful to have only one bag that he could easily manage for himself. Other travelers were in disarray as they scrambled for the limited number of available baggagemen.

Finally, the carriage stopped outside the main entrance, and the driver opened his door. Nick stepped into the bustling, noisy atmosphere and wished even more that he could be at sea. He tipped the driver generously, then headed inside.

He'd not gone far when he spied a line of wanted posters on the wall near the ticket counter. The drawing of the first man closely resembled Booker Duran.

Wanted—Robert Wayfair, he read, *for murder in Buffalo, New York.*

Wayfair. The name was wrong, but the image was very similar. There were things that didn't quite fit, but it was close enough that it made Nick wonder. Then again, maybe Duran had a brother who used another name.

Nick frowned as he continued to stare at the poster. Or maybe Duran used another name.

Elise congratulated herself in having kept well away from Booker Duran during the short trip to Toronto. She made sure they were never alone together. Even so, in Nick's absence, Duran felt he had the right to do as he pleased and more than once had managed to touch her as he passed by her in the galley. He had even gone so far as to feign a hand injury. Wounds and injuries were generally treated by Elise, but when Duran suggested he might have broken one of his fingers, it was the captain who took charge and declared it nothing more than a sprain. It was easy to see Duran wasn't happy with the arrangement, but there was nothing he could say without bringing more attention to himself.

Elise had prayed continuously for safety and for some way to see Duran taken into custody if he truly was the murderer. One thing was certain: he wasn't a good seaman. Her father had taken him to task for being lax in his duties, but Duran always had some excuse. Papa wasn't taken in by his explanations. He knew the man was untrustworthy. At their last confrontation, Papa had even told Duran that he would be put off in Oswego upon their return if things didn't improve. Since then, Duran had been a model crewman.

She couldn't help but wonder why. Why not just escape them rather than go on threatening Elise and Caroline? If he was going to betray Caroline's secret, he'd have more opportunity by leaving the crew in Oswego. She just couldn't figure out his game.

Their return trip from Toronto was without problems until they were nearly to Oswego. That was when they started having trouble with the rudder. Ollie Johnson was a good mechanic and rigged the rudder to endure a little longer, but he made it clear they'd need to lay over for more extensive repairs once in port.

Now that they'd arrived, Elise was more concerned with her sister's welfare and what Duran might do. If her husband realized Caroline was on the *Mary Elise*, he would no doubt find a way to legally force her to come home.

"Your uncle is waiting for us on the dock. I hope there isn't more trouble," Elise's father said as he joined her at the rail. He waved, and Elise did too when she spotted Uncle James.

"I fear for Caroline," Elise said, turning to him. "She can't leave the ship without revealing herself. And since we'll be here for a week for repair work, it would be horrendous for her to have to wait hidden in the cabin. We'd have to stay here with her."

"I've already thought of that, which is why we now have a large trunk that must be taken with us to your uncle's house."

Elise's eyes widened. "Caroline?"

He grinned. "None other. It was her suggestion when I mentioned the situation."

A giggle escaped her lips. "Won't the staff be surprised when they open the trunk expecting clothing and find my sister instead? I'd like to be there to see that."

"I have already planned that you will be."

She swept her gaze back and forth along the docks as she'd done since drawing close enough to see them. Nick was nowhere to be found. "I wonder where he is."

Her father didn't pretend not to know who she was talking about. "We have no way of knowing when he might return to us. If his father is as bad as he feared, it could be a quick death or a lingering one. There's no way of telling."

She sighed. "I know. I was just hoping he'd be here. You said yourself that this might be our last trip to Duluth, given all the extra problems and the changing weather."

"The weather's been pretty good for November. Thankfully, we've not had any major storms."

"Yet. But we both know they're coming, and so too the ice."

"Relax," he said, patting her arm. "I've already arranged with Nick to join us in Duluth if he returns and learns that the ports are closed. He'll take a train to Duluth and winter there, helping me make further repairs to the *Mary Elise*."

Elise felt her fears ease. "That was a very smart thing, Papa. Thank you."

"My pleasure. Can't have my future son-in-law lost, now, can I?"

"Why do you call him that?" Instead of joyous thoughts, Elise remembered Duran's threats.

"Because I believe if he has his way, he'll be just that. Oh, look. The men are bringing your sister." He nudged Elise's arm and quickly moved aside for Ollie and Sam, who were carrying a very large clothing trunk. "You go ahead to the house with her and see that she gets unpacked first thing." He chuckled and pulled Elise with him down the gangplank.

Uncle James looked surprised by the huge trunk. "Are you planning a lengthy stay?" he asked.

Elise's father leaned close. "Your niece is in that trunk, lest her husband have spies watching for her to disembark."

Uncle James's eyes widened. "Well, I'll be. Very smart of you, because Nelson has been nothing but a problem. He brought the authorities to my house, and I had no choice but to allow them to search it from top to bottom. When they didn't find Caroline and

I assured them she wasn't there, Nelson was livid. Apparently, his father will not allow him his grandfather's inheritance until Nelson can prove he's still married. Rumors abound, since they've seen nothing of their daughter-in-law."

"Sounds like this will be a very difficult situation," Elise declared, leaning up on tip-toe to kiss her uncle. "I'm going to go with Caroline and see her carefully managed. I'll see the two of you at the house."

Booker watched Elise leave the *Mary Elise* for her uncle's carriage. Her ability to escape him had been carefully crafted, it would seem. Throughout the trip to Toronto, she'd managed to keep herself almost constantly in her father's company, and if not his, then one of the trusted crewmen. Duran had no possible need to speak with her privately, and so there had been no opportunity to further threaten her, nor to get her alone. She had even stopped her evening strolls, which would have afforded him the perfect opportunity to steal a kiss or perhaps more.

The captain and his brother-in-law headed for the deckhouse. No doubt to speak with Elise's sister, Caroline. He decided to maneuver himself somewhere nearby to overhear their conversation. Once he had as much information as possible, he intended to hunt down Nelson Worthington while they were in Oswego. Elise would regret not cooperating with him.

He headed to the deckhouse on the pretense of getting coffee, but when he arrived, he found the kitchen deserted and the coffeepot nearly empty. The captain and Mr. Monroe were no doubt in the captain's cabin. Booker eased his way toward the door. He figured if anyone said anything or caught him at it, he could say he was there to ask the captain something.

The men were definitely inside the room. He could hear their voices but not very well. He pressed his ear against the door.

"Nick telegraphed that he'd join you tomorrow."

"It'll work out perfectly," the captain replied. "The repairs shouldn't take more than a day or two. Ollie talked to the shop, and they believe they have the parts we need."

"That is good news. The sooner you can get out of here, the better."

"I agree. Did you make arrangement for the offloading?"

"It's all set. I have—"

Duran heard someone outside the deckhouse and quickly made his way back to the kitchen area. He grabbed some wood to put in the stove just as Ollie came down the steps.

"Coffee?" Duran asked. "I was gonna make a pot."

"Sounds good. Where's the captain?"

Duran shrugged. "Nobody here but me." Some laughter came from the captain's cabin just then. "Well, I stand corrected."

"No problem." The big Swede went to the door and knocked. "Captain?"

Wright opened the door. "What is it, Ollie?"

They began to discuss the repairs, and Duran felt it was impossible to hang around much longer than it took to make coffee. Besides, he was supposed to be working at the offloading of the machinery by helping with the hatches.

He thought of one last ploy after stirring up the fire and putting in a few small pieces of wood. He went to Elise's cabin door and listened for a moment. There wasn't the slightest sound.

"What are you needing, Duran?" Captain Wright surprised him by asking.

Duran turned, trying not to look upset. "I wondered if your daughter would like some coffee. I'm making a pot."

Wright looked at him doubtfully but then turned toward the stove. "She won't want any, but we'll take some. Let me know when it's ready."

Duran nodded. He felt frustrated that someone always seemed to be there to interfere with his plans, but it was just the way things were. He wasn't going to spend a lot of time worrying about it. He'd simply get his work done and then go find Nelson Worthington. Someone was bound to know where he lived. Duran just needed to find that someone.

Nick arrived in Oswego eager to leave the train. He checked for wanted posters but found none in the station. He considered going to the police station, but he really had nothing of evidence to offer. He could tell them the sketch resembled Booker Duran, but he had no other proof. Maybe it'd be best to discuss the matter with the captain first. Captain Wright was a reasonable man with a good head on his shoulders. He'd know what to do.

With that matter resolved in his mind, Nick went directly from the train station to the *Mary Elise*. He learned quickly about the repairs being made and that the family was staying with James Monroe. He hated to impose himself on the family, but he longed to see Elise and tell her all that had happened, as well as tell the captain about his suspicions. Wasting no time, he made his way to the Monroe estate and found himself readily admitted to the house.

The housekeeper went to announce him to the family, and it was only another minute before Elise appeared. She wore a beautiful silk gown the color of a dark plum. Her black hair had been pinned up with ribbons and pearls, and she looked very much the part of a proper socialite.

Nick bowed and straightened with a grin. "I'm here to see Miss Wright."

"And I was looking for Nick Clark. Perhaps you've seen him," Elise replied in amusement.

He glanced down and chuckled. "I was so anxious to get back here that I left directly from my lawyer's office in Boston."

"Lawyer?"

His smile faded. "My father died. The day after my arrival, but we had time to talk and to repair our relationship."

Elise appeared to be trying to take this in. "I find myself both happy and sad to hear your news."

"It's really all joy. My father accepted Jesus as his Savior in my presence. I know I shall see him again one day."

"Of course. I'm glad you have that assurance." She nodded toward the formal sitting room. "Why don't you join us, especially since you're already properly dressed? I know my father will be eager to hear what happened."

Nick followed her into the room, where her family, including Caroline, was already gathered. He gave a nod as Elise announced his return.

"He came directly here when he found no one at the ship."

"You're more than welcome, Mr. Clark. I must say, I was surprised to hear from my brother-in-law that you were from Boston," Mr. Monroe declared. "Elise mentioned your family is into textiles. Your father isn't Frederick Clark, is he?"

Nick was surprised by the question. "He was. I'm afraid my father passed away."

"I'm sorry to hear that," Monroe replied.

"As am I, Nick." Elise's father rose in greeting. "Did you know him, James?"

"Not well, but I did business with him in the past. His mills produce some of the finest cottons. When I invested in that number of hotels, I searched many of the mills for just the right bedding, and his company had the best."

"I'm glad you thought so." Nick knew his father's sheets were the finest to be had.

"I'm sorry to hear about your father, Nick." Elise's father motioned for him to join him on the couch.

Nick nodded and took a seat. "We set the past to rights, and Father made his peace with God. We had a good talk, and he let me know that he had already reinstated me in his will. I was no longer disinherited."

"So now you're a mill owner. Will you give up the sea?" James Monroe asked.

"No. In fact, I gave the mills to my sisters. Their husbands have been running the mills for many years. It seemed only right, since I have no interest in them."

"That's a lot of money to give away."

Nick looked at Elise, who was smiling. "It seemed the right thing to do. My heart is still with sailing."

"Well, perhaps you could work for me. You're rich enough now to buy your own ship, and our freighting company is always looking to expand."

Nick pretended not to see the way Elise's expression fell or the thoughtful look her sister was giving him. "I appreciate your offer, sir. I haven't yet had time to consider what I'll be doing with my future. For now, I'm going to winter in Duluth and help Captain Wright make repairs on the *Mary Elise*."

"Do keep it in mind."

They asked him a few other mundane questions about his travels and Boston, and then the conversation turned to the Monroes' two sons, who were absent from the family gathering. Nick was exhausted and longed for a bath and bed. He needed to get settled for the night and figured he'd splurge on a hotel rather than make do on the *Mary Elise*.

"If you'll excuse me, I should leave. I need to get some sleep."

"Please stay with us," Mrs. Monroe declared. "We've plenty of room and you are most welcome."

"Yes, do," James Monroe agreed. "I'll ring for the servant to take your bag up. Would you like a hot bath?"

"Very much," Nick replied. "Thank you for your generosity."

A maid arrived, and James Monroe stood and directed her attention to Nick. "Take Mr. Clark's things and put him in the far north room. Have my valet prepare him a hot bath and get one of the boys to build him a fire."

"Yes, sir."

Nick rose. "I guess I will see you all in the morning. I'm sure someone should probably wake me." He grinned. "I'm so tired I think I could sleep for a week."

Chapter 21

Nick awoke with a start. Something didn't seem right. Although the curtains were still drawn, he sensed the presence of someone in the room. Pushing back the covers, he noticed someone bent over the fireplace. It was a decidedly female figure, and she was stirring up the embers and adding wood to the grate. No doubt a maid.

He didn't want to startle her, but at the same time, he needed to acknowledge her presence. He cleared his throat. "Who's there?"

"It's Caroline—Elise's sister." She straightened, then moved toward the bed.

"What are you doing here?"

"Building up your fire." She paused by the footboard and gave him a smile.

Nick pulled on his robe and got up. "Can't a servant do that?"

"Listen to you. You sound like a wealthy man of means rather than a ship's first mate."

"What time is it?"

"Not even five thirty," she replied.

He noted her open robe. "Well, thank you for the fire. You should go now."

She smiled and came toward him. "Not until we have a little talk."

Nick was very uneasy having her in his bedroom. "Why don't you go back to your room, and we can talk later today?"

"But I want to talk now," she said with a pout. "I might not have another chance to be alone with you."

He was growing increasingly more uncomfortable. "I don't think it's proper for us to be alone, Caroline."

"I like the way you say my name. In fact, I like you very much." She sauntered around the corner of the bed and came to stand directly in front of him. Reaching up, she pushed back his hair. Nick flinched. "What's wrong? Don't you like me?"

Nick pushed her away and moved around her toward the door. "I am in love with your sister. I thought you knew that. You should go now."

She went back to the hearth instead of following him to the door. "I know you're in love with Elise . . . or think you are. But that doesn't mean we can't be something to each other."

"If I have my way, you'll be my sister-in-law." He opened the door. "Now, however, I'd like for you to go."

"But since we'll be in the same family . . . it wouldn't be difficult for us to be close to each other."

"You don't need my closeness, Caroline. You need the Lord. After all you've been through, God is the one you should draw close to."

She frowned and looked away, saying nothing. Nick wasn't sure what her game was, but he wasn't about to play it. He knew her husband had a mistress and that this had hurt her tremendously, and why shouldn't it? He felt sorry for her.

Leaving the door wide open, he crossed to where she stood in her lacy white gown and open robe.

"Caroline, I know you were hurt by your husband, and perhaps that's why you think it all right to hurt your sister. But not all men are like Nelson Worthington. I'm faithful and true to one woman, and that's Elise. Come breakfast, I intend to tell her about this encounter. Now, however, I'd just like for you to go."

For a moment she did nothing, but then he heard her sniff. Was she crying?

"You don't have to say anything. I plan to tell her about this myself," Caroline said. "I was only testing you. Papa said you were going to ask my sister to marry you, and I know she will say yes so long as you promise to remain on the *Mary Elise*. I just wanted to know for sure that you wouldn't take a mistress. Nelson said all men do."

"And you believed him?"

She shrugged. "I also believed he loved me."

"Yes, but you surely don't think your father took a mistress."

"Mama always said he wasn't just married to her, but also to the *Mary Elise*. Perhaps there was a woman as well. Can a man truly love just one woman and devote himself to her?" She used the back of her sleeve to wipe away tears. "I don't want Elise hurt. She deserves good things, because she's a good woman. Better than any other I know."

"I agree, and I love her. Only her." He paused for a moment, wishing he could ease the young woman's pain. "Caroline, I'm sorry that your husband has a mistress and that he hurt you, but you needn't test me. I belong to Elise and only Elise."

Caroline nodded. "I'll go, then. And I do plan to tell her what I've done. I don't want there to be any servant rumors about me visiting your room in the wee hours." She went to the open door and paused. "Please, please be faithful to her."

The pleading in her voice was heartbreaking. Nick might have gone to comfort her except for the situation. "I promise. I will be."

"You what?" Elise asked, raising her voice in shock.

"I tested him," Caroline said. "I wanted to make sure he wouldn't take advantage of you."

"How could you act in such a wanton way?" Elise lowered her voice. "And in your condition?"

Caroline sat on the window seat in Elise's bedroom. "It seems foolish now, but all I could think about was making sure he was worthy of your trust. I figured if I snuck into his room and offered myself, we would know for sure what kind of man he is."

"But I already know what kind of man he is." Elise didn't know whether to slap her sister or kiss her. The heart behind her escapade was a good one, but it was unthinkable that she would do such a thing.

"I thought I knew what kind of man Nelson was." Caroline turned away from Elise and gazed out the window. "I didn't want this kind of pain for you. I'm so humiliated and heartbroken. I haven't been a good sister to you always, but I wanted to be one in this. I don't want you sorely used as I have been."

Elise went to the window seat and sank down beside Caroline. "I know you're concerned. I appreciate that you care for me in such a deep manner. But please, no more testing of anyone."

Caroline turned to face her. "I'm sorry. Please forgive me."

Elise wrapped her arms around her sister and pulled her close. "I do, and I promise I'm going to see you through this . . . no matter what."

"Thank you. Thank you so much. Sometimes I just don't know what will become of me."

"You'll be fine . . . the baby too. We'll take care of you."

Caroline pulled back. "I don't think I can keep this child. I certainly don't want Nelson to have it, but this baby was created in a violent act, Elise. There was no love or even tenderness. How could I ever love it?"

Elise looked at her sister. "But the child had no part of that violence. He or she is just as innocent of that as you are. You mustn't punish the baby for the sins of the father."

"I know. I'm just afraid that every time I look at it, I'll only remember the pain."

"Then we'll pray about it and what you're to do. I won't force you to raise a child that brings you constant sorrow, and neither will Papa. But remember, this baby is as much a part of you as it is Nelson Worthington."

"Nick said I needed to draw closer to God." Caroline began to pace. "His words really made me think. I know I've pulled away from God over the years while living with Uncle James and Aunt Martha. Not because they don't believe in Him, but the focus is different. We go to church on Sunday, and that's pretty much it. We don't even pray over meals unless you and Papa are here. God always had such a presence on the ship that I don't have here."

"We are reliant on God out there in the middle of the lake. He is our only hope on so many occasions."

"I remember." Caroline stopped and turned. "I lost that. I don't spend time in my Bible or prayer anymore. Maybe that would help me."

"I know it would. It offers me constant consolation. Papa always comes in while I'm cooking breakfast for the crew and shares some Scriptures and prayer while I'm cooking. It starts the day out right." Elise went to her sister. "Caroline, no matter what happened in the past, I have prayed for you and I will continue to do so. Nick is absolutely right. The one you need right now is your Heavenly Father. Draw close to Him, and He will draw close to you."

As she planned a trip to town to pick up some travel things for Caroline, Elise was still contemplating her sister's comments. She was no longer shocked by what she had done to poor Nick, but she was still concerned by Caroline's intention to give up her child. Given her desire to hide the child from Nelson, it probably would be better to give the baby up for adoption, if she could do so privately. On the other hand, was it right to keep the knowledge of the baby's existence from Nelson? There was no way Caroline would be given an annulment or divorce if the judge knew her to be with child. Elise wished she could seek counsel on the matter, but she had promised Caroline she wouldn't tell.

"Well, I'm going to head down to the docks to check the repairs," Papa said.

Uncle James helped Aunt Martha from the breakfast table. "And I must get to my rat killing," he said.

"Jim, I told you I hate that phrase."

He laughed. "Sorry, my dear. Our old cook used to say it all the time."

"Mama said it too." Elise looked at her sister. "I always wondered where she got that saying."

"Now we know," Papa declared.

As the family all went their separate ways, Elise started after her father. "Papa, do you suppose we'll be able to head home tomorrow?"

"I believe so. The boys are hoping to have everything finished today. If they get it done early enough, we could leave yet this afternoon."

She nodded. "Then maybe you could escort me shopping. I'm certain Caroline will need some warmer things for the trip home, and since she can't be seen in public, I must be the one to go."

"I'm not sure I'll have time, Elise."

"I could take her," Nick said, seeming to come out of nowhere.

"There. That would be acceptable, wouldn't it?" Her father smiled. "I'm thinking more than acceptable."

"Yes." Elise glanced at Nick. He'd been strangely quiet at breakfast. She wondered if her sister's shenanigans had left him upset with the entire family.

"Good." Elise's father bent and kissed the top of her head twice. "Give one of those to your sister."

She laughed. "I will." She waited until he'd left to turn to Nick. "Thank you for being willing to take me shopping. I'll go find Caroline and—"

"Wait," Nick said, taking hold of her arm as she started past him.

She stopped and lifted her face to his. She couldn't help smiling. Nick made her feel happy. "Yes?"

"I need to talk to you."

"I want to talk to you too. I want to hear all about your trip home. I figured we could talk on our walk to the shops."

He looked worried. "I . . . your sister came to my room . . . and . . ."

Elise nodded. "Yes, I know all about it. I'm so sorry." She sighed and gave a shrug. "I know her intentions were good, but it was wrong of her to do that to you. Please forgive her."

"I was afraid you'd hear about it and think I was having a tryst with her. You must know that I only have eyes for you."

If Elise had ever doubted his feelings for her, she had only to look into his eyes. "I know. You needn't fear my reaction. Caroline confessed all, and my first thought was how startling it must have been to you."

"Yes. I must admit it was. I figured a servant had come to tend the fire, but instead I found your sister wanting to play games."

"But you will forgive her . . . won't you?"

"Of course." He looked at her for a moment. "What about you?"

"I'll admit I wasn't happy she would do such a thing, but given her state of mind and her situation, I suppose I understand it. You made an impact on her when you told her she needed to draw closer to God. She's giving it a lot of consideration. She said she'd been ignoring God for the most part, and your comment made her think. She was raised to know the truth of our need for God, but it had gotten away from her over the years. I pray this will bring her back to him."

"God has a way of beckoning to us. I'm glad I could play a part in that. I'm glad too that this matter can be put behind us."

Elise nodded. "I want us all to be close, and if you have anger or resentment toward Caroline, I know that will cause conflict." The hall clock chimed the hour. "It's nine. I'll go speak with Caroline and see what she would like me to purchase for her. Oswego will have a much better selection than Duluth."

"I'll busy myself, never fear," Nick declared.

Elise took to the stairs with a light step. She was so glad Nick felt the need to tell her what had happened with Caroline. It was one thing for her sister to admit what she'd done, but for Nick to see the need for complete honesty blessed Elise.

"Caroline?" she called, knocking on her bedroom door. Elise opened it, figuring her sister would be putting on the finishing touches to her ensemble. She'd been absent from breakfast, but Aunt Martha said that was often the case when she'd lived with them. "Caroline?"

"I'm back here . . . behind the screen. Stay there. I'm sick."

Elise could hear her heaving and went to her anyway. "Morning sickness?"

"I suppose so, but mine happens all the time. It's making me miserable. Just when I think I've finished with it, it comes again." Caroline covered the ceramic pot with a towel.

"What does the maid say about it? She must be suspicious of your condition."

"I told her I always react like this under duress. You know that's true, so I told her no lie."

"Poor sweet sister. I had quite forgotten that about you." Elise recalled many times in their youth when nervous situations sent Caroline to the ship's rail. "I've come to see what articles of clothing I might purchase for you. I know you'll need warmer and simpler clothes for life in Duluth, and Nick is going to take me shopping. Since you obviously can't go, I will pick up anything you need."

"Has he forgiven me?" Caroline left the pot behind the screen and straightened.

"He has. He hopes, as do I, that there will be no further tests."

Caroline went to sit by the window. "I give my word. I really can't believe I did something like that. I don't know how I would have handled it if he'd wanted to take me up on my behavior. I hope you both will just forget about it."

Elise heard the embarrassment in her voice and felt sorry for her sister. Caroline had once been confident to the point of arrogance. Now she was a defeated soul. "That's exactly what we plan to do."

A commotion rose from downstairs.

"What in the world is going on?" Elise went to the door and opened it to better hear what was wrong.

"And if not here, then where?" a man's raised voice demanded.

"That's Nelson," Caroline said, trembling. "I hoped he'd stay away from here, but with the *Mary Elise* in port, he's bound to know I'm here."

"I'll go see what's going on."

"No, just stay with me," Caroline said, grabbing Elise's arm. "He's vicious, and if he should demand to search the whole house again, I don't know what I'll do."

"I understand. I'll stay."

Elise wished their father were still here. Uncle James and Louis were also gone. At least Nick was at the house. He knew the circumstances and would keep Caroline's whereabouts a secret, but how long could he manage if Nelson Worthington got violent?

"I swear," the man began again, "I will storm this place with the authorities again if need be."

Aunt Martha rushed into the room. "It's your husband," she said in a hushed voice.

"I know," Caroline replied. "I'm so sorry, Aunt Martha."

"He's making me a nervous wreck." She entwined her arm with Caroline's. "Whatever are we to do? I sent the maid to the stables to tell one of the groomsmen to go get your uncle. He's not been gone that long and probably hasn't even arrived at his office. Hopefully he can just get the driver to turn around and come home." She pressed a hand to her chest.

"I'm sure Nick can keep Mr. Worthington under control." Elise patted her aunt's shoulder. "We'll just wait it out and see what happens."

The minutes ticked by, and they no longer heard the harsh voice of Worthington booming through the house. It seemed to take forever, but finally Uncle James's voice could be heard as he came into the house, demanding to know what was going on.

Elise edged toward the stairs to hear better. It seemed the men had gone into the sitting room.

"Stay here," she told Caroline and her aunt. "I'll go see what's happening."

She slipped down the stairs, reaching the ground floor just as Nelson Worthington came from the sitting room. He was angry but paused to give her a quick once-over, as if to assure himself she wasn't Caroline. Then he threw open the door and left without so much as a backward glance.

Elise looked toward the sitting room and saw her uncle and Nick in the doorway. "Well, he was certainly loud."

"He's threatened us with the law again," her uncle said, shaking his head. "I fear we're going to need to get Caroline out of town in some way other than the *Mary Elise*. Mr. Worthington has promised to have the authorities search the ship."

"She could go by train. Perhaps Louis could accompany her," Elise suggested. "She can go to our house when she arrives in Duluth. Our neighbors will see to her safety, and Louis can come back."

"That does sound like a reasonable way to move her, but surely Worthington will be checking the train station as well," her uncle said.

"Maybe Louis could travel alone . . . with a large trunk," she said, smiling. "As soon as the train got on its way, he could arrange with the baggage keepers to set Caroline free."

"It's a good thing your sister is so petite," Nick said.

"Mrs. Cavendish, go upstairs and let my wife and Caroline know that he's gone for now," her uncle instructed. The housekeeper nodded.

Elise turned to her uncle. "Nick and I were going downtown to shop. If you're returning to work, perhaps you would give us a lift?"

Aunt Martha descended the stairs. "I would rather you remain home, Jim. Let them take your carriage. I cannot manage alone if Mr. Worthington should return."

Uncle James looked at Elise. "By all means, take the carriage. My driver will take you wherever you need to go."

"Thank you, Uncle James. Meanwhile, it might suit our situation if you were to have one of the servants go to the train station and buy Louis and Caroline's tickets to Duluth. Perhaps even a private compartment—that way no one needs to see much of Caroline. The train should leave tomorrow because that's when it's planned for us to go. I fully expect Nelson will be at the docks."

"Or they could leave tonight. That might be better still," her uncle suggested.

Elise saw the wisdom in that. "She'll arrive in Duluth before we do either way, unless there are problems in making her connections, so it doesn't really matter. I just figured Nelson would be at the docks watching for her if he knows we're leaving, and thus the train station would be clear."

"Oh, he knows. He mentioned that his man had already talked to some of the crew on the *Mary Elise* who were fairly confident of leaving at first light tomorrow."

"So we must act quickly. Maybe even leave tonight. Nick and I will go buy the things she needs for the trip and be home in time for lunch. You can let us know what you've managed to arrange then."

Elise and Nick left in Uncle James's carriage. Elise was uneasy and knew her sister was in more trouble than the others realized. She felt that she should tell someone—see if they could offer better insight. Nick was the only person she had available. Dare she tell him?

"I'm glad we have some time alone," he said. "I know you want to shop, but I need to tell your father about something I saw in Boston and again in Buffalo."

"What are you talking about?"

"A wanted poster. You might not be familiar with it, but the train depots often display various wanted posters. The police always check on the station and the comings and goings of people, and having the posters at hand makes it easier to identify criminals. When I was on my way back to Oswego, I noticed a poster in Boston and another in Buffalo. I didn't see the same one here, but they might have failed to post it. The drawing of the man looked very similar to Booker Duran."

If he hadn't had Elise's full attention before, he did now. "What was he wanted for?"

"Murder. The bill stated the killer's name was Robert Wayfair, but the drawing looked too similar to Duran to be ignored. Especially when we have concerns about what he might have done in Duluth."

Elise wanted to tell Nick about Duran's threat, but to do that, she would also have to tell him about Caroline's condition. But hadn't she already been considering that?

She took a deep breath. "I need to tell you something, but you will have to pledge to me that you'll say nothing—not even to my father."

Nick looked at her in surprise. "You're keeping secrets from your father?"

"Only for now. I don't want him to have to lie about . . . well, about something important." She knew her tone was pleading and hoped Nick would understand from that just how desperate the situation had become.

"I won't lie, so maybe you shouldn't say anything."

Elise considered this. "I don't want anyone to lie, but this is a matter of life and death, as far as I'm concerned. I'll just tell you part of it." She thought through her words before speaking. "Duran overheard my sister and I talking on the *Mary Elise*. Information was shared that could cause Caroline much grief. Booker threatened me regarding his bloodied shirt. He told me not to mention it to anyone or he would expose Caroline. When I told him I'd already mentioned it, he demanded I recant or at least make it clear that my timing was wrong. He went on to say that if I was asked by anyone,

I should say I was with him that evening in Duluth—the night the man was killed."

"So he did kill him?"

"I don't know for sure. He didn't confess to it, but he was determined I should give him an alibi. He also said I needed to let him . . . take liberties with me."

"And your need for secrecy gave him the feeling that he could make this demand and you would oblige?"

Elise let out a heavy breath. "Yes. But I haven't let him. I *wouldn't*. I've made sure never to be alone when on the ship."

"And he hasn't assaulted you?"

"He's . . . well, he's touched me a few times. Usually in trying to get past me in the galley. Others are always present, so he does it just innocently enough not to be questioned, while still reminding me of his demand."

"Of all the nerve. He needs to be kicked off the *Mary Elise*."

"But if he is, he'll tell Caroline's husband where she is."

"Well, he's not going to know much longer, is he? After all, we just made arrangements for your cousin to escort her by train. Duran won't have the ability to tell Worthington anything."

Elise leaned back against the carriage seat and sighed. *Only that she's carrying his child.*

Chapter 22

When Elise and Nick returned to the *Mary Elise* to speak to her father, they were surprised to learn he was already gone.

"Said he had something to take care of," Sam said, shaking his head. "I don't know what it was, Miss Elise."

"That's all right, Sam. We'll just drop off these things and talk to him later." She motioned Nick to follow her to the deckhouse.

She'd no sooner opened the door to head inside, however, than she came face-to-face with yet another problem. Booker had poor Tom up against the wall. He was just about to land a punch when Elise and Nick made their appearance. Both men looked rather surprised.

"Stand down, Duran. What's the meaning of this?" Nick demanded.

"It's between the boy and me," Duran replied. "Stay out of it."

Nick tossed aside the packages he'd been carrying. "As first mate on this ship, I am in charge in the captain's absence, and I demand to know what's going on."

Duran's eyes narrowed. "And I said stay out of it. You shouldn't be allowed any authority after killing most of your crew. I've heard you're from a rich family, so why not go back where you belong? It might be safer for everyone if you did."

Elise was livid. She tried to move toward Tom, but Nick held her back. "What happened, Tom?"

"He threatened to throw me overboard one night." Fear edged the young man's words.

"To kill you?" She looked at Duran. "For what reason, Mr. Duran? Or do you even need one?"

Duran remained silent. It wasn't at all like him. It was apparent Tom was the only one they could count on to tell the story.

"He hates my harmonica," Tom said, pushing out of the corner to get away from Duran. He went to stand between Nick and Elise.

"That's what this is about? A stupid harmonica?" Nick asked. "You'd take a life because you don't like his harmonica-playing?"

Duran's already hateful expression darkened even more. "I'm not answering to you, Clark. You have no say over this, and if you dare raise a hand to me, you'll be sorry. Just ask her, if you don't believe me."

Elise felt her cheeks grow warm. "Tom, go on and do whatever it is you're supposed to be doing. If you find my father, send him here."

"Are you ready to reveal all your secrets?" Duran looked at her with a slight raise of his brows.

"I am. I'm not going to live with you trying to control me. You're an evil man, Mr. Duran."

"You won't say anything, or your sister will pay the price. I've already talked to her husband."

"You what?" Elise felt her knees weaken. She only wanted to keep Caroline safe.

"I told him I had information on her whereabouts." He grinned. "He paid me well. I didn't say anything about . . . well, you know. But I will if you don't just forget about this."

"And how will you go and tell him if I lock you up?" Nick asked.

"I've made arrangements," he said, smiling. "You don't think I'm stupid enough not to have someone help me? I have a lot of friends who are always willing to do anything for money."

Elise wished Nick would say something about the posters. She might have herself, but she wasn't the one who had seen them. Now Duran was threatening to let Caroline's husband know about her condition, and since her sister wasn't yet out of town, Elise couldn't let that happen.

As if reading her mind, Nick looked at her and shook his head. "I don't think we can do anything to him at this point. He only threatened Tom and didn't hurt him. I'll have a talk with the boy. Your father will probably want to dismiss him for threatening Tom's life."

Duran looked at Elise. "You know the price of my silence."

This angered her. "You already told him where to find her."

"And why not? She's his wife. I think we both know that's only fair. Besides, we know he won't be able to take her by force. Your father would never allow that, but it does stir things up and keeps everyone busy and away from the ship."

"What purpose does that serve, Mr. Duran?" Elise knew if she stayed here much longer, she'd say something she'd regret.

"With the authorities busy with that, they

aren't concerned about me." He smiled and crossed his arms.

"I believe you have work to do, Mr. Duran," Nick said, dismissing him.

Duran sauntered past them. "I expect you to honor our bargain, Miss Wright. Otherwise, Nelson Worthington will know everything."

"I made no bargain with you, Mr. Duran. That would be akin to making a bargain with the devil himself, and that will never happen."

He paused at the stairs and gave her a smirk. "We'll see about that." He left them and made his way on deck.

"Why didn't you say anything about the posters?" Elise asked in a whisper.

"I think we need to have the authorities at hand when we do that. I'm more and more convinced that Duran is the man they're searching for. That makes him very dangerous. Too dangerous to risk not having help."

Elise felt a terrible sense of dread. She gathered the packages Nick had earlier dropped to the floor. "Let's go back to my uncle's house. I worry that my sister's husband will return. Maybe with the police." She put two parcels on the table, then went to her cabin door with the others. "Take those, and I'll leave these here." She disappeared into the cabin for only a moment, then returned quickly. "I have a terrible feeling things are going to get much worse."

Nick nodded. "With men like Duran, they usually do."

~⁓~

There were several carriages on the half-circle drive at the Monroe house when Nick and Elise arrived. Elise had no idea what was happening, but something felt very wrong.

She gripped Nick's arm as they made their way up the walk. "Let's go in through the servants' entrance."

"Do you think something has happened?"

"As far as I know, we weren't expecting company, so this must be Nelson's doing."

Nick nodded and shifted the parcels he carried. "The servant's entrance is probably wise."

They made their way around back and entered the kitchen, only to find the cook and several of the household staff standing at the doorway, looking out into the dining room. There was some loud arguing going on toward the front of the house. Elise could hear her sister shouting.

"I will not come back to you, Nelson. You're a beast, and after what you did to me, I will not be left alone with you."

"If this is how it's to be, Nelson, you will not receive another cent of your grandfather's money."

"That must be Mr. Worthington, Nelson's father," Elise said.

At this, the staff realized they weren't alone and turned in unison. At the sight of Elise, they hurried back to their positions.

Nick set the packages by the back stairs. "Perhaps we should get out there. I don't know who else might be here, but your sister may need your support."

Elise didn't need to be encouraged. She hurried through the dining room and into the music room. From there she came out into the hallway that ran behind the stairs.

Everyone stood at the base of the staircase. Her father was there, as well as Uncle James. Nelson and his father were there with another man she didn't know. The latter was older and quite distinguished-looking— perhaps a lawyer. Caroline stood on the first step and looked grateful when Elise came into view.

"I think we've heard more than enough from both parties," the older man said. "I believe, Mr. Worthington, that it is time for us to discuss this further in my office." He spoke to Nelson's father rather than Nelson.

"I won't leave here without my wife, Judge

Marcus," Nelson declared. "We are legally married. She is mine."

"She doesn't have to come back to you unless she chooses to do so," Papa said in a calm and precise voice. Elise knew it was a sign of his increased anger when he spoke like that.

Caroline turned on the step and started back upstairs. "I won't ever come back to you, Nelson, and there is nothing you can do about it."

Judge Marcus waved a hand. "It would be better to discuss this apart from the others."

Caroline was nearly to the top of the stairs when Nelson broke from the group and charged up after her. He grabbed her roughly by the elbow. "You're coming home."

She jerked free and attempted to push him away, but he dodged her shove, and Caroline lost her balance. She fell backward down the stairs.

Elise screamed but could do nothing to save her sister. She pushed her way through the men and rushed to Caroline's side as soon as she landed at the bottom of the stairs. Blood immediately began to pool around her head.

"Someone send for the doctor!" Elise cried. "Hurry!" She took Caroline's hand. "Caroline. Please say something."

"That wasn't my fault," Nelson said, staring down at them. He didn't even try to care for his wife. Not that Elise would have let him touch her sister. "You all witnessed it. She pushed me. She tried to kill me," he continued in his smug, superior way.

Elise looked up at him. She had never hated anyone as she did this man. She tried to pray, but in her rage, she had no words. She knew in that moment that if she could have pushed him down the stairs, she would have.

⁓

Papa carried Caroline to her bed. The wound on the back of her head didn't appear all that big, but there was plenty of bleeding. Elise refused to leave her sister's side. She shooed the men from the room and even asked Aunt Martha to leave. When they were gone, Elise and Etta undressed Caroline and put her in a simple nightgown. Etta had already placed several towels under her head to soak up the blood.

"Please wake up, sister. Please," Elise whispered against Caroline's ear. "You must live."

When the doctor arrived, Elise asked Etta to leave. She followed the maid to the door. "Don't let anyone else come in. The doctor will need privacy."

"Yes, miss." Etta looked concerned but said nothing more.

The doctor was already examining Caroline, who was starting to come to. "What . . . what happened?" she asked.

Elise rushed to her side. "You fell. You fell down the stairs."

"Just lie still," the doctor ordered.

"She's with child," Elise blurted. "She doesn't look it, I know, but she's five months gone." She looked to Caroline in apology, then glanced at her sister's relatively flat stomach. "I'm sorry. He needs to know in case you miscarry."

The doctor continued his examination, and after nearly half an hour looked more puzzled than conclusive.

"You have a concussion and a cut on the back of your head. I will need to put stitches in the head wound," he explained to Caroline. "I don't know quite how to ask this, but what made you suppose you were with child—much less five months along? I find no evidence of that. Your abdomen is soft, and there's no sign of a baby. At this stage I should be able to feel the formation, especially in one as thin as you."

"Perhaps she miscarried." Elise looked at her sister. "Have you bled?"

"No. Not since before our wedding. In

fact, I stopped bleeding a month or so before. You know how nervous I get, and the stress was so great."

"You left us when you were fifteen. I hardly know anything about such things with you." Elise tried to remember. "I do recall that you were given to throwing up when you were nervous. Even when you were young. Mama thought it was the motion of the water."

Caroline looked at the doctor. "She's right. I am often given over to my nerves in such a fashion. Is it possible that what I've thought of as morning sickness was nothing more than my nerves?"

"It's very possible," the doctor said. "You have obviously not been eating right. You're skin and bones."

"She hardly eats at all," Elise declared. "My aunt has often said as much."

"I find it difficult when I'm upset. It usually just makes me feel worse. I generally eat little bits throughout the day in order to avoid becoming nauseated. Especially when I'm anxious."

"And have you been anxious these last months?" the doctor asked.

Caroline nodded. "I have. It's been most brutal—life-changing."

He rubbed his chin and nodded. "Then I

would say that is our answer. You presumed because you were a new bride that you were with child."

A look of relief crossed Caroline's face. "But I'm not. You're certain?"

"Quite certain. I'm sorry."

"You don't understand. I did not wish to be." She smiled at Elise. "One day I will desire children, but I am most happy not to be expecting a baby at this time."

The doctor shook his head. It was clear he hadn't expected this. "I need to stitch your head. Perhaps your sister could let everyone know that you're all right. You have a concussion and will no doubt be sore from the fall, but otherwise you are fine."

Elise felt as if a weight had been lifted from their shoulders. "I'll let them know."

She walked to the door and paused to look back at Caroline. There were tears in her sister's eyes.

"I'm sorry, Mr. Duran, but I have no choice but to dismiss you from this ship," Captain Wright declared. "After speaking to the first mate and Tom, it is clear you threatened the life of one of my crew. That, I will not tolerate."

Duran wished he could kill both the captain and his first mate. Then he'd go take care of that troublemaking boy once and for all.

The captain shook his head as if dealing with a child. "Go get your things, and I'll have your final wages ready and waiting."

Duran looked at Nick and then the captain. "You'll regret this. I don't let anyone push me around."

"I already regret ever hiring you on," Captain Wright said. "I believe in giving all men a chance, however. One day, I hope you'll decide to change for the better, Duran."

"There's no need for change. My way suits me just fine."

Duran left the captain and Nick and went to the forecastle to get his things. The most troubling thing about all this was the location. Had this happened in Duluth or even Toronto, he would have felt better about being stranded. Now he wasn't even sure he had enough money for a train ticket.

The Wrights had caused him no end of trouble, but he still had the knowledge that Elise's sister was pregnant. He'd find Nelson Worthington again and tell him that he had something more important to tell him regarding his wife . . . but it would cost him.

Chapter 23

"I'm glad Louis was able to change the train ticket for later this week. I think, given what's happened, Nelson will surely stay away for fear of someone filing charges against him." Elise leaned over and kissed her sister's head.

"I hope he does. Uncle James said he plans to threaten him with it if he refuses to sign the annulment papers." Caroline smiled. "You know, I think this is the first time I've been happy in months."

"Even though you're moving to Duluth?" Elise smiled. "It really has become quite a nice town. I think this winter will be a good time for both of us to explore."

"Are you going to marry Nick?" her sister asked out of the blue.

Elise shrugged. "I want to, but I believe it's important for Nick to get back to captaining his own ship. I can't leave Papa and the *Mary Elise*, so I'm not sure what to do."

Caroline frowned. "You can't give up your life for our father. He's a good man, and he's strong and capable. He wouldn't want that for you."

"Yes, but I promised our mother." Elise went to the window and looked out. The skies were growing dark, and soon she'd need to be on the *Mary Elise*. Papa had decided it would be better to sleep on board since they were leaving early in the morning.

"Did Mama ask for that promise, Elise? I doubt she did, because she was never that selfish. You know that very well. She wouldn't want you to forsake true love."

"I know she would want me to find happiness, Caroline. However, I know she would also like to know that Papa is happy. We shall have to pray on it, for God has all the answers."

"I've thought about that ever since talking to Nick. I've been praying more and reading the Bible. I see how He answered my prayers, and I know I must put aside my selfish ways. I don't know what God has planned for me, but I want to change."

"You already have," Elise replied. She stepped back from the window. "I'd better go bid everyone good-bye. I'll see you in a couple of weeks." She went to Caroline and kissed her again.

"Don't tell him no," Caroline whispered against her ear.

"What?" Elise straightened.

"Nick. When he proposes, don't tell him no."

Caroline's words echoed in Elise's thoughts. The more she came to know Nick, the more she felt certain he wouldn't feel whole again until he held the command of a ship. But her father would never give up the water and command of his own vessel. It was a dichotomy she found herself thinking about more and more. What could she do? To say yes to one was to deny the other.

"There you are," Uncle James said as Elise came down the stairs. "Your father and Nick are ready to return to the ship. They plan to leave by midnight. We were just starting to look for you."

"I was telling Caroline good-bye." Elise embraced her uncle. "And now I will bid you the same."

"Just remember, you are always welcome here. Your sister too, although I know she wants to be as far away from here as possible. Poor girl. I'm afraid society will not be kind."

"Probably not, since they don't know the truth."

Uncle James shrugged. "They probably know about Nelson and his mistress, but I doubt they care. Things like that are done all the time by men of power and wealth."

"Well, it isn't right, and it's certainly not of God." Elise glanced back up the stairs. "It's my deepest desire that you can keep Nelson Worthington from doing any further damage to her. The rest will heal in time. Caroline is a lot stronger than you might think."

He chuckled. "Oh, I know how strong she is. You're both your mother's daughters, and you inherited her strength and love."

A pounding sounded at the front door, and Mrs. Cavendish appeared in her mob-cap and pinafore apron. Without waiting to be invited in, Nelson Worthington crashed through the door as the housekeeper started to open it. Mrs. Cavendish fell back against the wall, and Elise rushed to her side. She steadied the old woman as Nelson began to rail at her uncle.

"I will sue you for every dime you have for alienating the affections of my wife and keeping the knowledge of my unborn child from me," he yelled as he shook his fist at Uncle James.

Elise felt her stomach tighten. Duran was responsible for this. But why? This information was his only hold over Elise. It must have become more beneficial to him to tell the news, and that somehow made the situation all the more worrisome.

She let go of Mrs. Cavendish and stepped forward. "My sister isn't with child. You can ask the doctor who was here earlier."

"I don't believe you. I have it on good authority—"

"You have it on the authority of a man who is most likely wanted for murder in at least two states," she countered. "Booker Duran is nothing more than a vicious beast who enjoys threatening those who seem weaker and helping those who appear as evil as himself. Especially if money is involved."

Worthington looked at her in surprise. "I said nothing of Mr. Duran."

"You don't have to. I already know it was him. He overheard Caroline and I discussing something and took it upon himself to use it as a threat to get me to do what he wanted. But Caroline is not with child, and I am not going to allow him to force me into any compromise."

"But he said that she admitted she was pregnant. He overheard it himself."

By now Louis, Nick, and Elise's father had joined them in the foyer. They all seemed more than a little surprised by the discussion. For their sakes, Elise explained.

"Caroline feared she might be with child because she hadn't bled since before marrying you. Added to that, she was frequently vomiting and thought it was morning sickness. But the doctor examined her and assured her she isn't with child. The condition is something she's dealt with most of her teen years and into adulthood. When she is suffering a large amount of stress and fear, she has problems in these areas. She is not, however, expecting your baby, Mr. Worthington." Elise looked around at the men and decided it didn't matter that she was going to be shockingly bold. "Furthermore, unless you want her going very public with the circumstances of her wedding night, I would cooperate and give her a quiet annulment. Otherwise, I fear we will have no choice but to share the story with the newspapers. After all, Caroline has nothing to lose." She smiled. "It seems to me that you're the only one who has anything to lose."

Worthington paled at this. "You wouldn't dare. A scandal like that would ruin me— ruin my family."

"You should have thought of that before you took a mistress, then raped and beat my daughter," Elise's father said, stepping forward. "I've only remained silent out of respect for Caroline, but don't think I wouldn't like to beat you to a pulp. Now, I suggest you leave before I forget my manners."

Elise took hold of her father's arm, hoping to calm him.

Worthington backed a couple of steps toward the door. It was clear he didn't want to have to deal with the well-muscled ship captain.

"I'll send the lawyer around tomorrow first thing," Uncle James said. "With assurance from the doctor that your wife is not in a family way, as well as the papers you'll need to sign for the annulment on grounds of misrepresentation." He stepped to the door, and Worthington eased across the threshold to the porch beyond. "You will sign the agreement for annulment, or our next meeting will be with the owner of the *Oswego Daily Palladium*."

Worthington held Uncle James's gaze for only a moment more before turning on his heel.

Elise's uncle shut the door and turned to the others. "I'd say we have him right where we want him."

"Well, there are other places I can think of to throw him," Elise's father declared, "but I suppose this will have to do."

Elise crossed her arms, still contemplating why Duran would give up the information about her sister. "I was surprised Booker Duran has played what he supposed to be his trump card."

"Your father fired him. Put him off the ship," Nick explained.

Papa looked at her. "He threatened you and you didn't come to me?"

"I wanted to tell you both," she said, looking at Nick and then back to her father. "He threatened to tell Caroline's husband about her belief that she was with child if we said anything about his bloody shirt. He wanted me to convince you and anyone else necessary that he'd been with me that night in Duluth. I believe he must be the killer of that poor man."

"Not to mention the wanted posters from Buffalo. The sketch of the suspect was a rather good likeness of Duran," Nick declared.

"Yes, but as I said, we have no real proof. We can offer him up as a possible suspect, but little more," Papa reminded them. "But rest assured, I will speak to the authorities and tell them our suspicions."

"I'm just glad he's gone." Elise let go of her father's arm. "Poor Tom was so scared."

"Speaking of which, I suggest we get back to him and the others. I asked Sam to stick around while Tom is doing his watch duty. No sense risking Duran coming back to get even." Elise's father turned to his brother-in-law. "Thank you for everything."

"Of course. I will see to this annulment and be in touch. Hopefully before Christmas, but otherwise shortly thereafter. And Louis will take good care of Caroline on the trip to Duluth. Have no fear for her safety."

Papa smiled at Louis. "I know she'll be safe in his keeping. Nick, why don't you and Elise head on back to the ship? I'm going upstairs to tell Caroline good-bye."

"It's much too cold out there to walk. I'll have my driver take you back to the ship," Uncle James said.

Elise's father laughed. "You forget, we live our lives on the open seas. The wind and cold are just old friends."

"We'll be just fine," Elise told her uncle. "We know how to bundle up. Look, I even bought some of those bloomers for riding—or in this case, staying warmer on a ship." She raised her skirt to the knees in a most unladylike manner, revealing dark blue bloomers beneath. "I shall be quite warm."

The men all laughed.

Later, as she and Nick made their way back to the ship, Elise was still contemplating the choices she had to face regarding her father and Nick. He hadn't yet asked her to marry him but had implied that he would.

382

She had no idea what she would say when the time came.

"You seem awfully deep in thought. Are you thinking about your sister?"

"Actually, no. But the thoughts are every bit as important. Even more so."

"Perhaps I can help. You could share the problem with me."

She laughed. "You are the problem."

He looked stunned. "What has made me a problem to you?"

"I've fallen in love with you."

His expression changed to pleasure. "Yes, I know. But that's not a problem. You see, I'm in love with you, as well. So it seems we are in full agreement rather than contemplating a problem." He put his arm around her as the wind picked up.

"But I also love my father." She let him pull her close. "And I made my mother a promise to take care of him."

"Again, I see no problem unless he dismisses me from working for him on the *Mary Elise*."

"But, Nick, you are a ship's captain. You need to have control of your own ship again. I see your restlessness. I know you're unsettled."

"I was unsettled. In fact, I wasn't at all sure what I was going to do. Everything I have done for the past ten years has been to impress my father. I wanted him to see my worth, my value. I didn't realize he already did. Our parting was so bitter and hurtful, and all I could think about was showing him up—teaching him a lesson. Instead, God taught me a lesson about pride and self-assurance."

"But you need a certain amount of that to lead. Papa always said as much. He too is sometimes prideful and always self-assured."

"Yes, but he's tempered too. He knows the dangers of making decisions based on pride. I've learned those as well, but it cost men their lives."

"You can't let that defeat you from returning to take charge of your own ship."

"Let's just say I'm content to be a first mate for now. The rewards for such a position are great."

"But it won't always be enough, and I don't want to feel forced to choose between my father or my . . . husband."

"I pledge to you, Elise, I will never put you in that position. If I have to remain a first mate for the next thirty years, then so be it. I love you." He paused and pulled her into his arms to face him. "I want very much to marry you."

"I want that too, but I won't desert my father."

"You'll never be asked to. I promise." He

reached into his trouser pocket and produced a ring. "This was my mother's. I brought it back from Boston knowing that I wanted to ask you to marry me." He gently unfastened Elise's glove and pulled it from her hand. "Elise, will you marry me?" He slipped the ring on her finger and stepped back to watch her. "I pledge before God always to be there for you and your father . . . and never to ask you to leave him."

She looked up at him and smiled. "Thank you, Nick." She held her hand up to the light. "Yes, I will marry you."

His lips had barely touched hers when someone began yelling.

"Fire! Fire!"

"Thankfully it wasn't a bad blaze," Nick told Elise's father as they stood at the rail of the *Mary Elise*, looking down on the portion of the dock building that had been burning only an hour earlier. The fire department had done an excellent job of getting the fire under control before it could burn the entire area. "Someone was thoughtless with their smoking, or perhaps a bum tried to make a fire."

"It's certainly possible. Fire's a terrible threat—one of the biggest fears for sailing men," Captain Wright declared.

"God was definitely good to us." It was Nick's watch, and he knew the captain would soon head off to bed.

"He is. Despite all that we've endured these last few days, God has offered great protection." Elise's father looked at him and smiled. "I see my daughter is sporting a new ring. I presume you asked her to marry you."

"Yes. Just as I asked you permission to do." Nick's smile faded. "She was very concerned, however, about you."

"I told you she would be. She's all caught up in that promise she made her mother."

Nick nodded. "So she said. But I assured her I was content to act as first mate for as long as you needed me. God is teaching me valuable things here, and I will not take them lightly."

"And as I've already told you, I intend to retire from the *Mary Elise*. It isn't the same without my Mary, and now that Caroline will need me, I want to be there for her. I could never leave her to fend for herself in Duluth, so at least for a time, I'll quit the lakes. But I have a feeling it will be permanent."

"I can't imagine you sailing for most of your life and then just giving it up."

Wright rubbed his beard. "I never thought that day would come, but isn't it funny how a man can, after yielding all to God, find himself moving in directions he never thought possible?"

The question tugged at something deep in Nick's heart. "God always manages to have His way."

"And aren't we grateful for that?" Wright said, laughing.

"This is going to be a shock for Elise."

Still chuckling, Wright nodded. "I'm thinking she'll get over it, since you'll be there to draw her focus."

"No matter what, I'll be there for her. I give you my pledge."

"And I will hold you to it." Wright slapped Nick on the back. "For now, however, I am still the captain, and I need to prepare for our departure."

Nick watched him go. He was a good man, better than most, and yet from their talks, Nick knew he had once been godless and difficult. In his case, the accidental meeting of a young woman had begun his transformation, and God had completed the rest. Nick felt he could claim the same story for himself.

Booker Duran stretched out as best he could and opened the bottle of whiskey. He would have revenge on the *Mary Elise* if it was the last thing he did. He smiled and thought

of all the times others had crossed him or
gotten in the way of his plans. He never let
one of them get off without some form of
punishment.

"They'll learn," he muttered to himself.
"Never cross Robert Wayfair, no matter what
name he goes by."

He took a long drink and then another,
hoping the whiskey would warm him against
the chill of the night. He closed his eyes and
eased back against his pack.

They'd pay. They'd all pay.

Chapter 24

Nick didn't like the looks of the deteriorating weather, and neither did the captain. The snow had started after they'd cleared the Soo Locks earlier in the day. It had fallen lightly for hours, but as the day progressed toward evening, the snow increased. Both men knew that November storms on the lakes could be some of the worst. Both also knew the odds were great that the ship would take on damage if they couldn't get to safety.

"The wind has been gusting up to twenty knots with this front movin' in," Captain Wright declared to Nick as he came to check in. The captain was going over the charts, and Nick joined him at the table. Elise was busy in the galley, making supper.

The entire trip had seemed cursed. One thing after another had gone wrong, and strange things had been happening. Food had gone missing, ropes had been cut. Tom had fallen and nearly gone overboard when breaking up ice at the bow. He'd been alone and the snow had gotten heavy. He'd lost his footing on the icy deck and fallen back against the windlass. As he struggled to stand, the ship dipped low and threw him forward. He said it felt as if someone or something was actually trying to push him over the rail. In his position, all he could do was hang fast to the rail, and when he was finally able to get upright with the help of Sam, no one else was there. Sam hadn't seen a soul.

Just today, while everyone had been at lunch, something had brought down one of the sails. Everyone was spooked.

Now it was obvious this cold front was going to bring more than the light snow they'd experienced all day. Nick had felt uneasy since early that morning, and he knew Captain Wright had too. They'd discussed several ports where they might take cover if things turned bad, but since the snows had been light and the sailing uneventful, they had pressed on.

"We will take cover, but this is a rough area," Wright said, still studying the map. "There's just not a lot of choices to be had."

"I'm sure it's best to wait out the storm," Nick said. "What about here?" He pointed to a place on the map. "The depth is good and there's a hint of protection from the winds."

"I was thinking the same. If we can reach it." Wright looked at Nick and then back to the map. "I told you I was just as guilty of bad decisions as others. I hope and pray this isn't one of those times."

"There was no reason to stop before now. The snow was light, and the wind was too. This storm front is what's bringing us trouble. We had no way of knowing. When we checked with the folks at the locks, it looked safe enough to proceed, and the Weather Bureau wasn't concerned."

"I trust my gut more than I do that newly formed group of scientists. What do they know about the taste of the wind or the feel of dropping pressure?" Wright asked. "You and I have both felt there was trouble coming. This trip has been a problem from the beginning. Anchors don't just drop, and ropes don't cut themselves. Someone is causing this."

"But who? You said yourself you'd trust any of these men with your life."

"And I do." The captain shook his head. "If Duran were still on board, I'd think it was him."

392

"And that would be a natural assumption, but he's not here."

The captain rubbed his bearded chin. "Or is he?"

"What are you saying?" Nick thought maybe the stress of things had gotten to be too much for the captain.

"That fire in Oswego . . . it made a good diversion. Anyone could have snuck on board. It wouldn't be my first stowaway."

"By why would he want to be on the *Mary Elise*?"

"Who's to say? It could be nothing more than the law was closing in on him. I'm sure I don't know."

Nick considered that. "Let's say he did stow away on the ship. Where would he likely be?"

"There are plenty of hiding places on the *Mary Elise*. He could slip out and cause havoc, then disappear again. No one expects him to be here. No one is looking for him."

"Then maybe we should." Nick was beginning to see his point. Duran had promised to get his revenge. "I'll get a couple of the boys, and we'll start searching the ship. We'll make a pretense of trimming the cargo and go below."

"The way these waves are building, a pretense won't be needed. I'm sure the load has shifted. I can feel the slight list to the port side." Captain Wright shook his head. "I'll let Elise know our suspicions. You let the boys know as you can without making a formal announcement. If Duran is on board, he already has the advantage. Let's do what we can to take that from him."

Nick nodded and pulled his thick knit cap back on his head. "Aye aye."

He headed for the stairs, wishing he could stop and speak with Elise for a few moments. Instead, he opened the door and stepped back into the freezing snow and ice. It was clearly worse than when he'd come indoors.

He made his way to Sam, who was at the wheel with Ollie, keeping watch for him.

"Sam, I need to speak to you and Ollie."

Elise was certain her father had come to tell her to let the stove go cold. She smiled up at him as he crossed the galley. "I've already stopped feeding the fire. It's dying down."

He nodded. "That's good. We're going to find a place to hole up, but that's not why I'm here." The waves sent the ship rocking hard to starboard. Elise stumbled, and her father caught her. "We think we have a stowaway. We think it's Duran, given the things going on."

Elise pulled back. Her eyes widened. "Well, that would certainly answer a lot of questions."

"I don't want you walking the ship unless Nick or I can be with you. Stay completely away from the rails." He paused, as the rocking was clearly growing worse. "Better still, lock yourself in your cabin. Don't come out unless Nick or I come for you."

She nodded. "As soon as the stove is completely out."

"Douse it. We can clean it up later."

"All right."

"Be quick about it, sweetheart." He kissed the top of her head. "I have to go."

"Please be careful, Papa. I love you."

He nodded but said nothing more.

Elise watched him leave, wondering how Duran could have gotten back on board without the watch knowing. Then she remembered the dock fire back in Oswego. Everything had been out of control, and the watch had left the ship to try to help with the fire, as had she and Nick. Duran could have used that time to get on board.

It was a terrible feeling to imagine him there, watching . . . waiting. He had promised to seek his revenge, and she'd been foolish to think it had ended with telling Caroline's husband about the baby.

She doused the stove, secured the food, then put out the lamps one by one. She lit a lantern, then went to her cabin. Her nerves forced her to check through the room for any place even the smallest man could hide. There was no one. She locked the door, went to her tiny desk, and took a seat. Papa had built a secure slot for the lantern, and she placed it in this apparatus and turned the flame low. If the waves grew worse, she would blow it out, but for now she needed the light.

She pulled out her Bible and held it close. The room was already growing much colder. She opened the Scriptures. She had a special marker for times like this.

"'God is our refuge and strength, a very present help in trouble,'" she read from Psalm forty-six. "'Therefore we will not fear, though the earth be removed, and though the mountains be carried into the midst of the sea; though the waters thereof roar and be troubled. . . .'"

But this time it was neither the sea nor the storm that troubled her most. It was Duran. The very thought of his being on board to torment them—perhaps even to kill them—bothered her most. She'd seen her father manage the bad weather and difficult seas, but this was an evil man intent on revenge.

Her gaze fell again on the start of the

psalm. *God is our refuge and strength, a very present help in trouble.* She sighed and hugged the Bible close. "Oh, God our Father, You are the only refuge we have. This is a very bad situation with Booker Duran and the storm around us. Please, please deliver us."

Nothing about this storm was normal. The winds whipped from one direction and then another. The snow turned to icy pellets and beat them fiercely as thick ice formed around the ship. The men fought to get the ice off while seeing to other instructions the captain gave. And all the while, they kept watch for Booker Duran in the fading light.

Bill knew he'd faced tougher times, but at the moment he couldn't remember when. Whether it was God's forewarning or his own natural senses, Bill knew somehow that this storm was going to be his undoing. The ship wouldn't be able to survive. Prayers or no prayers.

The men had searched as best they could, but the storm had worsened so fast that there was no hope of checking everywhere for Duran. Bill and Nick were now consumed with steering the ship, and worries about Duran had to be set aside.

Bill had tried to steer them into a small

cove, but the weather had gone out of control much quicker than he expected. Such was the way of winter storms on Lake Superior.

The coast was very close, and the rocky cliffs that shot up out of the lake were like foreboding sentinels. They had to make certain they stayed away from the rocks, but their control was rapidly slipping away.

As the waves pushed them ever closer to the shore, Bill ordered the anchor dropped with fifty fathoms of chain, but it didn't help. When the bottom of the *Mary Elise* scraped against the rocks, his foreboding of destruction was confirmed.

They were in trouble. They all knew it. Even Elise, who was locked in her cabin, would know the horrible danger they faced. He wished he could be with her to tell her all would be fine, but he had no assurance of that. In fact, the opposite was true.

The waves whipped them back off the rocks. Bill dreaded the results. "Ollie, take Russ and see what damage we have," he yelled above the storm.

Just then the waves seemed to lift the ship high in the air and then toss her aside like a child's toy. The ship hit the rocks hard, and the waves shoved the *Mary Elise* higher onto the rocky ledge. There was a distinct tilt to the deck, and Bill knew without a doubt that they were breaking apart. He looked at Nick, who was trying to right himself. He'd nearly gone over the rail with that last wave.

Ollie and Russ were hurrying across the deck. If they were back already, it couldn't be good.

"We're taking on water fast," Ollie reported. "We're doomed for sure."

"Stand by to abandon ship," Bill called above the roar of the wind.

Nick knew the captain was right. But how to do it? Where were they to go? He studied the rocks and the cliffside. It might be possible to get up there. He could tie off a rope on the ship and then find a place to tie it to the rocks so the crew could climb to safety. That was probably their only hope.

With the ship stuck on the rocks, Captain Wright motioned for Nick to follow him inside. The captain's beard and mustache were caked in ice, as were his eyelashes.

Elise appeared at the door to the galley. She had on her warmest coat and a thick knit cap and gloves. "Are we leaving the ship?"

"We are, if I can figure out how," her father answered.

There came a horrendous noise from outside, and the trio left the deckhouse to see what had happened. The waves washed over the ship's deck, and Nick reached out to keep Elise from losing her footing. She clung to his arm, meeting his gaze. The fear he saw there matched his own.

"The main is gone," Captain Wright said, pointing.

The main mast had broken away and now lay half on the deck and half off. It was as if it were reaching for the cliffs. It might offer them a way to get to the rocks. But then what? They'd have to climb to the top.

"I'll take ropes," Nick told the captain. "I'll tie them off on the mast and the rail and then climb the rocks and hopefully tie them off on top. Then the crew can use them to climb up."

The captain looked uncertain but finally nodded.

Nick motioned to Tom to come help him. The wiry boy was able to maneuver the deck quickly despite the wind and ice. He and Nick tied two ropes to the ship, and then it was time to climb.

Nick crawled out on the mast as far as he could before grabbing onto the slippery, ice-laden rocks. There was no possible way for this to work unless God interceded.

"Lord, help us," Nick whispered.

He had no way to tie the rope to the rocks.

He'd seen mountain climbers use hooks of some sort, but a schooner on the Great Lakes didn't have anything like that. He would just have to risk it. He would get to the top of the rocks and somehow tie it off up there.

Even then, Nick wasn't sure the men could manage, much less Elise.

Elise clung to her father as he gathered the men. "Nick's doing what he can to provide us a way off the ship," he told them. They were listing hard to starboard, and no one knew how much time they had left. "When the rope is secure, you'll have to do what you can to climb to safety." He looked at Elise, the fear in his eyes clearly directed at her.

"Don't worry, Papa," she whispered against his ear as she hugged him close. "I'm strong."

They watched and waited as the storm bore down upon them.

"Two of the men aren't here," her father said after a moment. "Where are Seamus and Russ?"

Somehow the others heard his question and glanced around. They shook their heads.

"I'll go find them," Ollie said, pulling up his collar.

"I'll go too," Nils Hanson declared.

Without waiting for permission, they grabbed lanterns and headed toward the bow. Elise whispered a prayer for them, then strained again to find Nick in the storm.

Tom appeared through the sleet. "He gave me the signal. The ropes are secure." He was yelling. "We have to walk the mast and then get onto the rocks by using the rope. It won't be easy, because then we have to climb."

"Women and children first," her father declared. "Tom, you help Elise. Go now. Sam, light more lanterns."

The entire group moved toward the fallen mast. Everyone was eager to get to safety, although they knew great peril awaited them before the slightest hope of security could be had.

Elise soon found her skirt was dragging her down. It was heavy with ice and snow. She climbed upon the mast, taking hold of the guide rope, but her balance was precarious because of her skirt. She hesitated only a moment, then unbuttoned the waistband and let the skirt drop to her feet. The bloomers she had on beneath were still fairly dry and in no way encumbered her movement. She held fast to the rope and kicked the skirt aside, then continued up the mast.

It was like nothing she'd ever done before. When she was younger, she had at times climbed up into the rigging, but this was different. The wind seemed to push and pull her from every angle.

Tom was right behind her to offer whatever help he could. He held on to the second rope so as not to cause any interference with Elise. He clearly wanted to be close at hand if she needed him.

When she reached the rock face, Elise knew she didn't have the strength for what was required. She stared up toward the top of the cliff.

God is our refuge and strength, a very present help in trouble.

The words came to her from the depth of her soul. She swallowed hard, wondering how her mouth could possibly be dry in the midst of this storm. She looked upward again . . . then began to climb.

Once she left the mast for the rocks, Elise felt a sense of loss. She glanced back to see her father talking to Ollie and Nils. Seamus and Russ were nowhere to be seen. Had they been swept overboard?

Elise slipped and realized she needed to give the rocks her full attention. Night was falling, and the darkness would soon make this task doubly difficult. She drew a deep breath and felt the rocks. She searched for footholds as she held fast to the rope with her gloved hands. The icy wind stole her breath, making it all the harder to concentrate.

She felt Tom take hold of her foot and guide it to a small nook. She pushed upward. The next step was a bit easier, but there was such little security that she dared not stay in one place. Again, when she paused for too long, Tom helped her, and again she made progress up the icy rock. It was almost helpful that the wind was at her back, pushing her into the cliff.

Her arms burned, and her hands slipped constantly on the rope. Despite the bloomers being intended for such adventures, Elise could feel them weighing her down. Still, she pressed on, knowing that if she didn't keep moving, the others would never have a chance to come behind her.

The ice no longer stung as much against her face and hands. She thought the wind might be weakening but couldn't be sure. She forced her focus to remain on the task at hand. Nothing else mattered but getting to the top of this rockface. She found a ledge on which to rest, but the sense of urgency pressed her on. She had to be nearing the top, even if she couldn't see it.

Onward she struggled, knowing that her strength was nearly gone. "Oh, God, please help me!"

She reached upward on the rope but lost her grip and slipped. Tom caught her before she fell very far. She hadn't even had the time to scream in fear. She tried again to pull herself up, but she didn't go very far, and it was almost impossible to find a foothold. Then, just as she knew she had nothing left to give, Elise felt a hand clasp around her wrist and pull upward. It was Nick. It had to be Nick.

She didn't know how to help, so she tried her best to find a place for her feet to push up from. And then, without warning, she felt herself being pulled over the edge and onto flat land. The effort to fight gravity and the storm was gone. She was exhausted, almost unable to move.

Tom soon joined them, practically climbing over her. She couldn't just lie here. She struggled to her hands and knees, but before she could go far, Nick had her in his arms. He kissed her frozen face and held her close for a few heartbeats.

He pulled her to her feet and led her to a grouping of rocks. "Stay here."

She nodded and tried to tuck herself into the rocks to block the wind. She was alive. She hadn't fallen to her death or drowned in the deep. She was alive. Now, if only the others could get to safety. She dropped to her knees and began to pray in earnest.

Bill Wright felt Booker Duran's presence before he saw him. "The ship's sinking, Duran. Best to take the rope and get to land like the others."

"Not until I take care of business. I've already lit this load on fire, and the *Mary Elise* will soon be no more."

"You lit the ship on fire? Are you mad? Don't you realize the danger to yourself as well as the others?"

"I don't care. My life is already forfeit. It's only a matter of time until the authorities catch up with me. One more death isn't going to make my punishment any worse, but it will satisfy a hankering in me."

"So you did murder that man in Duluth?"

"That man and one in Buffalo, another in New York City. Two of your crew, although I did try for more. There's so many I've lost count." He laughed against the wind. "And now I'm gonna kill you."

He lunged for Bill, but the captain merely stepped aside. Duran went crashing against the rail. He stood and slipped on the icy deck just as flames from below broke through the hatch.

"Where's your pretty daughter? I have

plans for her." Duran regained his footing and charged again.

Bill took hold of Duran's coat at the shoulders and tossed him aside like a sack of grain. The bigger man gave a yell that was quickly swallowed up in the wind.

The two men fought unseen by the others. Bill didn't want to kill the other man, but Duran was bent on this fight being to the death, and Bill would oblige. His anger at the way Duran had endangered them over and over fed his rage. Duran would see them all dead, and Bill knew he was the only one who could resolve the situation.

The flames were growing against the ice and snow. The waves crashing against the ship didn't seem to have any effect on the blaze. They were taking on water, so surely that would help stifle the fire. But Bill didn't think on the matter long, as Duran came charging at him once again.

This time Duran took Bill to the ground with the full blow of his body. They slid across the icy deck until they smashed up against the side. Duran pulled Bill to his feet as another fierce wave hit the ship.

The loud cracking sound was no doubt proof that the *Mary Elise* had only moments before completely breaking apart. Bill did his best to put Duran down on the deck, but it was as if the man were possessed.

The ship shifted, and so did the men. They were thrown against the rail, and with each man embracing the other in a death grip, they were hurled over the side and into the lake.

Bill's last thoughts were of his daughters.

"The ship's on fire," Elise heard someone yell above the wind.

She got up from where she'd been huddled against a group of rocks to walk back to the edge of the cliff. She could see the eerie scene below as flames rose from beneath the hold of the *Mary Elise*. She looked at the small group of men pointing and commenting. Two other men were on the ground at the edge of the rocks, helping someone finish the climb. Elise prayed it might be her father.

When Ollie Johnson came over the ledge, Elise tried not to feel disappointed. She wanted each man to be saved. However, with the ship on fire and the storm raging, she wanted to know that her father was safely making his way up the ropes. She searched for Nick. He was with the group of men, doing his best to make a plan.

"We're going to need help, but we'll wait

until first light. There's no sense trying to make our way in this storm and the dark."

She took hold of his arm. "Have you seen my father?"

He looked down at her. "I told you to stay put. I haven't got time to worry about losing you." He walked her back to the rocks. "Please stay here. I'm trying to account for everyone. I haven't seen anything of your father yet. Russ and Seamus are missing, as well."

"Father will be the last to leave."

"I know."

A sense of emptiness washed over her. Papa would wait until everyone else was off the ship, including Duran if he could find him, before ever trying to seek safety for himself.

She sat back down, shivering against the bitter wind. She tucked her feet up under her and made a tight huddle against a large rock. If they didn't get better shelter soon, they'd freeze to death, and their escape from the water would mean nothing. She had no idea where they were. Were there cities close by, or even a small farm? Would any of the men know where to seek help?

Tucking her face against her knees, Elise pulled her coat up over her head and prayed.

"Please, God, save my father," she whispered. "Save us all."

Chapter 25

They were freezing to death. The water wouldn't take them down to its depths, but the icy cold would claim their lives if they weren't able to get to shelter. Elise didn't want to leave, however. She felt certain her father would join them. He couldn't die like this.

The storm had passed, leaving a gloomy red horizon as the sun came up. Below the rocks, the still-smoldering remnants of the *Mary Elise* sat broken and battered. Just pieces of her former glory. Papa had been so proud of that ship.

Elise tried to reconcile herself to the idea that he was gone. Nick had braved a journey down the rocks to the *Mary Elise* to search for her father but found nothing. He salvaged the ship's log and a photograph of Elise's mother and returned to confirm what Elise already feared must be true.

"We're gonna walk to find help. The walking will keep us from freezing further," Nick told her. He put his arm around her as she gazed out on the lake.

"I can't believe he's gone."

"I know, but the last thing he would want is for you to freeze to death. Come on. We have to seek refuge."

"But what if . . ."

Nick shook his head. "Elise, he's gone."

"But you didn't see Booker Duran or Seamus or Russ. Maybe they got off the ship."

"And went where? The only way was up. We would have met up with them." He touched her frozen face. "Come on. The men are waiting."

As they began to walk in hopes of finding a house or a nearby town, Elise could hardly feel her feet or hands, but her heart most assuredly ached.

Papa would have told her to stop feeling bad, for he had died just as he lived. The lake, he had always said, would be his death, and he was all right with that because it had also been his life. Elise, however, couldn't imagine how she would tell Caroline or Uncle James or even Carter and Mina in Duluth.

The sun rose higher but offered little

warmth. Nick said the temperatures to be no more than twenty degrees, if that.

It was nearly noon before one of the men spotted smoke rising in the air. They pressed on toward the place and found a single cabin. The owner welcomed them readily and put more wood on the fire. The old man had little to offer them, but what he did, he gave freely.

Tom and Ollie volunteered to go on to the small town some two miles away and bring back more help. The old man gave them the use of his large draft horse along with explicit directions.

Elise was so tired and cold that she couldn't stop shaking.

The old man came to her with a mug of hot coffee. "Drink this down. It'll warm your insides."

She did as he suggested, grimacing at the bitter taste. Papa had always had his coffee black, and she'd teased him about the awful flavor. How she wished he were here now.

By the time the sun was setting again, Tom and Ollie were back with several towns-folk and a couple of wagons with blankets, food, and dry clothes. The crew of the *Mary Elise* was fed and clothed, then driven back to town, where it had already been decided they would be allowed to sleep in the church for the night before pressing on for the next town and the railroad.

Elise lost track of the time and slept. She rallied only briefly in the night at the sound of the wind. Apparently, another storm was upon them. Exhaustion kept her from dreaming, and when she awoke the next day, her body didn't hurt nearly so much as it had.

Before they were to head out on two sleighs, the town's doctor came to see to their needs. He looked over the men first, then came to Elise. "How are you feeling?"

"I believe I'm starting to thaw." She gave him a smile. "Thank you for what you've done for the crew. I know my father would have appreciated it."

"Your father was the captain? One of the men lost?"

"Yes." Elise let him examine her hands.

"Let me see your feet."

She unfastened the leg bands of the bloomers, then unrolled her stockings.

"Mr. Clark said everyone warmed their hands and feet gradually after rescue. That was wise. You'll have some pain for a while, but I don't think you'll lose any toes. You're fortunate."

"What about the crew?"

"A man or two might yet lose toes. It's hard to say. I've instructed them on what to do and to see a doctor as soon as they reach the city. You're all very lucky."

Elise didn't feel lucky. "We are blessed, but we also lost four men."

"The first mate told me. Word will go out in case the bodies should be recovered, but you know yourself the odds are . . ."

"Yes. I understand." She clutched her hands together. No one had to tell her about the unlikeliness of finding her father.

The doctor looked at her for a moment as if he intended to say something more, then stood and left the room. Perhaps he was just as much at a loss for words as Elise.

She sighed. It just didn't seem real. She kept expecting to wake up and find it was all nothing more than a bad dream. Why couldn't it be that and that alone?

She pulled on her stockings and then covered her feet in the thick wool socks that one of the women of the town had given her. She pulled on her boots and was tying them up when Nick entered the area that had been quartered off for her.

"We're just about ready to go. How are you?"

"The doctor thinks I'll be just fine." She looked up at him after securing her laces. "After all, you can't do much for a broken heart."

She fastened the leg bands on her bloomers. The same woman who'd given her the socks had also brought her a wool skirt, but Elise couldn't remember what she'd done with it.

"I can't find my skirt. Where's my skirt?" She patted the bed sheets, thinking it might have gotten tangled within. She looked nearby and still found nothing. "Where is it?" Tears came to her eyes. She hadn't yet wept for her father. Why was she crying over a skirt?

Nick pulled her to her feet and held her close. He didn't try to speak away her pain, he just held her. Elise clung to him and sobbed.

Nearly a week later, Elise was still contemplating what was to become of her and her sister. Should they go to Oswego and live with their uncle as he had suggested was best? At least there, they wouldn't have to worry about food or shelter. They had the little house here in Duluth, but it had also suffered damage during what Dr. Thomas Foster, editor of the *Minnesotian*, called "The Storm King: The Most Terrible Storm Ever Known on Lake Superior."

The storm had flooded Minnesota Point and other low-lying areas, and the wind had wreaked havoc as well. Nick had been making repairs to the house with the help of Mina's husband, Carter, but Elise had no idea how they would pay for it. And, should more repairs be necessary, that would require more money. She supposed she could ask her uncle for help.

Caroline had been surprisingly strong. She comforted Elise with her constant presence and genuine concern. She was there whenever Elise wanted to talk and silent when Elise wanted to be left to contemplate all that had happened. Nick was a constant in their life as well. He stayed with Mina and Carter in order to keep everything appropriate. Elise hated to see him go at night and had even suggested that marrying right away would take care of all proprieties. But he wisely wanted to give her time.

The storm damage to Duluth and the harbor was extensive, and word was trickling in of other ships that had been lost. Elise hadn't felt like attending the services being offered on behalf of the lost, but knowing that her father was one of them, she felt she had no choice. So she found herself among the congregants that Sunday, singing a song of God's mercy.

The church was packed with men, women, and children who knew all too well the dangers of life on the lakes. They had gathered many times for their families and friends, for neighbors and strangers. When loss like this came, they were all one family.

The song concluded, and they all took their seats. Elise was comforted by the fact that Nick was on her right and Caroline on her left.

Pastor Johnson took the pulpit, Bible in hand. "We have gathered here today in loving memory of those who have perished at the hand of the most recent storm. These men and women will never be forgotten. Their duties put them in danger, often for our benefit, but this life was the one they chose and loved. They were vibrant and loving people who feared not what might come upon the morrow."

Elise knew that was true of her father and mother. They had loved sailing and had loved each other. They had given Caroline and Elise the best life possible, despite the doubts of her aunt and uncle.

"As children of God, we need not fear the hour of death, for while that hour represents loss to our loved ones, it is indeed a glorious moment for those who are called home. In the Bible, we are given so many examples of the hour of death. I believe our Lord did this in order to acquaint us better with a situation that must come to all men but has absolutely no power over the child of God. That power was defeated at the cross, and because of it, death for the true believer is but a door that we pass through—out of this world and into the presence of God."

Several people murmured their amens, while the sobbing of others grew a little louder. Elise thought of the many times she had sat in similar crowds with her mother and father. They were true believers, and all of her life they had taught Elise not to fear death or even mourn it, and all for the very reason Pastor Johnson just stated.

"Death holds no power over you, Elise," her father had assured her.

"These earthly bodies will die, but never our spirit," Elise could hear her mother say.

"Jesus died on the cross, setting us free from the laws of sin and death," Pastor Johnson continued. "He was victorious over the grave, and so too are those who belong to him. Yet here we are in our sorrow, and it is the natural state of those who have lost someone dear. I do not condemn your grief, but merely encourage you to dwell on the love. To know that everyone here shares somehow in that sorrow and will happily help you bear it. You are not alone. Just as our loved ones were not alone in this storm. Not even for a moment."

Elise had been more upset over the idea of her father dying alone or with Booker Duran than anything else. She had wanted to speak final words of love, but there had been no chance. But they'd had a lifetime of love. Her father had no doubt of her feelings. She had been willing to give up her life for him. There was no need for spoken words. And her father hadn't been alone. Jesus had never left him alone for even a moment.

After the services concluded, the people greeted one another with hearts of genuine compassion and love. Elise felt completely enveloped in their concern and kindness. Several of the women promised that meals would be brought to the house, while the men sought Nick to hear the story of the *Mary Elise*'s final hours.

When they were able to slip away to catch the ferry, Elise let go a heavy sigh.

"You sound so tired," Caroline said, taking her arm. "When we get home, I'll make you some hot cocoa and then tuck you in bed."

"I'm afraid this kind of weariness won't be helped by sleep. I've spent a week trying that, and it hasn't helped at all."

Nick took Elise's other arm. "It will take time to endure this sorrow, but I'd like to share something with you, if I may."

Elise looked up at him as they waited for the ferry to take them back to Minnesota Point. "Of course."

"Your father didn't want to tell you yet, but he had plans to quit the *Mary Elise* after we were married. He figured this winter he and I would work on fixing her up, and then come spring thaw, you and I would sail her, and he'd remain here to oversee matters in Duluth and look out for Caroline's needs."

"Father intended to quit sailing?" Elise shook her head. "He mentioned it once, but I thought it was just his grief talking. I didn't think he truly meant it."

"He said it wasn't the same for him since losing your mother. He also felt that with Caroline returning home, it would allow him to spend some time with her. He loved you both so much and just wanted to make sure you both knew that. Before we left, your uncle suggested needing a representative here in Duluth for the shipping company, and your father had decided to take that on."

Caroline dropped her hold on Elise's arm and reached for her handkerchief. "I wish I'd sailed with you. I could have spent that much more time with Papa."

"No," Elise said, shaking her head. "It was horrible, and I kept thinking at the time how glad I was that you had taken the train.

I know Papa was glad too. He was so worried about me. I could see it in his eyes."

"And for a good reason," Nick said, "but God delivered us."

"I wish He would have delivered Papa." Elise dabbed her tears with gloved fingers.

"But as Pastor Johnson said, he *was* delivered, just not in the way we hoped. We're going to miss him for a long time. He was a good man, and he taught me a lot about faith and trusting God. I will never forget him. And I'll have you by my side as we continue his tradition."

Elise looked up at him. "What do you mean?"

"We'll continue sailing in the spring. I think he'd want us to, don't you?"

"But we have no ship," Elise said. "The insurance on the *Mary Elise* will go to my uncle to compensate for the loss. I have no idea if he'll want to purchase another ship or not."

"I'm sure he will, since he was planning for a bigger operation. And even if he doesn't, I intend to keep sailing. I would have taken on the *Mary Elise*, but now that she's gone, I will buy a new ship that is even now being built. That is . . . if you'll join me on it. Be my cook and companion. Spoil our crew as you always have."

"Do you really think the others will come back to join us? They've scattered to their own homes and families."

"I've asked each one to meet us here in the spring . . . or sooner. They all agreed they would sail with me."

Elise considered this as the ferry approached. She said nothing for a long while, even after they'd boarded for the short ride to Minnesota Point.

"I was born on the water," she finally said. "I sometimes feel such a love for the lakes, and other times I want to curse them. Still, I cannot bring myself to leave." She looked up at Nick and smiled. "I'll join you, no matter where you lead. As your wife, it will be my duty and my joy." She turned to Caroline. "But what about you?"

"You don't worry about me," Caroline stated with a confident air. "I know how to fend for myself. I will deal with Nelson and this annulment, and then I will seek God's counsel rather than my own. And, if you'll allow me, I'll keep our little house well while you are gone. After all, Mina and Carter will be there if I should have need."

Elise met Caroline's gaze and smiled. "You are truly stronger than me in so many ways, and here all these years I was certain I was the strong one."

"You have infinite strength, Elise, but there is no reason we can't both be strong."

The next May, standing on the deck of their new schooner, *My Refuge*, Elise fought back tears of joy as Tom handed Nick her wedding ring. Nick slipped it on her finger and held her fingers to his lips.

"With this ring, I thee wed," he whispered, then kissed the ring as if to seal it on her hand.

Caroline handed Elise a handkerchief to wipe her tears as the ship slowly rocked in the water. Elise dried her eyes and tucked the cloth up her sleeve as Nick turned her to face their small audience. The men who had formerly crewed the *Mary Elise* stood watching with smiles alongside their Duluth friends. Elise could imagine her father standing there with them.

"I now pronounce you husband and wife." Pastor Johnson looked at Nick. "You may kiss your bride."

Nick raised Elise's veil and gave her a wink. He took hold of her face and pressed his lips against hers in a tender kiss of promise while their friends broke into loud cheers.

Elise cherished the moment. She had been waiting on love all her life, believing that perhaps it would never come because of the promises she'd made others. But it had been there all along. First in the love of her parents and now in the arms of her husband. And wrapped around all of it was the love of God that never failed nor deserted.

"Are you ready for our new adventure, wife?" Nick whispered against her ear as he stepped back, grinning.

She met his gaze and smiled. "I am."

Tracie Peterson is the award-winning author of over one hundred novels, both historical and contemporary. She is often referred to as the "Queen of Historical Christian Fiction," and her avid research resonates in her stories, as seen in her bestselling HEIRS OF MONTANA and ALASKAN QUEST series. Tracie considers her writing a ministry for God to share the Gospel and biblical application. She and her family make their home in Montana. Visit her website at www.traciepeterson.com or on Facebook at www.facebook.com/Author TraciePeterson.

Sign Up for Tracie's Newsletter

Keep up to date with Tracie's news on book releases and events by signing up for her email list at traciepeterson.com.

Also from Tracie Peterson

While caring for her grandmother, Kristin encounters the brother she long thought dead. In shock, she volunteers to care for her brother's injured friend, Ilian. As Ilian recovers, an attraction sparks between them, but both are dealing with problems that have no easy answers. With no clear way forward, can love ever thrive and the past be forgiven?

Forever My Own • LADIES OF THE LAKE